I0728784

OATH BOUND

SPELLBOUND MURDER BOOK 1

AMANDA BOOLOODIAN

Printed in the United States of America
Copyright © 2018 by Amanda Booloodian
Published by: Walton INK

ISBN-13: 978-1-947382-91-6

Walton INK
www.Booloodian.com

Book cover designed by Deranged Doctor Design.

Dedicated to Adria Waters. Thank you for joining me in this adventure!

CHAPTER 1

T HE HARKER NAME HAD EARNED a wary regard from the Supernatural Community long before Bram Stoker ever wrote his book. Rumors of deals with demons and unbridled power faded as the family became less involved in worldly affairs. The name became nothing other than a legend fallen from time. At least until Emmit Harker showed up in the city and people in the Community started dying.

Mira caught sight of Emmit several times during the conclave of supernatural groups. His presence had caused a stir at less formal events, but she hadn't expected to find him in her shop.

She drummed her fingers on the counter, unsure of whether to approach Emmit or treat him like any other customer.

"Miss Owens, may I have a word?"

Internally, she cringed. "Mr. Benton, I didn't notice you come in." She mentally berated herself for not seeing him right away. Usually, she made an effort to meet him as close to the door as possible to discourage him from staying any longer. "How can I help you?"

"I'm stopping by to leave that proposal I mentioned." He dropped a folder onto the counter.

"Oh." Several phrases passed through her head starting with, *I told you I'm not leaving,* which somehow expanded to, *you can't force me out of here, you little bastard.* She settled on, "That wasn't necessary. My partner and I are very happy with this location."

"Huh," he scoffed. "Well, my *lawyers* have already drafted it, so it wouldn't hurt to take a look."

Mira tried to tell herself that she wasn't going to be intimidated by an implied threat of lawyers. "I'll take a look when I get the chance." Brian Benton had been trying to force her out of her shop since the day after his father's funeral, but her lease was still standing its ground against any legal action. "Can I get you a cup of tea or coffee?"

It crossed her mind that if he drank something, she might be able to spell him to the point that this whole mess would go away. It was an ugly thought and one that no witch should ever have. Still, the idea lingered. For some reason that made her look toward Emmit. One of her employees, Ana, was speaking with him.

"No, thank you." Brian Benton responded in answer to Mira's offer. "I'll stop back in a few days to see what you think of the proposal." He didn't bother waiting for a response.

Flipping open the file folder, Mira glanced through a couple of pages. It was written in legalese, a foreign language far from the scope of her normal one. Luckily, Della Yates, her best friend, happened to work for the attorney general and spoke the language well.

Looking around the shop, she saw that Emmit was watching Brian leave the store. There was no way Emmit could know what was going on, but he glared at the back of the man until Brian was out of sight.

When Emmit turned away, he noticed Mira. The harsh look he had given Brian was gone. His gaze wasn't exactly friendly, but his face had softened, and for the first time since Mira had seen him, she realized he didn't seem intimidating. Why were people whispering his name in dark corners, as though afraid of what might happen if they were overheard?

Emmit turned his attention back to the wall of ingredients that could be mixed together to make unique flavors of tea. Was he looking for something to drink or spell ingredients? The best thing about running the *Essence of Tea* was the fact that she had an ample supply of materials for witches throughout the city. She'd even started to supply witches living further away through online sales.

Tearing her eyes away from Emmit, she flipped through the folder again. The sight of it only made her stomach queasy, so she shoved the documents under the counter and out of sight. She helped a few customers, those coming in for coffee before the lunch rush. Once they left the store, she found herself face-to-face with Emmit.

"Mr. Harker," Mira said, smiling broadly, "did you find everything okay?" Her face began to turn red when she realized that she had never been introduced to Emmit, and he probably had no idea who she was.

"Your assistant over there," he gestured to Ana, who was working with another customer, "gave me a wonderful introduction to your tea. You would be Miss Owens, correct?"

It was the first time Mira had heard his voice. She knew he was British, but she had had no idea his smooth voice would make her toes curl. "Yes, but you can call me Mira."

"And you must call me Emmit," he said.

"It's nice to meet you, Emmit." Mira felt like she was grinning like an idiot, so she tried to dial it back. "What brings you into the shop today?"

Standing this close to him, she realized his voice wasn't the only thing that was seductive. He was tall and handsome, but his eyes were what lured her in. They were a beautiful shade of green, and he wasn't looking at her or through her. Instead, he was looking into her, with all his focus.

"Tyler insisted that I stop by your store should I ever find myself in the vicinity," Emmit said.

"That was nice of him." Mira struggled with what to say. Tyler had never mentioned that he knew Emmit. She now had a million questions for her friend. "Um, have you and Tyler known each other long?"

"We met shortly after I came to town. He speaks very highly of your work away from the store."

The words broke Mira's thoughts away from her amorous attraction to Emmit. Tyler and Mira regularly spent hours working on spells together. It wasn't like Tyler to talk about witchcraft outside of witches, friends, or family members. It made Mira uneasy to know that he'd been discussing her work with Emmit.

Too late, Mira realized that she had been quiet for too long.

"Will I be seeing you tonight at the conclave?" Emmit asked.

"What? I mean… I didn't know there was a meeting tonight."

"I only heard word of it moments before entering your shop. It appears to be a last-minute decision."

How did someone that was practically a stranger to town know before she did? "That's strange. Thank you for letting me know, though."

"I take it they don't often call an assembly together on such short notice."

"No," Mira said. She tried to puzzle together a reason they would call a meeting with no notice. The only thing she could think of was that someone must have been discovered. Maybe a werewolf in the park or a warlock conjuring something? "We usually have a few days' notice at least."

"Will I see you there?" Emmit asked.

"Yeah, I'll be there." There wasn't much that would keep Mira away. What could have happened?

"I'm glad to hear that. I look forward to the opportunity to chat with you outside of your work."

"That'll be nice." Thoughts about the last-minute gathering filled her mind.

"It was nice meeting you," Emmit said.

"You too," Mira said.

It wasn't until after Emmit had disappeared into the street that Mira thought about what he had said. He wanted to talk to her outside of work? Was he making polite chitchat, or did he mean something else?

Mira shook the thought out of her head and tried to stop thinking about Emmit's voice. What little she had heard about him was that he was formal and polite, which is exactly what she had seen.

Emmit had somehow created an invisible barrier around them as they spoke. Now that he was gone, customers from the back of Ana's line moved to Mira's register, and Mira lost herself in her work. A few hours later, the store was mostly empty again, and she joined Ana.

"They tore through the coffee," Ana said as she wiped down the machine.

Mira had learned early on that people loved the shop, but outside the supernatural community, the coffee was what brought customers in. "It was a long rush," Mira said. "Before we got busy, I was talking with someone—"

"The British guy. I noticed," Ana said. "I'd kill to listen to that voice longer. I tried to talk with him, but he seemed distracted."

"Did he buy anything?"

"Tea. One of the premade blends. Speaking of distractions…" Ana caught sight of their newest customers.

Mira rolled her eyes, not that Ana would notice, and looked at the newcomers.

Wow. Distraction was the right word. Mira thought Emmit was handsome, but hot was the only way to describe the two newcomers. They weren't overly muscled, but the way their clothes clung to all the right places confirmed time spent in the gym. One brunette, the other blond, and both were looking around her shop with interest.

"I've got this, boss," Ana said, not tearing her eyes off the men.

Seeing her employee ogling the two made Mira realize she was doing the same. She shook her head and brought her thoughts back to the real world. Ana could handle their customers, since Mira needed to make some calls.

When Mira grabbed her cell phone, it vibrated for a moment, letting her know she had missed messages. She ignored the call from her mother and went straight for the texts. Sure enough, her sister Robin started with, *Dad said he couldn't reach you....* Della and Tyler wrote as well, but Robin tended to get bent out of shape if Mira didn't answer her texts first.

Mira might have been a better spell caster than her older sister was, but Robin tended to have oddball talents that you didn't often see in witches. Most people wouldn't think that knowing someone had put off reading your texts would be a part of witchcraft. A quirk of Robin's power was that she knew every time Mira avoided her messages. Being a coven witch, Robin was all about family and coven first, which meant she took the avoidance personally.

The conclave has been called for tonight. No one knows why, do you? I'm coming into the city with Dad. Call me.

Mira looked at the almost empty store and contemplated calling back, but she saw that Ana was gesturing at her as she spoke with the men who had entered. Knowing that Ana was going to need her for something, Mira let Robin know that she couldn't call and that she'd see Robin at the meeting.

Before she could get interrupted, Mira checked the texts from Della and Tyler. Neither said why the community was gathering, but they at least let her know where the meeting would take place.

"Mira," Ana said, keeping an eye on the customers as she approached her boss. Ana didn't look as happy about their presence as she had earlier. "There are two detectives that would like to speak with you."

Frowning, Mira shoved the cell phone into her pocket. "Did they say why?"

"Only that they wanted to ask you a few questions."

Mira's stomach clenched. "Can you get us some coffee?"

"Coming right up," Ana said.

The two men didn't look familiar, but Mira could guess why they were there. She stood a little straighter and marched over to the two, ready to get this over with.

"Can I help you?" Mira asked.

"Are you Miss Owens?" The brunette asked.

"I am," Mira said.

"I'm Detective Burke and this," he said, indicating the blond man, "is Detective Flint. We would like to ask you a few questions."

"Is this about Sally?" It was abrupt, but if it was about Sally, Mira wanted it over with. It had been a month and although the loss of Sally was still raw, the gaping hole her absence had created was starting to heal. Mira knew that more questions would threaten to rip everything back out into the open.

CHAPTER 2

"WE HAVE A FEW QUESTIONS relating to Miss Hayes, if you have the time," Detective Burke said.

"Of course," Mira said.

Ana appeared with a tray. "Mira, here's your tea, and I wasn't sure what you'd like," she added, turning to the detectives, "but this is black coffee. We also have a station over there if you'd like to add cream or sugar."

"Join me at the table in the corner when you're ready," Mira said before either of them could protest.

Sitting at one of the few tables in the store, Mira watched the detectives while she made sure she was mentally prepared for questions about Sally. There had been many interviews over the past few weeks, and very few details released about what happened beyond the fact that Sally had been stabbed three times and her body was found in the park.

A month later, and they still didn't have the killer in custody.

It wasn't until Detective Burke moved toward the table that Mira realized he looked familiar. Had she met him earlier on the case? It was unlikely she would forget anyone that looked like Detective Burke, but Mira didn't remember a lot about the few days following Sally's death.

She gripped her cup as the detectives sat down at the table. "How can I help?"

"First, we wanted to say that we're sorry for your loss," Detective Burke said. "You were close to Sally, correct?"

"She was one of my best friends," Mira said, frowning. Were they going to ask the exact same questions all over again?

"How long had you been friends with her?" Detective Burke asked.

"Since high school, but you all know this already." She hadn't meant to say it out loud, but she was glad she had.

Detective Burke nodded, but it was Detective Flint that replied. "We needed to confirm a few things."

Mira tried not to look dejected. Could asking the same old questions bring about anything new?

"What can you tell us about her relationship with Martin West?" Detective Burke asked.

"Not a lot, really," Mira said. "She was happy with him. They'd been seeing each other for around five months."

"And they were living with each other?" Detective Burke asked.

"Yes." Her eyes narrowed as she mentally dared him to turn that into something negative about Sally.

"Did Sally and Martin appear to have any trouble once they moved in together?" Detective Flint asked.

Mira move her attention to Detective Flint, trying to relax. "No."

"You sound very confident about that," Detective Flint said.

"I am." Mira's thoughts turned inward as she thought of her friend. Sally was… had been… happy with Martin, Mira was certain about that.

"You're positive she would have told you if something was wrong between them?" Detective Flint asked.

A sad smile turned up as she remembered Sally's past experiences with dating. "Sally would have told Della and me. When she wasn't getting along with someone she was pretty vocal about it."

"Would Martin have known that?" Detective Flint asked.

Mira sniffed and tried to drag her thoughts back to the present. "I have no idea."

"We understand that Sally kept a routine appointment one evening each month or so," Detective Burke said. "What do you know about those appointments?"

"Was it for work maybe?" After Mira said the words, she connected the dots. The supernatural community in the city held a conclave once a month. With so many supernaturals living so closely together, it was the best way to settle disputes while staying hidden among the humans. "Did Martin tell you about the appointments?" Martin hadn't been a part of the community, so there was no way Sally would have told him.

"It's been mentioned during the course of our investigations," Detective Burke said. "Did Sally have any religious affiliations?"

Okay, that was a new one. "Are you asking if she attended church?" Mira didn't really care what the question was as long as it moved away from discussion about the conclave. "I think she went with her parents a few times a year, but I wouldn't call her religious."

"Did Sally know a Dennis Simmons or Helen Kassell?" Detective Burke asked.

Mira tried to keep her face impassive, but she could feel her forehead crease in her confusion. "Dennis Simmons or Helen Kassell? I—" Mira didn't know how to continue. She'd never heard the first name, but Helen was a werewolf, so of course Sally had seen her, but had she ever seen her outside of the meetings? "The names don't sound familiar," Mira lied. That was one of the ground rules: if you didn't know the supernatural outside of the meetings, you didn't know them. "But Sally met a lot of people through work. Maybe check with her boss?"

Detective Flint crossed his arms and Mira noticed his eyes narrowing in on her as though she was being studied.

"Was one of these people involved in Sally's death?" Mira asked. Even if they had known each other in the outside world, Sally couldn't have been close to Helen, or Mira would have known about it.

After a moment's hesitation, Detective Burke cleared his throat and leaned forward. "It's unlikely, but we believe that there is a connection between the two. It's important that you tell us how they knew each other."

Mira shook her head and tried to sound confident. "As far as I know, Sally didn't know Helen."

"Do you know Helen Kassell?" Detective Flint asked, still giving Mira the same look.

"I told you," Mira snapped, "the name doesn't sound familiar." But Mira could tell that Detective Flint didn't believe her.

"Are the names Yvonne Childs or Karen Green familiar?" Detective Flint asked.

"They aren't," Mira said. Karen Green. Had she heard that name before? "What makes you think Sally knew these people?"

Detective Flint shook his head, but didn't say anything.

Mira couldn't think of a way to fill the silence that was lingering beyond comfort.

Detective Burke cleared his throat and went on. "We might have a more—"

"We would like to get a more formal statement," Detective Flint said, interrupting his partner.

She shifted in her seat. Mira knew what that meant, but she was hoping she was wrong. "Do you need me to sign something here?"

"Actually, Miss Owens, we were hoping you would accompany us to the office. We have some follow up questions and you could sign a statement there."

Mira's stomach knotted. She'd been to a station when she wasn't working with the police—on the wrong side of the desk you might say—and she hadn't enjoyed the experience. "Uh, is this something we can do here?"

"We'd rather you come with us," Detective Flint said.

Detective Burke frowned at his partner and Mira wondered if the request to do this at the station was one sided.

Mira ran a hand through her hair. "Sure," she said, "my car is parked a few blocks away, but if you give me the address, I can follow you."

"We'll give you a lift," Detective Flint said.

Mira's stomach was clenched tight and she bit her lip. Looking around the store, she couldn't find a good enough excuse to refuse.

"Okay," she said, "I'll need to grab my coat and talk with my employee, and then I'll be ready." Not bothering to wait for a response, Mira left the two officers at the table.

After writing a quick note to the manager coming in, Mira grabbed her purse. While she spoke with Ana, she watched the two detectives out of the corner of her eye. They were waiting by the door and neither one of them looked happy, but Mira got the feeling that Detective Burke was aggravated with his partner. Clearly, taking her to the station for a statement had not been a part of the plan.

Mira took one last look around the store before she approached the detectives again. "I guess I'm ready to go."

"This won't take long," Detective Burke said while holding the door open for her.

The frigid air wrapped around Mira, sucking out all the warmth of the store. She pulled her coat tighter, noting that both men appeared unfazed by the cold. Even Detective Flint, wearing what could barely be called a jacket, didn't seem to notice. Thankfully, they hadn't parked far away.

Detective Burke held the back door open for her and she slid in. It was a normal car, not a police vehicle, which helped to calm her nerves some.

They were mostly silent on the way to the station, so Mira took the opportunity to text Della. *Detectives came to the store to ask me more questions. They are taking me to the police station.*

Della's response wasn't as immediate as Mira would have liked, but a few minutes later, she received a message. *Have you been arrested???*

No, Mira quickly wrote, *they wanted to ask me more questions and sign a statement. They asked me to come with them.*

This time, Della's response was immediate. *Why on earth did you go with them?*

Mira frowned, feeling that she was being admonished. *Because they asked.*

You should have called me first. I'm going down there. Which station?

Shoot. That was the last thing Mira wanted. *Don't. It's fine. I'm fine.*

"Everything okay?" Detective Burke asked, turning from the passenger seat.

"What?" Mira asked, staring at her phone, hoping for Della to tell her she wasn't on her way. Then Detective Burke's question sunk in. "Oh, I'm fine. I'm just trying to convince Della not to come to the station."

"Della Yates?" Detective Burke asked. Mira noticed the sideways glance he gave his partner.

"Yep," Mira said, trying to keep the satisfied smile off her face. Knowing a friend that was a lawyer in the distinct attorney's office would definitely work in her favor.

"Why did you tell her if you didn't want her to come?" Detective Flint asked. It sounded like he had a bad taste in his mouth.

"We're meeting up a little later," Mira said. "I let her know in case I ran late."

Detective Burke sighed audibly.

Mira was pleased he didn't seem any happier with the situation than she did. Detective Flint was unhappy, too, but that wasn't a change. Mira had the idea that he was upset for a whole host of other reasons.

An aggravated silence permeated the front seat, but Mira kept her eyes on her phone, waiting for Della to respond.

Traffic was turning thick as people began leaving the city or returning to the city after their workday. It was a bad time to be driving through town.

Mira began watching the traffic outside her car window. Tailpipes were fuming and brake lights blinked off and on, as cars rolled a few feet and stopped. Her phone vibrated again and she welcomed the distraction.

One hour, Della texted. *If you're not on your way out, I'm coming down there. Will you be at the meeting?*

Shoot. She'd almost forgotten about the meeting. *I'll probably be late, but I will be there. Do not tell my mother or sister where I am.* Mira knew her father wouldn't blow things out of proportion if he found out where she was.

NP was Della's only response.

Mira waited, hoping Della would offer some unsolicited advice, but slid her phone in her pocket when nothing else came through.

"Is your friend joining us?" Detective Burke asked.

"Depends on how long I'm here," Mira said.

Light dimmed as the car moved into a parking garage.

"It won't be long," Detective Burke said again. He shot his partner another look, which Detective Flint either missed or ignored.

The parking garage had quite a few police cruisers and other cars. They wound their way up a floor before Detective Flint parked.

As the detectives led her through a door and down a maze of hallways, Mira tried to build some confidence. It wasn't as if she had done anything wrong.

They led her into a 'conference' room. It was marginally nicer than the rooms she had been taken into during college, but it was what it was; an interrogation room with a dressed-up name.

Detective Flint sat opposite Mira, while Detective Burke stood, leaning against the wall behind his partner. Flint went over her previous statement and asked if she had anything to add.

Mira shook her head, thinking she was getting off easy if they just wanted to rehash what she'd already said.

It was a short-lived thought.

Detective Flint started asking questions about the statement. The questions were slow and casual at first, but then he got more serious.

"We've had some interesting facts about this case come to light recently," Detective Flint said. "It appears that your friend Sally had made herself unpopular with a lot of people. What can you tell us about that?"

Mira thought over his puzzling statement. "Sally was one of my best friends," she said carefully, "but I don't know of anyone that didn't like her. Maybe an ex-boyfriend or two, but she was friendly and social."

"What can you tell me about Sally's relationship with her boss, Mr. Leer?" Detective Flint asked.

"Uh," Mira thought about anything that Sally might have said about work, "she was one of his top sales people. She said she was selling more cars than just about anyone else."

"She never said anything specific about Mr. Leer?"

Listening more carefully to the questions and attitudes of Detective Flint made her think through her answers slowly. His body language was eager. He wanted to know more.

"Sally won an award at work not long ago," Mira said.

Detective Flint let a flash of frustration cross his face. "And Mr. Leer gave her this award?"

"From what Sally said, she received the award from Mr. Leer in front of everyone. I'm sure that wouldn't be hard to check out."

The detective shook his head. "Did she mention anything about Mr. Leer specifically? About his habits or his family?"

"No."

"What about her boyfriend, Martin West? Did Martin say anything about Mr. Leer?"

"I didn't really talk to Martin much," Mira said. "We barely spoke."

"Did Sally have an interest in anyone else?"

Mira knew the question had been left wide open for a reason. "I'm not sure I understand what you're asking."

"Did Sally say anything about secrets that others may have? Maybe something that she had found out."

Mira thought over the question carefully. Sally had been a clairvoyant and had a great many secrets about other people, but she never shared them. Well, sometimes they played games to find out interesting bits of information about their server at the bar or about a guy they were hitting on, but nothing serious. It was also something that Mira couldn't tell the detectives.

"Sally never said anything about anyone else. She wasn't the type to gossip much." Despite the pause, Mira said this with confidence. The detectives were fishing, but she had no idea what they were trying to find out. Finding other suspects, maybe?

"I find it hard to believe that, as her best friend, she never shared any information with you. Did Sally tell you how she bought her new car?" Detective Flint asked, getting more aggressive.

"I assumed she bought it at a discount from work."

"And the clothes and jewelry?" He scowled at Mira.

It didn't do any good. Mira had no idea what he was looking for. "I assume she made good money where she worked. Sally worked hard."

Detective Burke moved forward a bit and cleared his throat. Detective Flint, who had been leaning forward in his seat, sank back and switched tactics.

In a calmer voice, Detective Flint asked, "Did Sally practice witchcraft?"

"What?" Mira asked, hoping confusion masked her fear.

"Did she ever have an interest in the occult?"

CHAPTER 3

MIRA USED GREAT CARE WHEN trying to come up with a response. "How are you defining the occult?"

Flint sighed. "Did she believe in magic or witchcraft?"

They had to have looked at Mira's file. Why else would they ask her something like that? Now, how did she play this?

"You do know that there's a lot more to the occult than that, right?"

Smug satisfaction played across Detective Flint's face. "Are you into the occult?"

That was enough to satisfy Mira that Detective Flint had no idea about her past experiences with the police, but she didn't know if that would work for her or against her. "I know a great deal about the occult, if that's what you mean."

"So you know how to perform sacrifices?" Detective Flint asked.

Her nose scrunched up in distaste. "What are you talking about?" Mira looked at Detective Burke, who didn't appear happy with the direction the interview was taking. "Why are you asking that?"

"Can you please answer the question?" Detective Flint asked, sounding far too nice.

"Fine," Mira crossed her arms. "A sacrifice for what purpose?"

"For sacrificing," Detective Flint said.

She rolled her eyes and shook her head. "Are we talking devil worship, voodoo, hoodoo, generic black magic, or any number of other belief systems that may involve sacrificing?"

"It sounds like you're an expert," Detective Flint said.

"Isn't that why you're asking me?" Mira asked mockingly. "Because of the other cases where law enforcement has used me as an expert?" Saying cases, plural, was pushing it, but she didn't care. Technically, it had been more than one case, but it also, *technically,* had been only one incident.

Apparently, neither of the detectives knew what to do with that.

"Miss Owens—"

"She's not lying," Detective Flint said, cutting off his partner. He didn't sound happy about it, though.

He knew she wasn't lying? Mira looked at Detective Flint closely, past his good looks and his frustrations, trying to figure out what he might be thinking.

Damn, he was cute.

Well, that wasn't helping anything. "No, I'm not lying. Why would I lie about something like that?"

"There was nothing in your file…" Detective Burke said.

"Did you do a federal background check?" Mira asked.

"I put in the request today," Detective Flint said.

"Right," Mira said, checking the time on her phone. "Why don't you get back to me when you have that information?"

"We have other questions," Detective Flint said halfheartedly.

"So do I," Mira said, "starting with why you're asking the questions you're asking."

Detective Flint crossed his arms and leaned back in his seat. "Where will you be tomorrow?"

"I'm not sure," Mira said, "but you should have my contact information."

"Thank you for your time," Detective Burke said, moving forward.

"Wait. Before I go, why has the case changed hands? You

look familiar," Mira gestured to Detective Burke, "but I know the case was being handled by someone else."

Mira noticed the sideways glance that Detective Burke gave Detective Flint.

"The case has grown in scope," Detective Burke said. "But the original investigators are still involved."

Grown in scope? They had asked about Helen and the occult, and then they said the case had grown. And who were those other people they mentioned?

This wasn't good.

Mira glanced at her phone. "I'm running late, can I go now?"

Detective Flint looked at his partner, but Detective Burke said nothing.

"You're free to leave," Detective Flint said. "Thank you for your help."

It sounded like he was saying something by rote without the meaning ever really sinking in.

Mira snatched up her bag and left the room. She was halfway down the hall before she realized she had no idea how to get out of there.

"Let me give you a ride to your car," Detective Burke said.

"I don't have time to go back to work," Mira said. "I'll just take a cab."

"I'll drop you off wherever you need," Detective Burke said.

Mira thought about her other options. She could call Della or spend a fortune on a cab.

"We did bring you here, after all," he said when she took too long to decide.

"Um, I guess," she said. Oh well, at least she wouldn't be too late.

"Follow me," he said.

To Mira, the silence was awkward as they walked through the building, though Detective Burke appeared more at ease than he had when they'd arrived. They went down a flight of stairs and out into the parking garage. It struck Mira that she was following an unknown person. Law enforcement or not, she was pretty sure that horror stories started that way.

Still, when he held the car door open for her, she got in. More silence greeted her, and she struggled to find something to say to fill the void.

"Where are we going?" Detective Burke asked.

Taking anyone to Lance's house would be a bad idea. The people gathering would definitely not want the police to be around, even if it was just to drop someone off.

"My house," Mira said, pulling out her phone again. "I'll pull it up on my GPS."

"Sorry we made you late," Detective Burke said.

Mira shrugged, and then realized that wasn't helping the awkwardness. "I'm still not sure why you did. It took longer to bring me there than it did to interview me."

Detective Burke followed the voice telling him to turn left. "I'm not sure you'd believe me even if I told you why."

Mira's entire world was filled with stuff that others wouldn't believe. "Try me."

Detective Burke took his time answering. "Gabe has this knack for telling when someone is lying. It sounds strange, but I've never known him to be wrong."

"He thinks I'm lying?" Mira asked. "About what?"

"It's hard to say."

"Huh." Mira looked out the window. She had noticed he'd caught her in a lie, and he'd known when she told the truth, but that could still be coincidence.

"I told you that you wouldn't believe me."

Mira didn't say anything. She did believe—she just didn't want to.

"Anyway," Detective Burke said, "the questions would have taken longer, but you threw us for a loop."

"Glad I could help out," Mira said.

He chuckled.

"Look, Detective—"

"Ian," he said.

"What?"

"Call me Ian. It's not like we're complete strangers."

Mira frowned and looked at him in profile. "We're not?"

He grinned. "Your name sounded familiar, so I looked you up."

"And?" Mira said when he didn't continue right away.

"We had a few classes together in college."

"Oh." To Mira college had been one big blur, and she'd really like to keep it that way. "Sorry, I don't remember."

"You looked busy," Ian said. "We talked at a few parties as well."

Ugh. Mira really didn't want to remember the parties. Her addiction had sprung up around those parties. "What classes did we take together?"

"I remember you in logic and reasoning, abnormal psychology, and statistics. I'm pretty sure we were in the same calc class, but I dropped early and took it the following semester instead."

Maybe that wasn't all bad. By the time Logic was over, she had been getting her life back on track.

"How do you remember me?" Mira asked. "Those classes weren't exactly small."

"Quinton Franks was in the same fraternity as me. I think you two knew each other."

"You know the mayor's son?" Mira bit her lip. Quinton was the reason she had worked with the police. She had pulled herself out of addiction and away from a group of friends, which were a cult when it came down to it. Then she'd jumped back in to pull Quinton out, though not for any noble reason. It had kept her out of jail and out of trouble.

"Yeah. He said you helped him out of something when I asked him about you."

Helped him out of trouble? Well, yeah, you could say that, even though he resented her for doing it.

Wait, what?

"You asked him about me?" Mira asked.

"You're surprised?"

"Well, yeah. I was a mess in college."

Ian shrugged, but kept the grin.

Mira joined him, but wanted to kick herself when she felt her face turn red.

Then she thought about the file that Ian and his partner might receive tomorrow. It was enough to kill any lightened mood.

"Um, I really was a mess in college…" She had no idea what was in that file and wasn't sure what she should tell him.

"Who wasn't?" Ian said.

Maybe saying nothing was the best bet. "I guess so." She forced a smile. "Small world, though."

"It is," he said, glancing over at her.

Her insides felt fuzzy at the look. "I guess that means you should call me Mira."

Ian was cute, but that smile set him over the top. Knowing the weirdness that he was about to see in her file, Mira tried to cement the picture in her mind. It might be the last time she saw it. At least directed at her.

"Nice house," Detective Burke said as he pulled into the driveway.

She looked up at the big house as they drove beside it, toward the back. "Thanks, but, um, I rent the apartment over the garage." She pointed to the top of the three-car garage that had been built to match the house. "Will I see you tomorrow?" Mira asked, thinking what Ian might discover about her and Quinton the next day.

Ian appeared to think that over. "It's hard to say. I guess that depends on what turns up."

"That's understandable," Mira agreed. "But after… well, after you get more information on me, you may have some questions."

"I'm sure we both will," Ian said, looking more serious.

"Yes, but yours might be more… specific and not about the case. No offense to your partner," although Mira privately thought she wouldn't care about offending Detective Flint, "but I don't think I'll feel as comfortable answering your questions with him around."

"Gabe's a good guy when you get to know him," Ian said. "Don't get put off by the whole lie detector trick he does."

"I think I'm more put off by the fact that he thinks I'm guilty of… I don't even know what. But guilty of something."

"I shouldn't be saying this, but you'll find out soon anyway. There's been another death that may be related. We've been given the case and he thinks you know something you're not telling us." Ian hesitated as he stopped the car next to the stairs to her apartment. "If there is something you're not telling us, you need to let me know what it is."

Mira sighed. "I didn't hurt Sally, if that's what you're getting at. And I don't know who did."

"I don't think you killed her."

"And your partner?"

Ian didn't say anything.

"Well, I'm sure I'll see you tomorrow." Mira opened her car door.

Ian got out as well. "I'll walk you to your door."

"You don't have to." Mira spoke more quickly than she'd intended. She only planned on being here until he left. Lance's house wasn't too far away. She could walk there.

"Be careful," Ian said as Mira rushed upstairs.

"You too," Mira called. She opened the door and flipped on the inside light. "Thanks for the lift home."

She dashed inside before he could say anything else. Hopefully he would only assume she was in a hurry. Being rude wasn't her intention, but more than ever, she wanted to rush over to Lance's and see what was going on.

Alchemy, the larger of her two black cats, wound around her legs as way of greeting. Oracle stood in the window, barely glancing up to acknowledge that she was home. Mira went over and patted him on the head anyway. It wasn't like him to ignore her.

There had been another death and they had talked about the occult. Mira couldn't get those two facts out of her head as she fed the cats. She watched the clock, letting five minutes go by before she went back out into the dark evening.

CHAPTER 4

T HOUGHTS ABOUT THE GROWING CASE filled Mira's mind. Was it Helen that had died? She should have asked, but they likely wouldn't have told her anyway. When she stepped into Lance's palatial house, Mira ignored the grandeur, for once, and sought out Della after hanging her coat in the coatroom.

If it had been Helen, she'd find out tonight.

There were more people present than Mira had expected. Maybe ten people were in the parlor, and she knew more would be in the ballroom. Many avoided meetings that were held at Lance's house. Most hear the word vampire and either run away or show up with the torches and stakes.

There's good reason for it. Vampires were vicious monsters, for the most part. It was a little-known secret among the supernatural community that there was such a thing as a non-feral vampire. Lance was one of the few known civilized vampires, but he hinted at others.

Still, the word vampire conjured certain images.

The buzz of curious energy was strong among the group. There was a wide gap between three elves and others in attendance. They seemed bouncy. An energetic elf isn't necessarily a good thing.

Although Mira was looking for Della, Robin was the one who found her when she stepped into the ballroom.

Mira loved her sister, but found her awkward to be around. Robin had joined a coven, and after Mira's bad experiences with other witches in college, Mira no longer liked the idea of being that dependent on others.

"This is quite the crowd," Mira said, glancing nervously at the twenty or so people milling around. "Have you found out anything?"

"I was going to ask you the same thing," Robin said.

"How does something like this even get called?"

"The elders are the only ones that can call an emergency meeting of this size. Even the humans are here." Robin gestured to a group of people that seemed packed together a little tighter and keeping a little further away than the others, much like everyone else was staying away from the elves.

Mira barely glanced at them, noting that it was only the older humans, and calling them human was a stretch. Looking around more, she saw that William Strike, a witch hunter, and John Parnell, a psychic, were chatting with other races. They weren't exactly the run-of-the-mill humans on the street.

"Have you seen Della?"

"Some of the other sorcerers are in the corner," Robin said dismissively. "She's probably with them."

The idea of the instant power that sorcerers had available to them had always been an affront to Robin's sensibilities as a witch. Mira had seen the aftermath of sorcerers using their magic and thought it was an equal exchange. Work magic fast and fall on your face from exhaustion afterwards; plan, create anchors, and take time on your magic, as witches do, and you can go for days.

"I don't see her," Mira said. "How are the kids?" Mira asked as she moved back toward the parlor again.

"They're doing well. You wouldn't believe the amount of stuff they do after school." Robin filled her in on the family while waving and saying hello to people as they walked through the rooms.

"Oh my," Robin said, catching Mira's attention.

"What?" Mira asked.

Robin lowered her voice. "Mr. Harker is here."

Mira followed her sister's gaze and spotted Emmit. He gave a polite nod in her direction, a gesture she repeated, adding a smile, before looking away again.

"Of course he's here," Mira said, keeping her voice light. "Everyone is."

"Who's here?" Della asked.

Mira turned to the fiery redhead, glad to see her.

"Mr. Harker is," Robin said. "Everyone's been talking about him."

"What are they saying?" Mira asked.

"He's mysterious," Robin said.

"And gorgeous," Della added with a sigh. "He looks tense, though."

"People want to know what he's doing in town," Robin said, not commenting on his looks. "I mean, he's a Harker."

From Robin's tone, she could have been talking about her favorite celebrity.

"He *is* cute," Mira admitted.

"And he's coming this way." Robin gripped Mira's arm for a moment, but then seemed to remember that she was an adult and didn't want to be caught fawning over someone.

Mira looked around, surprised to see Emmit was already upon them. She worried for a moment that he might have heard what she had said, but dismissed the idea.

"Miss Owens," Emmit said, "it's a pleasure to see you again."

"And you," Mira said, falling once again for his distinguished British accent. Then her sister poked her in the back. "Um, this is my sister, Robin Lake, and my friend, Della Yates."

"It's nice to meet you both," Emmit said. "May I join you?"

"Of course," Mira said, trying not to betray her nervousness. "But only if you call me Mira." She thought of her conversation with him that afternoon. She had assumed he had been being polite about wanting to chat with her, but maybe he'd meant it when he said he had hoped to see her.

A small smile appeared which seemed to make Emmit look lighter. "Of course."

Seeing an odd sparkle in Della's eyes when she looked from Mira to Emmit, Mira rushed to choose a subject, afraid of what her friend might say. "Does anyone know why the meeting was called?"

Della's face fell. "I think so." She leaned in and lowered her voice. "I think someone else in the community has been murdered."

Robin gasped, apparently caught off guard.

Mira tensed. "Helen." She whispered the name the detectives had mentioned.

"Helen Kassell?" Della asked, dropping her voice even lower. "What have you heard?"

"Nothing really. But earlier, when, you know," Mira really didn't want to say she was questioned by the police in front of her sister, "Earlier Helen's name came up, along with a few others."

Della started to say something, but three loud knocks sounded out, seeming to come from everywhere at once, reverberating and filling the air.

The noise was followed by a few seconds of complete silence before voices filled the void once again.

"Who was it that questioned you?" Della asked, not catching the hint, as several people began to file out of the room.

Mira purposefully avoided looking at her sister. "Detectives Burke and Flint. One of the questions they asked is if Sally knew Helen." Mira tried not to sound defensive, but she felt uncomfortable about bringing Sally up, and she knew Della wasn't happy that she went to the police station.

"You were friends with Sally?" Emmit asked slowly.

"Della and I both were," Mira said.

Emmit nodded as though making up his mind about something. "I believe that you and Della should join me in the meeting."

"We have representatives in there," Mira said.

"And today, you'll be my guest," Emmit said.

Mira hesitated. "Do you usually attend the meetings?"

"The offer has been extended to me as the only apparent member of my race in the area. Please join me."

Mira looked at him for a moment, frozen in indecision, and then her sister gently shoved her forward.

"Um, sure." Mira looked at Della, who nodded. "We'll join you."

Although they were running late, Emmit appeared unconcerned. The meeting of the elders was being held in Lance's formal dining room. Emmit graciously opened the door for Mira and Della.

As soon as Mira stepped into the room conversation stopped, and all eyes fell on her. Most didn't look happy with the interruption.

Mr. Contrey stood and leaned forward. "This is not—" He stopped what was sure to be an angry diatribe when Emmit moved forward.

Emmit was such an unknown that all he had to do was look intently at Mr. Contrey. Although Emmit appeared more passive than unfriendly, Mr. Contrey sat down.

"We were just getting started," Ms. Vears said. "I'm afraid the matter is delicate. Typically, only one of each race is represented on the council."

"That was my understanding," Emmit said. "I was invited to join you."

"Of course, Mr. Harker, but…" Ms. Vears response trailed away as she glanced to Mira and Della.

"Yes?" Emmit asked.

Twelve different races were represented tonight—thirteen, now that Emmit had joined. Working together, all of them were forming a silence that became more uncomfortable as each second ticked by. Even Lance looked uneasy, which was something that no one expected to see in a centuries-old vampire.

Mira admired the way Della stood, as though she had every right to be there. She didn't bother trying to emulate Della, however, knowing that it was bound for failure.

Emmit appeared unconcerned. Maybe he was used to the scrutiny of others.

Mr. Contrey cleared his throat. "Have a seat while we explain the situation."

"This is a meeting about the death of one of your own, correct?" Emmit asked.

Mira found it interesting that he was speaking directly to Noah Tate, who was a werewolf, same as Helen had been, and wondered how well Emmit knew everyone.

"Yes," Noah said shortly.

Emmit took a close look at the man. "I am very sorry to hear about the loss of your clansman."

Noah appeared to hesitate before giving a curt nod of acknowledgment.

"Since this is the second member of the community to meet an early end," Emmit continued, "I thought it prudent to invite Mira and Della—they were friends with Sally. It should also be noted that Mira was questioned by the police today."

Once again, Mira found everyone looking at her. She could feel her face getting warmer and wondered why she had agreed to this.

"What did you say?" Mr. Contrey demanded.

Emmit gave him a cool look. "Why don't we let Miss Owens tell us the whole story."

Mira took a deep breath and tried to ignore the looks on the faces of those around her. Fear, anger, and loss bored down on Mira while she spoke, telling them everything that had occurred earlier in the day.

"They are trying to find a link between the two women," Ms. Vears said. "Which means they are connecting the cases."

"Shouldn't they be connecting them?" Noah asked.

"No," Mr. Contrey said tersely. Several others in the group echoed his sentiment.

"How are they supposed to find the person responsible if we are hiding things from the police?" Noah asked, his voice raising.

"And what would we say to them?" The scorn was thick in Mr. Contrey's voice. "The two had no connection outside the conclave."

"There has to be some way to tell them the truth," Noah said.

"Not at the risk of exposing all of us," Mr. Contrey said.

"And if one of us is behind the murders?" Anger was beginning to fuel Noah.

"We handle our own business," Mr. Contrey snapped.

"Do we know anyone on the police force that we can trust?" Ms. Vears asked, keeping her voice level, not rising to match the tempers of the two men.

"We don't have any supernaturals on the force," Della said.

"Is there something you can do from your office?" Ms. Vears asked.

Della looked at her blankly. "I'm sorry. If someone was arrested, I could keep an eye on things, but there's nothing I can do for an investigation."

"Then we are back to handling the situation on our own," Mr. Contrey said, still having an edge to his voice.

"We want this killer caught!" Noah yelled.

"Of course we do," Ms. Vears said. "We all want that."

"There's still a possibility that these deaths are not related at all," Mr. Contrey said.

"We don't have any solid information," Della said. "But it sounds like they are investigating the cases together."

"Then we have to find a way to give the police the information they need," Noah said.

"We don't know *what* they need," Mr. Contrey said. "And I won't let our community be exposed."

Arguing broke out around the table. Mira watched for a while and wondered if she should make her escape.

"This is a lively bunch," Emmit said. He didn't sound happy about it. "But the response is hardly effective."

Mira shrugged. "The council gets things sorted out before it gets to the rest of us."

"The problem is," Della said, "there's no way to get around it. The police have to know, but they can't know."

"I think there *is* a way around it," Mira said.

Emmit looked closely at her. "Do you think there is, or do you know there is?"

It was an uncomfortable question. Emmit was watching her, seemingly expectant of a positive answer. If there was one thing Mira was certain of, though, it was that she was a talented witch. If given enough time, a witch could get around almost anything.

"I'm positive," Mira said.

She received a calculating look from Emmit before he stepped up to the table. Those sitting next to and across from where he stood went silent. Like a chain reaction, voices died around the table.

Mira looked closer at the elders. Emmit hadn't actually done anything, but he had expected them to pay attention—and they did. Was she doing the same thing? Paying attention to him because he expected it?

"There is a solution to the issue," Emmit said. "Mira, would you please explain your idea?"

That same expectant look from Emmit was now directed at her, but in a good way. He had taken her words at face value, without even knowing what she had in mind.

Was that a good thing or bad?

Whichever it was, his expectations made Mira feel more confident. "Yes. We really only need one person involved in the case to know the truth, right?"

"We can't trust a human that we don't know," Mr. Contrey snapped.

"It's not a matter of trust." Mira wasn't about to be deterred. "It's a matter of keeping them quiet."

Mr. Contrey let out a sigh, but Ms. Vears leaned forward, clearly interested in the new direction.

"How do you propose we keep the person quiet?" Ms. Vears asked.

Mira glanced quickly at the one person in the room she wanted to avoid. Mr. Singer, the elder witch in the room, might not be too happy with her suggestion, but she knew it would work.

"We bind someone." Mira hurried on before anyone, especially Mr. Singer, could interrupt. "If we bind the human in the *singular* area of not letting our secret out, we could work with that person."

"Is that possible?" Mr. Contrey asked the head witch.

Mr. Singer tapped his fingers on the table while his eyes bored into Mira. "It's a slippery slope. It must be a talented witch, and there might be repercussions that the witch would face."

"But the witch could work with the police then, right?" Noah asked.

"How would it look from the outside?" Ms. Vears asked. "The witch would look like a random civilian leading someone around. We know that Della could show up, but she couldn't work on the case closely."

"It would have to be the witch that worked with the police," Mr. Singer said. "A person of strong mind could eventually break the spell. The witch would be the only one able to sense the weakening and do something about it."

"You know all the witches in the area," Mr. Contrey said to Mr. Singer. "Are there any that would work?"

"We should go," Della whispered low enough that only Mira and Emmit could hear. Della could sense the direction things were turning.

Mira didn't bother with a response.

"I have one in mind," Mr. Singer said.

Mira bit her lip. She had meant to give the idea and then let them work it out, but she could tell from the way Mr. Singer was watching her, sizing her up, that he had Mira in mind.

She could do it. She was certain of that. It was her idea and it would work.

"The repercussions are very real, though," Mr. Singer said to Mira.

She knew they would be. Binding was one of those spells that fell in the gray area between good and bad, but it dipped more than a toe in the dark side and there was no way to avoid it.

"But if it helps us find the murdering bastard who did this to our people, isn't it worth it?" Noah half asked, half yelled at Mr. Singer. It was difficult for a werewolf to get over their anger.

He was right. If it helped find a killer, it would be worth it, right? It wasn't the first time that Mira had tripped over the line and fallen into the darker side of magic. The first time, it was addiction that painted her black. If she had risked throwing everything away on selfish reasons, she could risk this.

Finding Sally and Helen's murderer could even balance the scales.

"The karmic backlash could be large if the person bound fought the spell. Only the witch doing the binding can say if it's worth it," Mr. Singer said. It was the first time he had looked away from Mira since she had shared her idea. "And it must be voluntary. Karma can kill. There will be no intimidation and no coercion."

He was adamant, but it surprised Mira that the others took it as a fact. No one disagreed or argued.

"Is there someone on the case you would suggest binding?" Mr. Singer asked Mira.

She thought about Detective Burke and Detective Flint. Detective Flint was out of the question. He didn't like her, and she wasn't fond of him. Having to follow him around and work with him was out of the question.

"There's a new lead," Mira said. "I'd need to find out more about him, but right now, I'd suggest Detective Burke."

"Are we moving forward with this?" Mr. Contrey asked.

Mr. Singer drummed his fingers on the table again.

"Barring any other options," Emmit said, "I think Miss Owens' idea would be ideal if you find a likely candidate."

"Mira?" Mr. Singer asked.

It was one word, but Mira knew what it meant. Was she prepared to make the sacrifice?

Mira nodded.

"We'll explore other possibilities, but you'll hear from me later tonight," Mr. Singer said.

"Let's go." Della didn't bother keeping her voice down this time. She grabbed Mira's arm and pulled her toward the door.

"Mr. Harker," Ms. Vears said. "Would you care to join us for the rest of the meeting?"

"Thank you for the offer," Emmit said, "but I only thought it prudent for Mira to share her interview with you. I'll take my leave."

Della had Mira out the door before Emmit had finished talking, and she didn't stop pulling on her until they were well away from the room.

"Ouch," Mira said, trying to gain back access to her arm. "Why are you pulling on me?"

"You've obviously lost control of your senses," Della snapped. "I'm getting you out of here before you decide to do something else stupid."

Mira sighed, not wanting to fight with her best friend. Once they reached the empty sunroom, Della dropped Mira's arm and rounded on her.

"What were you thinking?" Della asked, her face a contortion of concern and anger.

Mira needed to put an end to this before it started. "If you could help someone find Sally's killer, wouldn't you do whatever you could?"

"It depends on what I had to do to help."

"That's a lie and you know it."

Della blew out a huff of air. "Tyler has the ability to do this. I'm sure there are others."

"They don't have an excuse to be there. I've worked with the police before, so I can work with them again."

The door to the sunroom opened and Della glared at Emmit as he entered.

"I'm sorry if I'm interrupting," Emmit said.

"This is your fault," Della snapped.

Emmit raised an eyebrow at her. It may have made others pause, but Della wasn't the type to stop until she was ready.

"Don't look at me like that," she said. "You had no right to say anything in there."

"I knew that Mira's information would be valuable and her idea would have merit," Emmit said. "It may have solved a difficult issue."

"You do realize that if this murderer is targeting supernaturals, Mira is basically jumping out in front of him, waving a red flag."

Huh. Mira hadn't thought about that.

"I doubt anyone outside the room will be told that this was Mira's idea. Unless you tell them, of course."

"You really are a special kind of stupid," Della said.

Emmit's face hardened.

"Della!" Mira had had enough. Her friend was treating her like a child and Mira wasn't going to stand for it. "It was my decision to make."

"What decision?" Emmit asked, not taking his eyes off Della.

Della crossed her arms and glared. "She's the one doing the binding."

CHAPTER 5

EMMIT'S FACE WENT BLANK. "I hadn't realized." Although his expression didn't give him away, Mira could see that he was thinking furiously. It was his eyes again. People say they are a window to the soul. Maybe that was especially true for Emmit Harker.

"I know that you are a very skilled witch," Emmit said. "But why were you chosen for this particular task?"

"I, um, managed to help on a case when I was in college." Mira really didn't want to go down that road, so she tried to find a way to cut the conversation short. "In the end, I became listed as an expert."

"What is your expertise?" Emmit asked.

"Certain ritualistic aspects of the occult," Mira said.

"How does that help?" Emmit asked.

"It will. Trust me," Mira said.

"And you believe this will make Mira a target?" Emmit asked Della.

"Don't you?" Della asked.

"It is a possibility," Emmit said.

"I'll be working with the police, not on my own," Mira said. "I'll be fine."

Della didn't look convinced, and it was hard to tell what Emmit was thinking.

"It's not as though I'm helpless." Mira sounded more defensive than she would have liked.

"Of course you're not," Emmit said. "Also, Della and I can assist in keeping you safe."

Mira's stomach tightened and it had little to do with the anxiety of the situation. Emmit wanted to help keep her safe. He barely knew her, but he seemed to have faith in her judgment and her skill as a witch.

Who was Emmit?

Della seemed to be thinking along the same lines. "We don't know you."

"Well, you shall have the chance to get to know me," Emmit said. "I was going to ask Mira to assist me with something, so I planned to be around. Now that this situation has arisen, I have twice the reason to keep myself available."

Mira's heart sunk. Emmit did have faith in her skills, but it was because he needed a witch.

"What do you need help with?" Mira asked.

"Never mind that now," Emmit said. "It can wait. I have a feeling the council will be wrapping up soon. Are you staying to talk to Mr. Singer?"

"No way," Mira said. "Not with my mother around. He can call me later."

Della frowned and tapped her foot. "I have to stay. Judge Wilton is here, and I need to speak with her outside of work."

"It's no problem," Mira said.

"It shouldn't take me long, if you want to wait," Della said.

There was no way Della could spend less than an hour talking about something work related, and Mira wasn't in the mood to stick around for that.

"We can catch up later," Mira said.

Della cast an apprehensive look at Emmit.

"You can't be worried yet," Mira said. "I haven't even done anything."

"I have a feeling that we all need to be worried," Della said.

"We should be cautious at least," Emmit said. "I'm sure the council will encourage vigilance."

"Well, I'm getting out of here before they do," Mira said, leaving the sunroom. "I'll see you tomorrow."

Once back among the milling supernaturals, Della disappeared into the crowd. While keeping a close eye on the people around her in an effort to avoid her mother, Mira went straight for the front door.

She made sure not to go too quickly, though. Mira could feel Emmit following. She had no idea what he intended, but she found that she really wanted to know.

Emmit was still behind her when she reached the coatroom. She walked into the long closet and noted that most of the coats were black, which made her blue one stand out. When she shrugged on the coat, she looked at Emmit, who had joined her.

He was watching her.

Mira struggled for what to say. The questions *why are you following me*, *why are you helping me*, and *what do you want from me*, all raced through her head. *Who are you*, was still in the forefront.

Those were such big questions.

"Thank you for your help inside," Mira said.

"I did more harm than good," Emmit said, "and that wasn't my intention."

"What were your intentions?" The question slipped out before she thought it through.

He looked uncomfortable with the question. "I was only hoping to get the chance to talk with you."

"Was it about something particular?" Mira asked.

A small smile appeared. "I have to admit that I was hoping to get to know you better."

"For this project you wanted to ask me about?" Mira asked.

The smile didn't fade. "The project slipped my mind once I got here."

"Oh." Mira had hoped for that answer, but now that she had it, she didn't know what to do with it. The one thing she couldn't do was keep the smile from her face. "Well, it was nice to see you again."

She hadn't realized Emmit had been tense until she saw him relax. Had he been worried about how she would respond?

The noise in the other room picked up.

Mira looked nervously over Emmit's shoulder to see if anyone was heading their way. "I really should go. If my mother finds out I'm the one doing this, she'll keep me here for hours."

"Would the council tell her?" Emmit asked.

"I'm not sure, but if I stay, I'm likely to trip up and say something."

"Would you like me to accompany you home?"

Mira cocked her head and frowned. "That seems presumptuous."

Emmit looked confused for a moment, and then light seemed to dawn and he stiffened again. "I didn't mean—what I meant—" His cheeks turned pink as he shut his mouth to stop the stammering.

Mira became even more enamored with his British accent now that he was tongue-tied, but she raised a questioning eyebrow waiting for him.

"What I should have said," Emmit continued once he had recovered his voice, "was may I see you safely home?"

"There's a lot for me to do tonight," Mira said uncertainly.

Emmit's voice was flat. "I understand."

Something in his voice made Mira nervous, and she discovered that his face was carefully constructed not to give a hint as to what he was thinking. There was once again something telling in his eyes, but she had no idea what they were trying to say.

Movement behind Emmit caught her eye.

"Hey," Tyler said from the doorway, "everything okay?"

"Good evening, Tyler," Emmit said, without looking around. "I was checking to see if Mira wanted me to follow her home to make sure she arrived safely. Would you mind if I borrowed your car?"

Tyler looked questioningly at Mira.

"Actually, I walked," Mira said.

Emmit frowned.

"We can give you a ride, then," Tyler said. "I'm ready to go if you all are."

"That would be wonderful," Emmit said, although he still wore a frown.

"I parked a block away," Tyler said, grabbing a coat. "I'll grab the car."

"Thanks," Mira called to Tyler's already retreating back. She was conscious of the fact that she was alone once again with Emmit and struggled to find something to say. "Did you come with Tyler?"

"No," he said, "but we were planning to meet here and leave together."

Mira nodded. "Do you mind if we wait for him outside? I have a feeling this room is going to get crowded soon."

He didn't say anything, which Mira took as an agreement.

Passing between Emmit and the line of hanging coats, she was close enough to him to feel the warmth radiating from his skin.

His hand wrapped around her arm and she froze. She hadn't seen him move. Since Emmit was a head taller than she was, she had to look up at him. It felt as though he were looking into her, searching for something.

"Yes?" Mira tried not to sound upset, but she had been taken off guard.

"Remember that it is possible someone is targeting the community," Emmit said. "You may have not done anything to make yourself stand out to the killer yet, but that doesn't mean he's not aware of you."

She let out a breath that she hadn't noticed was caught in her throat. "I'll remember."

His words felt foreboding, but Mira shook off the thought. When he didn't release her, she looked pointedly at his hand.

"Sorry," he said, letting go.

Mira swallowed hard and nodded. Now that she was over the initial reaction, her mind focused on how close Emmit was. She could have sworn his eyes were gray before, but they seemed to be turning green now. More importantly, they were looking at her.

"What brought that on?" She asked.

Emmit stepped back. "It was rude. I am sorry."

"It's okay," Mira said, taking a step towards the door. When Emmit didn't move, she glanced at him over her shoulder. "Are you coming?"

He gave her a small smile. "I'll be right behind you."

Mira peeked out in the foyer and found it empty of her mother. John Parnell was making his way to the closet, though.

"Hello, Mira," he said.

"Hi, John," she said, already moving towards the door.

"Be careful out there," he said. "Good evening, Mr. Harker."

Emmit already had his coat and gloves on. For a minute, he looked like he was studying John.

John nodded. "Thank you. You too."

"You…" Emmit started and then stopped.

"Yes," John said, nodding towards Mira. "Sorry for the confusion." Then John blinked and looked around.

Mira tried to hide a grin. "Emmit, this is John Parnell."

"It's a pleasure to meet you," Emmit said stiffly.

John nodded. "Thank you. You too."

"John is a psychic," Mira explained. "He sometimes runs a little ahead of everyone else."

"Yes," John said, nodding towards Mira. "Sorry for the confusion."

John hurriedly stepped around Emmit and disappeared into the coat closet. Emmit looked back and watched the man, his brow furrowed in contemplation.

"Come on," Mira said.

Emmit didn't turn around.

"Emmit," Mira went over to him and reached out to touch his arm, but Emmit turned to her and her hand dropped. She smiled up at him, seeing that he looked perturbed. "Come on."

She led Emmit outside and they walked down the wide but short set of stairs to the drive.

"John gets embarrassed sometimes when he gets ahead of everyone," Mira explained.

"I've met psychics," Emmit said stiffly. "They see flashes of events in the future."

"That's kind of what John does, but it's more like he lives it."

"Is the rest of his family like that?" Emmit asked.

Mira shrugged. "John is the only psychic I know."

"It usually runs in families," Emmit said.

"He's never talked about them."

"How far ahead does he see?"

"Most of the time it's only a minute or so. When he's living it, like he was inside, it can be longer."

Emmit looked back toward the house again, as though he could see John through the walls. "That sounds exhausting."

"It does," Mira said, shoving her hands in her pockets and pulling her coat tighter around her. The night was quiet, but she still strained to hear Tyler's car. "I wonder how far away Tyler parked."

"You look cold," Emmit said.

Mira nearly jumped. He was standing right next to her, yet she hadn't even noticed him move. She shrugged her shoulders in an effort to hide that he had startled her again.

"It's winter," Mira said. "Of course I'm cold."

"Would you like to step back inside?" Emmit asked.

"No," Mira said a little too quickly.

Emmit looked like he was trying to figure something out.

"Sorry," Mira said. "I don't want anyone asking any questions. There are some people that are going to disapprove of my suggestion."

"I see," Emmit said. "Your family?"

"It'll start there, but I doubt it will end there. The others… even if they agree with the suggestion, some of them will disagree with me being the one to do this."

"I'm not sure I understand," Emmit said. "The way Tyler explained it, you are an accomplished witch."

Mira shrugged away the compliment and wondered what it was that Tyler had been saying. "I think they're more afraid that I might be too good at it."

"At binding?"

"It's hard to explain," Mira said.

How do you tell someone that the other witches were afraid she'd slide too far down a dark path? A witch like that could turn on the others. At least, that's what they were afraid of, and the things she did in college hadn't gone unnoticed among the other witches.

Emmit scanned what little he could see of the streets. "I feel as though I am missing something."

"Let's just say that I'd rather wait out here," Mira said, hoping to drop the subject.

"As you wish. We are in luck anyway. Tyler will be here in a moment," Emmit said.

Mira looked for the car, but didn't see anything.

"Are you sure you want to be the one to cast the binding?" Emmit asked.

"If it helps find the killer it'll be worth it," Mira said.

"And if it doesn't help find the one responsible?"

She shrugged. "Then it will have been worth the try."

"Is there anything I can do to assist?" Emmit asked.

"No," Mira said without thinking. When she realized the response had been too rushed, she tried to explain. "Tyler and I usually discuss a spell if one of us gets stuck. I was going to see if he was free sometime."

"As I understand it, he is free tonight. If you'd like us to stay I'm sure Tyler wouldn't mind."

Mira bit her lip and thought that over. She liked Emmit. Considering she didn't know him, she liked him more than she should, but witchcraft is secretive by nature. Outside of covens, you usually won't find a spell swap and unless you were cooking, you wouldn't hear a debate on the best uses of sage. Sharing something with a non-witch was unheard of.

"Unless you and Tyler would rather be alone," Emmit added.

"We usually don't work with—" Mira stopped and glanced at Emmit. His tone of voice had been different, but the man was so hard to read. Did he think that she and Tyler were together in some way outside the craft?

For his part, Emmit was watching the car lights as they turned into the driveway.

Would it hurt to have Emmit around? In this day and age, even witch hunters didn't hunt witches. William and Tyler were actually good friends, something that would never have happened a century ago.

Did she want Emmit around? A witch's spells were like an extension of the witch. Mira knew all too well that if you shared a spell, someone might turn it into something you never intended.

"That was much too forward of me," Emmit said, his tone more formal as Tyler drove up. "I'll ask that Tyler drop me off first."

"No!" Once again, she was too fast and added more emphasis than necessary. She looked down, trying to think of a way to salvage the situation.

"He speaks very highly of you, and I know you wouldn't want to discuss things in front of a stranger."

Before she could make the situation worse, she shifted gears. "Actually, I was thinking that tonight I'd like to go over a few things on my own." She tried not to sound aggravated, but she was. Rubbing her head, she tried to figure out if she was aggravated with herself or Emmit. "It's been a long day."

"Of course it has been," Emmit said, his voice a little softer. "I wasn't even thinking when I made the suggestion." He opened the passenger side door and stood behind it for her to get in.

"Thank you," she said.

"I can't believe this is happening," Tyler started as the car door shut.

"Neither can I," Mira said, watching Emmit. He had paused before moving to the back door of the car, but he was turned away, so Mira couldn't see why.

"I didn't see you at the council's announcement. You or Emmit." Tyler grinned, but it looked uneasy.

"You could say we heard the news early," Mira said.

"The werewolves are pissed," Tyler said as Emmit got into the back seat. "I can see why this was held at Lance's house. Anywhere else and they may not have cared enough to keep themselves under control."

"It is understandable at the loss of one of their clansmen," Emmit said. "What did the council say in their announcement?"

"They said to keep an eye out for each other, don't talk to strangers. You know the gist," Tyler said. "They said to expect the police to ask more questions, but everyone was supposed to keep to the covenants. The only exception would be if a single detective came to them with one of the witches. They didn't say why, but they said they have a plan to *work cooperatively with law enforcement*. Must be a hell of a plan if they are breaking the covenants."

"The Bind spell is to be used on a detective," Emmit said.

Mira was glad he'd stepped in, because she wasn't sure what to say.

"No way," Tyler said, looking angry. "They can't ask someone to do that. It's too dangerous for the witch."

"I wish I had known that earlier," Emmit said.

Tyler glanced at him in the rear-view mirror. "You're not...I mean, can you even..."

"I made the suggestion," Mira said. "I offered to do the spell."

It was another block before Tyler said anything. "Why?"

"To help," Mira said. "I want to know what happened to Sally."

They turned into the driveway in silence, through the shadow of the large house.

"Are you sure you want to do this after—"

"I'm sure," Mira said quickly, interrupting Tyler. She tried to bring a lighter tone to her voice. "I was hoping you'd be free tomorrow sometime to go over a few things."

"Tell me the time and I'll come over," Tyler said, still sounding rather upset.

"Stop by around noon?" Mira suggested.

"I'll be there," he said.

Mira hesitated. "Emmit, would you—"

"I'll walk Mira to her door," Emmit cut in. "These are troubled times."

Feeling anxious, Mira slid out of the car after a quick, "see you tomorrow," to Tyler. Her emotions were tumbling around as they climbed the stairs, and she wasn't sure if she was leery because she was with Emmit, a complete unknown, or because she was with Emmit, a guy she was starting to fall for.

When she neared the landing, she decided to finish what she had tried to say in the car. "So, would you like to come over tomorrow with Tyler?"

"I believe I will be busy at that time," Emmit said.

"Oh," Mira said, and her stomach started to sink.

"I'd like to apologize for earlier. After being questioned by the police and then the council, I should not have suggested anything further for the day."

"It's okay," Mira said.

Emmit nodded. "Have a good evening." He turned to go.

"Wait," Mira said. "You mentioned that you wanted to ask for my help with something."

He seemed to hesitate. "I've already caused you to take up a rather heavy spell. I do not wish to add to your burden."

"It's no burden," Mira said. "I plan on getting this spell over with quickly."

"Please, do not rush on my account," Emmit said.

Mira gave him a nervous look. "The fact that someone else may get killed is what is causing me to rush. It has nothing to do with you."

A flicker of a smile passed over Emmit's face, making him look pleased for the briefest of moments. "If you are certain it wouldn't be a distraction…"

"It won't be," Mira tried to assure him.

"I'm not sure what time I will be free tomorrow evening. It could be late. Perhaps the day after?"

"I'll be up late tomorrow." Mira tried not to beam, but it was difficult. "Until at least twelve."

"Till tomorrow, then," Emmit said.

CHAPTER 6

ONE OF THE FIRST THINGS a witch learns is that magic should never be rushed. A carefully crafted, well-thought-out spell will always be more powerful, last longer, and in the end, will be easier on the witch.

The second thing they learn is how to get around the slow spells.

Well, maybe it wasn't the second thing, but for Mira it hadn't seemed far off. Maybe it was because she had an older sister, but Mira always felt like she was behind and trying to catch up. It wasn't until after college that she realized there was no race.

However, before that realization had taken hold, Mira had taught herself some wonderful tricks. Today, she was using every one of them.

Mira had spent almost an hour on the phone with Mr. Singer the night before. He had listened to her ideas, fed her warnings, and when pressed, he'd agreed with her choice of people to bind.

In her mind, the only option was Ian, but it felt good to have someone approve her decision. Binding someone without them knowing was treading a fine line between what she thought of as good and bad magic.

That was a simplistic description, of course. There was no such thing as good or bad magic.

It was about intention.

What Mira thought of as good magic brought the witch good karma, or at least warded off some of the bad. Bad karma, the kind where the world falls down around you, was the type of repercussion that Mira was facing.

The witch wouldn't end up with only her own bad karma. That was just the start. She paid the price for everyone that the spell affected.

That thought caused Mira's stomach to twist. If something bad happened, she could be taking the hit for every supernatural in the city.

And probably some of the humans, when it came down to it. It was a human that she was spelling, after all.

In theory, Mira had the day off. When you own your own business, however, you quickly discover that time off is some mythical beast that never shows itself.

When she walked into the store and saw Stella Dewley, she was glad she had decided to stop by work first.

"Stella, it's great to see you again."

"Look at you," Stella said, moving over to the counter with Mira. "You look radiant today." Stella always thought that those she liked looked some variation of wonderful and she meant it. Stella loved to compliment her friends.

"Thank you, Stella." Mira beamed a smile. "You're looking great. Have you been feeling better lately?"

"Oh, you know how it is. The cold gives me fits, but it's nothing that your tea won't fix."

"Well, I'll put together your order now." Behind the counter, Mira pulled out a tin. "You wait right here and I'll fix it up for you." Then she disappeared into the back room.

Stella was a wonderful woman, but her arthritis had started to worsen over the past year. Mira took a larger canister off the shelf in the back. The label said Anchor, and that's exactly what it did. It was one of Mira's methods for spelling in a hurry.

There were no shortcuts—Mira made sure of that. Each week, she put together what some people might call a base spell. The time and energy spent on its creation could be used to power other spells.

Mira took a scoop of Anchor and grabbed a much smaller container labeled Relief, sprinkled some of the contents on top of the tea leaves, and then mixed the two together.

Relief would keep Stella's pains at bay. After Mira closed the tin, she drew symbols on it with her finger. The Anchor and Relief would work together to make the spell last at least a week.

Since Stella was human, it was another case of spelling someone without their knowledge. The intent was good, however, so it balanced out, letting Stella make it through another week with less pain.

Mira wrote Relief on a small sticker and put it on the lid of Stella's tin. She was about to enter the main store again, when a note taped to the office door caught her eye. The sticky note on the envelope said, *Ms. Owens, I think someone pushed a letter under the door for you.* She pulled the note and envelope down and saw it had her name across it. She shoved it into her pocket to read later.

After Stella left, Mira went through the store's stock, including the back room, which stored ingredients that would never be sold to your average customer and certainly never find its way into tea. She spoke with her partner, another witch in the community, and then, once she paid for her purchases, slipped out before the store got busy.

Since this was such a tricky spell, she was thankful that Tyler would be meeting with her soon. When things got difficult it was always beneficial to bounce ideas off another witch.

The base of Bind is one of the most complicated spells a witch learns. Binding doesn't change a person's will. They can still want to do something. Binding just prevents them from doing it. It sounds like a simple idea. You see it from witches on TV all the time. A witch binds the person, and then, usually through some comedic results, the person can't do or say whatever the witch wanted to prevent them from doing or saying.

The real spell has layers and layers of craft behind it. In the end, the goal was to prevent Ian from telling anyone that supernaturals exist, or from writing about it, hinting about it, or from giving it away in a game of charades. If you just make the person tongue tied, they'll get around the spell. People are resourceful and cops even more so.

If a witch were to make it too restrictive... well, it was a slippery slope down into the bogs of darker magic. Mira didn't like the idea of bringing another witch in on spell like this, but Tyler's advice was invaluable.

She was going to need help from others as well. Binding Ian and telling him supernaturals exist is one thing. Proving it was altogether different.

When Tyler arrived, they set to work, Tyler reviewing her notes.

"You already have your base spell?" he asked.

"Yeah. I used a heavier version of Anchor," Mira said.

"This looks good," Tyler said as he read. "Why ammonite?"

"So the spell can stretch and grow to encompass what it needs to, but still leave the binding intact."

Tyler nodded and kept reading.

"What do you think a supernatural person may mean to a human?" Mira asked.

"What do you mean?" Tyler asked.

"Well, binding him is one thing. You know humans; they don't detect the subtle currents of energy. If a regular person took a tea with Fortitude added, they would assume the caffeine gave them a pick-me-up. Things like Clarity and Muse are spells that could easily be dismissed by someone thinking they were having a really good day."

"Same with Luck," Tyler added, "but if they took something like Bliss..." He stopped awkwardly.

"They'd think they'd been drugged," Mira said, trying to ease the atmosphere before gathering the currents of worry. Mira knew that Bliss was another story all by itself. She had spent a great deal of college Blissed out. Thinking back, she had probably been coming down from Bliss when Ian had described her as 'busy.'

"What I'm getting at," Mira said, redirecting the conversation, "is that I can use Bind, but the spell isn't going to make him believe me. Being subtle isn't going to work."

"Do you have anything flashy set aside for a rainy day?" Tyler asked.

"Nothing. You?"

"I have a few things that might fit the bill," Tyler said. "This could be fun."

"Just remember that we don't want to scar him or anything. We only need him to believe."

"I'm willing to throw out help in that area." Tyler was wearing an impish grin that made Mira worry about his intentions. "But it's going to take more than a witch."

"Do you think the werewolves…" Mira trailed off, uncomfortable with asking something that big from them.

"Hell yes. You didn't see them last night. If it helps them get closer to the murderer, they are all for it. I'll talk with Noah."

"Thanks," Mira said, starting to feel better about the idea. "I'm going to ask Della to help out as well. I don't think she'll go for it, but it's worth a try."

"The elves?" Tyler suggested.

"They might be convinced, but I'm not sure we'd be able to rein them in if they let loose, though," Mira said.

"Good point. I think we'd need to rule out Lance for the same reason."

"Agreed."

"With three of us, we can cover the convincing part," Tyler said. "I'll call Noah and then we can discuss your lack of lavender."

Mira grinned. "I'll go ahead and call Della as well."

Before Mira picked up her cell phone, it rang. The number was unfamiliar, but she answered.

"Hi, this is Ian."

Mira glanced at clock in the kitchen. "I was expecting a call from you or Detective Flint much earlier."

"That's why I was calling." Ian's voice sounded drained, as though he'd gone without sleep for days. "We haven't received your file yet."

"I bet that made Detective Flint a happy camper."

"Well, there's plenty of other things to do." Ian didn't sound enthusiastic about it. "Anyway, I know you thought I'd have questions this evening, but I won't. You can expect us to see you tomorrow, though."

Mira glanced around the kitchen with all the spell materials strewn about. She really didn't want to wait on this. Another day could mean another person's death.

"There are a few things I need to tell you," Mira said uneasily. It's vague suggestions like that, made to cops, that can get a girl in a lot of trouble.

"About the case?" Ian asked.

"It might be related," Mira said, trying to think of a way to get Ian to come without his partner.

"We can be over in—"

"No," Mira said, inventing quickly. "Look, it might not be related at all, and if it's not, I don't want Detective Flint all bent out of shape over it."

Ian sighed. "I told you, he's not a bad guy once you get to know him."

"Well, until that day, I'd rather talk to someone who isn't going to get all huffy with me."

"Huffy?" For the first time, Mira heard a grin in Ian's voice.

"You know what I mean."

"Okay. Where would you like to meet?"

"At the shop around seven-thirty tonight if you can make it."

"I'll be there."

Mira felt elated when she hung up. She instantly called Della and filled her in as surreptitiously as possible over the phone.

Once Della was recruited, Mira and Tyler finished dickering about the spell. When they finished and Tyler left to meet Della and Noah, Mira went to her store, confident that the plan would work.

The store had closed its doors at six, so when Mira arrived, it was empty, as she had expected.

She had a few minutes to get ready, but that was all she needed. Even with the base spell already created it had taken hours to get the spell ready. In theory, it should have taken days to complete the spell and Mira had put a lot of herself and her own energy into the spell to finish it quickly. She felt worn as a consequence.

Now, all she had to do was cast it. For that, tea was essential. She had it brewing when a knock sounded at the door. Something in her stomach was fluttering as she let Ian in.

"Hi," Ian said as he entered, "I wasn't expecting the store to be closed."

He was wearing jeans and a dress shirt, and she noticed as he walked past that he smelled like a dream. He looked tired, but seeing his handsome face made her smile.

After too long of a pause, Mira realized she was staring at him.

"Um, yeah, uh," she stammered, "we closed at six. Come in and have a seat, I made us some tea."

As Ian settled in, Mira snatched the two tea balls that she had specially prepared and served the tea with some leftover brownies that her partner had set aside for her.

"Thank you," Ian said, "I haven't had a chance to get dinner."

"Anytime," Mira said, pouring the tea.

The potion part of the spell was in both cups. Now all she had to do was activate it, which was the harder part. For this particular spell, he had to say his part. It was a small price to pay for a rush job, especially since the words weren't out of the ordinary, but he also had to mean them.

"It looks like you had a rough day," Mira said.

Ian shrugged. "It wasn't the greatest."

Seeing Ian made Mira second-guess her plan. She'd thought about it from many different angles, but hadn't really considered what having this secret might do to him.

"Do you think you're close to finding out who killed Sally?"

It felt awful leaving Helen's name out, almost as if she didn't matter. If all went well tonight, though, Ian would know how the two were connected.

"We're doing everything we can." He crumbled up a corner of his brownie, keeping his eyes on the food. "Listen, are you really an expert on the occult?"

"Why does that question keep coming up?"

Ian didn't respond.

It had to be something odd they had found out about Helen. "Yes, I'm an expert."

"How does someone become an expert in that?" Ian asked.

"It happened in college." Mira started choosing her words very carefully, knowing this was her chance to get him to say what was required for the spell. "Regarding me as being an expert, the file will tell you everything that Detective Flint will need for the case, but there's more to the story. That's the part that I think you'll have questions about."

"Do you want to give me an idea of what that might be?"

Mira looked him over. He appeared at ease, more so than she was, but he also looked worn down by the case.

Who knows, maybe this would help.

"The problem is," Mira said after her moment of hesitation, "that this doesn't only involve me. Quinton played a part." She tensed, hoping she was picking the right words. "Before I can tell you what happened, everything that happened, even if it doesn't help you with the case, I need you to swear that you won't tell anyone what I'm going to tell you."

"Gabe may need to know," Ian insisted.

"Everything related to the police case I worked is in the file. The rest is... more personal."

He looked at Mira for a few moments, really studying her. "Okay. I promise."

Mira had no idea what he saw in her and she wasn't going to ask. Instead, she smiled. "That's really not enough. Say, 'I swear I won't tell anyone'. "

Ian sighed. "I swear I won't tell anyone."

That had been easier than Mira thought. "How long did you know Quinton before you ran into me?" She watched the spell stretch over him.

Ian shifted uncomfortably in his seat. "About three years."

The spell needed time to sink in, so Mira told him about the past that she had kept hidden for so long. "I met Quinton about six to eight months before that Logic class. We didn't know each other well, but we sort of hung out together. You know?"

"Sure," Ian said, "he mentioned once that you helped him with something."

"Did he seem like he was having difficulties during that time?"

"It's hard to say. Most of the time I think he was happy." Ian looked lost in thought. "Sometimes, I wondered if something might be going on, though."

Mira nodded. "Happy may be an understatement. We were, um," she cleared her throat, "we were taking something called Bliss."

"Drugs?" Ian's face turned stern.

"Something like that. It did exactly as it describes. It makes you happy and you don't care about anything else. There was nothing I gave a damn about for almost nine months." Mira felt her face start to turn red. "Until you came down, of course. Then real life came rushing back and you found you had let your stress and problems pile up. Each time was a little worse, so each time, you wanted more Bliss to make it all go away again."

"I had no idea he was on drugs."

She shook her head. "That's not surprising." Mira checked the spell, seeing that tendrils were sinking in deeper, through the bone, through the soul, but were not yet anchored in place.

"And you helped him?"

"It was the least I could do." Mira looked down at her hands, twisting them together, but she really didn't see them. Her mind was cast back. "Bliss was something that I made."

When Mira chanced a look up, Ian's face had gone rigid.

CHAPTER 7

I

T WAS SOMETHING THAT ALREADY existed," Mira hurried to explain herself, as though that might make it better. "So I made some and... shared with a friend when they were having a hard time. That friend brought another, and then there were more people around."

"One of them being Quinton," Ian said.

Mira shook her head. "I stopped making Bliss after a month or two." She shrugged, still studying her hands. "Actually, I'm not exactly sure how long it was."

"Then how—"

"Someone else stole the... um... recipe. Being away from it was difficult and the group grew larger. I was shut out for a while, but it was always there. Always around. When I started taking it again, Quinton was there."

Ian had his arms crossed and was leaning back in his seat.

"The new stuff was harder to come down from," she continued. "The group was different, too. It was bigger and the person making the stuff, which you'll see in the file, was making all sorts of weird rules people had to follow in order to get some. For him, it wasn't about money—or even the Bliss—it was about the power."

This was harder to talk about than she'd thought it would be. She'd blocked so much of it away for so long that it was difficult to relive, so she fast forwarded a bit to get it over with. The spell was there. Ian was bound and it was time to get down to business.

"When I tried to come off the stuff again, it was noticeable. Not only to those outside the group, but those on the inside weren't happy about it either. I'm not sure who did it, but someone turned me in."

"We didn't see any arrests on file," Ian said, rather stiffly.

"It was covered up. Quinton's mom had a lot of pull, even then. I agreed to get Quinton out and turn everyone else over. If I did that, then the only thing the record would show was me being helpful to the police."

"How did you get Quinton out when you were already out?" Ian asked.

"They wouldn't let me near them until I begged and pleaded and found my way back in. They-" An involuntary shiver ran through Mira. "It was difficult, but once I was there, I was able to draw Quinton away." She clasped her hands together and rested them on the table, stiff, with her muscles clenched tight.

"You make it sound like a cult. You went back into that?"

"It was my fault he was there. It was my fault everyone was there. There's a price to pay for something like that and I paid it." Mira pushed the thought out of her mind. "Anyway, I got him out and testified when it went to court. Quinton wasn't involved with almost everything on file, but you will probably see his name in there somewhere."

Ian was quiet for a while. "How did you get him out?"

His hand covered her clasped hands and she jumped, startled. He carefully drew back, but the soft, concerned look on his face remained and threatened to melt her heart.

Mira felt wrung out. She was done with this. It was time to tell Ian the truth.

She checked the spells tied to Ian and went on. "Bliss was treated as a drug, and it was a drug of sorts, but it was so effective because it was a spell. I got Quinton out because I created another spell to counteract it. Slowly, so it wouldn't be as difficult."

"I don't understand." He looked confused and Mira didn't blame him.

Mira felt like a weight was settling in on her. "I'm not sure if this is making things better or worse for you."

"I'm not sure what it is you're trying to say."

"Supernatural people exist in the world." Mira took a deep breath and barreled on. "I'm a witch. Sally was technically human, but clairvoyant. Helen was a werewolf. They knew each other. We all know each other."

He looked like he was struggling hard with what to say. "I'm still not sure I understand."

"You'll understand in time," Mira said. "It'll take an adjustment, but it's important you know. We decided it was important for you to know. Sally and Helen have this secret in common and you had to know about it."

Ian shook his head and pulled away from Mira. "Look, I'm not exactly sure what this is about, but maybe I should head out for the evening."

This was the hardest part. Any supernatural that has ever told any normal person the truth about themselves faced this challenge. Normally, they'd ease the person into it, but Ian had to know everything all at once. He had a case to solve and the whole community needed him to get to work on it.

"Sure," Mira said, nodding, "I understand. Before you go, though, you should know that I put a Bind spell on you. You will not be able to tell anyone about this unless you know they are supernatural in some way."

"Look, Mira, just stop. Why are you doing this?"

She sighed. "We need you to know the truth."

"Is… this another cult sort of thing? Is that what you're trying to say?"

"No." She looked on him with pity. "I know you don't believe me and that's okay. After tonight, you will."

"Is that a threat?" Ian asked, his entire attitude turning ridged.

It was Mira's turn to look confused. "There's no threat. Remember that. No one is going to hurt you."

"Whatever. Look, I'm out of here."

"Be careful out there tonight," Mira said before he could get to the door. "Call me when you want to talk about it."

"You will definitely be hearing from me and Detective Flint tomorrow," he said curtly and left the store.

Mira slumped back into her chair and stared at nothing. She hated admitting it to herself, but she had hoped that things would go well with Ian. Maybe she shouldn't have gone into everything about Quinton, but she figured it was two birds with one stone. Now she had both pieces of knowledge out there to churn in Ian's mind.

Coming out of her reverie, she texted the others. *He's all yours.*

Mira didn't want to go straight home. After she drove around a few streets of the city, though, she realized she had nowhere else to go. Tyler and Della were both busy, and there was no way she could eat with all the influences of her past deeds floating through her mind. They stuck no matter how hard she pushed them back.

Before she made it home, she received a text from Della. *My part is done. I'm exhausted.*

When Mira parked her car next to the staircase to her apartment, she received another text. This one from Tyler.

I hope this worked. Noah had the grand finale.

Once she was ensconced in her apartment, she couldn't sit still. After giving Alchemy and Oracle as much attention as they deemed appropriate, she started flipping through her mail. She found an envelope in the pile that had only her name on it.

A text distracted her. She looked down and found another note from Tyler. *Noah's done. He's either a believer or too dense to be useful anyway.*

Mira wrote back, *Thanks for your help. We'll know soon.*

Frowning, she turned her attention back to the envelope and opened the note.

You're not wanted in this city. You'll regret it if you stick it out.

The envelope looked familiar, so she went to her coat and then searched the apartment until she found the envelope that had been left for her earlier in the day. Same envelope and paper. She opened it.

Ditch the store and leave the city.

Anger welled up.

Brian Benton did this. She knew it.

That slimy landlord was trying to get her to let go of her lease. Well, it would be a cold day in hell before she walked away. She wadded up the note and tossed it on the table, fuming. She dropped the other beside it.

Alchemy and Oracle watched from a distance as Mira paced the living room. Realizing that she continued to glare at the letters, Mira moved to the kitchen and began straightening things as a distraction. The cats padded to the doorway and watched, tails flicking and eyes bright as their person stalked around the room.

Mira's anger fell to a simmer. It dropped further when Oracle let out a yowl and leapt to the windowsill.

"What's up?" Mira asked.

He hissed and Alchemy joined him, which was rare.

A loud crash came from outside.

Seeing that it was after ten, Mira flipped on the outside lights and went to the deck.

"What the hell?" Mira's brain couldn't make sense of what she was seeing. Ian was there, looking not quite sober, but still on his feet. It appeared that he'd slammed himself into the trashcans beside the garage and crawled back out of it. The mess was everywhere and Ian looked disheveled and pissed.

The most striking part of this situation was Emmit, holding Ian up by the back of his shirt. Somehow, Emmit appeared to be supporting Ian, but at the same time, holding him at arm's length, not wanting the man close to him.

"I believe this person was attempting to call on you in a most inappropriate manner," Emmit said.

Mira went down the stairs to meet the men at the bottom.

"You!" Ian said, pointing at Mira. "This is your fault."

It took her a moment to figure out whom to address. Ian didn't look to be in the best of shape, so she ignored him and focused on Emmit.

"Hi, Emmit. Did Tyler pull you in to help the others tonight?"

"I did not take part in this evening's—presentations," Emmit said.

"This guy is one of those?" Ian looked like he was trying to glare at Emmit, but was having a hard time with Emmit holding him, arm still outstretched. "One of you?" The accusation was evident.

Which only made it easier for Mira to ignore him and talk with Emmit. "It's good to see you."

"You orchestrated this whole thing, Mira. You and your people. You lied and you obstructed justice. Hell, you probably brewed up the spell to murder your own people. That's what you do, isn't it?"

Mira's mouth dropped open and her eyes widened; surprised that he would make that kind of accusation. It hurt more than she would have expected. Why should she care what he thought?

Emmit shook Ian by the collar, still not allowing him to get any closer. "I had reservations about this when I understood that you would be performing the spell."

Mira detected a look of disdain on Emmit's face when looking at Ian. When he looked back up at her, his face was blank. "The others may have had their fun tonight, but it is you that has been placed in front of the line of fire."

Mira could feel a blush start to creep up on hearing Emmit's concern for her. "It's okay. Although you have great timing tonight."

"It's what you started to do in college to Quinton, wasn't it?" Ian accused. "But then you got caught."

Mira closed her eyes and rubbed her forehead. She hadn't expected him to use that against her and never wanted Emmit to hear the story. "Ian, you ass, shut up."

"Stop that," Emmit said, shaking Ian again. "Naturally, I was concerned for your safety. Adversity usually follows when a human is brought into our world. I'm glad I was able to take you up on your invitation this evening."

"I thought he might call or something," Mira said. "I never expected this, though."

"Sadly, retaliation is to be expected when the truth is exposed. One must always be prepared," Emmit said. "Now, what should we do with him?"

"You're one of them," Ian said, looking at Emmit. "Are you going to explode into a monster or do some other bullshit to try to scare me?"

Emmit pulled Ian close enough for Ian to feel Emmit's breath on his face. Emmit looked him square in the eyes, dropping his voice low. "You are wearing my patience thin." His voice was cold and the shadows appeared to grow darker. "I would not do such a thing in front of Mira. If I were to give you a display, it would be in the quiet darkness of your own home." Emmit dropped Ian.

His voice had been so menacing that Mira had taken a step back. The voice didn't even sound like his own. When he turned to her however, his mouth strained a bit when he noticed the extra space between them. "I am terribly sorry to show such a display, when I am already infringing on your time."

Ian was silent, breathing a bit hard, and he was edging away from Emmit toward Mira. Seeing Ian so fearful actually gave her courage.

Emmit was supernatural—one of her people. "I really appreciate you stopping by tonight." Mira stepped closer again to Emmit as Ian backed away. "You've made this whole thing much easier to deal with."

The slightest look of strain melted from Emmit's face. It may have been a trick of the light, but he looked relieved.

"Our friends seemed to have pushed Ian right up to the edge, if not over it," Mira said, dropping her voice in consideration for Ian. "I think I should talk with him."

"Do you believe that is a wise decision in his state?" Emmit asked.

They'd ignored Ian for so long that until he stepped in front of Mira, she hadn't realized that he was placing himself between her and Emmit.

He forced Mira back a bit as he faced off with Emmit. "Stay away from her," Ian said.

Emmit didn't look concerned in the least. "At least now he is giving proper respect to the woman he came to see."

Whatever Emmit had done when he spoke to Ian, it seemed to sober him up. Still, it was easy for Mira to dodge around him.

"Mira, there's something wrong with this guy," Ian said. "Move out of the way."

"You're being such an ass, Ian," Mira snapped. "Don't make yourself look like a bigger idiot than you already have."

Ian continued to glare at Emmit over Mira's shoulder.

"Go upstairs," Mira said, pointing Ian up to her apartment. "You and I need to have a chat."

Ian looked torn, seemingly not certain if he wanted to stay.

"Go," Mira snapped.

He rolled his shoulders, shot Emmit another dark look, and stomped up the stairs.

"Emmit, would you mind sticking around while I talk to him?"

When Mira faced Emmit once again, he seemed to be struggling with something. She wondered if his pride had been hurt when she'd stepped in between him and Ian, but dismissed the idea.

After a few moments, he pulled his face into his emotionless expression while watching Ian. "Forever at your service."

CHAPTER 8

MIRA FORCED IAN THE REST of the way up the stairs and into her apartment. Once she had pushed him into a chair, she got him a glass of water. Emmit gracefully declined an invitation for anything to drink. As they settled into the living room, Alchemy and Oracle joined them. Usually, they would show off for company or demand attention. Tonight, though, they sat down, one on either side of Mira, and watched Emmit. She scratched behind their ears before jumping into the conversation.

Ian was a mixture of pissed off and scared. That would have been a dangerous combination, but there seemed to be a little sadness mixed in, which calmed the issue down considerably.

For a while, he listened. Mira told him about the world that he had seen tonight and a little about the people.

"So you really are a witch." Ian said with a strained smile.

"I am," Mira said.

"And you know everyone?" Ian asked.

Mira could tell his mind was shifting toward the case. "Not everyone, but most of them."

Ian turned inward as he asked questions about people. They were cop questions. It was as though he had a list in his head and was working his way down it.

After about twenty minutes, Mira was beyond tired. "Ian, we can pick this up another time? I know you have tons of questions, but they're going to have to wait."

"I'm trying to catch a killer. I should be hauling you into jail for obstruction charges."

"That would be inadvisable," Emmit said. He'd been quiet through their talk and now his eyes looked pinched together.

"Would it?" Ian asked. He'd apparently heard a challenge in Emmit's voice and he was ready to meet that challenge. "Just what are you?" Again, there was an accusatory tone. "Mira said a lot, but she hasn't shared what you are."

Emmit rose to his feet with Ian shortly behind. They squared off.

"No, no, no!" Mira said, her voice rising. She again moved herself between the two. "Ian." He didn't look down at her, so she put her hand firmly on his chest.

He glanced down and tugged on her arm. "No." He tried to pull her away, but he was being much too gentle to make her budge. "I want to know. You did this for me to investigate, so now I'm investigating."

"Do not lay a finger on her," Emmit said quietly.

Mira glanced at Emmit. His eyes were dark and sucked light in. The air appeared to quiver around him.

Oh yeah, he was pissed.

"Chill out, Emmit," Mira said before facing Ian again. "Ian, I realize that you're new to all this, but you're being incredibly rude. You can't just walk up to someone and ask what are you?"

"Why not?" Ian asked.

"It's *intrusive*," Mira stressed. "Some people do not like others to know what type of supernatural they are."

Ian looked at me. "You don't even know what he is?"

"What he is," Mira said, crossing her arms, "is a friend of mine."

"Oh." Ian rubbed his hands over his face. "This isn't working out. I need to bring Gabe in on this."

"You can't tell him anything," Mira replied.

"He's my partner, so I have to bring him up to speed."

"You do remember how this evening started, don't you?" Mira asked. "Ian, I put a Bind spell on you. You won't be able to tell anyone. Not even Detective Flint."

"Yeah, I heard you earlier. You can say your little chants, but you can't stop me from filling my partner in."

"Little chants?" Mira's face turned crimson.

"Your manners seem to have reached a new low," Emmit said.

Ian rolled his shoulders. "Look, I'm sorry. I'm sorry to come here like this. Sorry for being rude or whatever. I have to go."

Ian left Mira and Emmit standing alone in her apartment.

CHAPTER 9

IRA AND EMMIT REMAINED STANDING, unsure of what to do now that Ian had left. Finally, Mira gestured for Emmit to take a seat.

"I am sorry this task has been placed upon you," Emmit said, sitting down.

"Once he cools off, I think he'll be alright. Better, anyway," Mira said. "Thanks for the help."

"You are welcome. I am happy I was of some assistance to you." Emmit hesitated, looking unsure of himself for the first time Mira had seen.

Emmit's reaction made Mira curious about what he might want, so she came out and asked, "You wanted to ask me something?"

Mira watched, as a part of Emmit appeared to shut down. As though by conscious effort, traces of emotion were chased from his face.

"Before we go into details, I must get your solemn word that you will not discuss the matter with anyone but me. Feel free to deny the request and I will not intrude on you again with the issue."

Mira contemplated the request. The usual day-to-day things she worked on never stretched her witchy abilities. Today, though, she had worked on an intricate spell and found that she'd missed the mental exercise. Emmit's request was intriguing, but

Mira really wanted to know more before making that kind of promise. Witches could do some pretty nasty stuff, and Emmit was practically a stranger.

"Before I can make that type of promise," Mira said, "I have to know more."

A small flash of irritation met Emmit's eyes. It was so brief that Mira thought she might have imagined it.

She dismissed the idea and pressed on. "Am I doing this for your own personal use or for someone else?" It was the nicest way she could think of to ask if he was going to be spelling another person.

"I assure you that it is for my own use and will only be used on myself."

Crimson began to creep up Mira's face. Apparently, Emmit had realized her intentions in the question and answered them fully.

Nevertheless, he hadn't sounded accusatory, which was a relief. That deadpan tone was something she could do without, though. It was as if Emmit had locked himself away for the discussion.

Since it was for his own use, Mira was less hesitant on the issue. She couldn't think of a nice way of asking if he was poisoning himself, but the spell itself would tell her that.

"Whatever it is you ask," she said, "I'll keep it to myself. Although, that doesn't mean I'll agree to do the spell."

Emmit looked at her intently, but his expression was unreadable. "I really must have your sworn word on the matter."

To many races of supernatural, words were important. Critical, even. Words could carry immense strength. Mira spent much more time contemplating his request than most humans would. Words have power and you had to use them carefully.

Mira couldn't think of any reason not to make the promise. If he didn't want her to tell anyone, well, that was his business.

"I swear on my name and my family." It was a shortened version of an old-fashioned promise that supernaturals made to each other. With her previous spell still on her mind, Mira braced herself for some sort of backlash in case the words bound her in some way, much as she had bound Ian, but nothing happened.

Emmit nodded. "Thank you, Mira. Know that I do not take this request lightly."

"So," Mira said, "how can I help you?"

Emmit studied her for a moment. "I am finding myself in need of Balance." It sounded as though he had carefully chosen his words.

Mira frowned. "That's usually something reserved for werewolves."

"Yes, but not exclusively. This type of Balance requires an adjustment. It will be used to balance myself between this world and the Ether."

Had she been standing, Mira would have taken a step back. The mere mention of the Ether was enough to make her want to put distance between herself and Emmit.

"Now you understand my need for secrecy," Emmit said.

"No one has been to the Ether in hundreds of years," Mira said.

"I realize that," Emmit said. "I assure you that I have not tried to travel those paths."

The Ether. The word itself could strike dread in some.

"No one does," Mira said sharply.

Another flash of irritation jumped from Emmit. "And I am not suggesting that anyone tries."

All the warnings that young witches receive when they were young welled up in Mira. She wanted to repeat them all to Emmit. Witches used to travel to the Ethereal Plane, but one day, they had stopped returning. Witches had wanted to unravel the mystery and find their people, but once they started to search the Ether, they too, didn't return. In the end, all spells created to travel to the Ethereal Plane were destroyed, but not before the witches were greatly diminished.

"I can see this was a mistake," Emmit said, rising to his feet.

"Wait." She didn't say it loud or with force, but it still stopped Emmit. She turned inward.

Balance for werewolves was internal, a difficult and rather invasive type of spell. Balancing the Ether with Emmit internally would be tricky. Mira's mind started rolling with the possibilities.

Emmit sat back down and watched Mira impassively.

"Werewolves use Balance monthly, or when they want to suppress the wolf," Mira said, almost as though talking out loud to herself. "It's physical, and some of the materials needed to balance the Ethereal Plane don't mix well with them." In her head, ingredients mingled, canceling each other out, enhancing one another, and even violently reacting.

"I understand that the undertaking of the spell will be difficult," Emmit said. "Especially working alone."

Mira's eyes snapped to Emmit's. "I would not bring Tyler in on something like this even if I hadn't made the promise."

Remaining passive, Emmit only nodded.

"You do realize that this will require blood," Mira said. "Your blood, I mean."

"If you agree to do the spell, I put myself in your hands. Completely."

Balancing between worlds. "This is not a spell that can be rushed," Mira said as she thought about all the things that could go wrong when dealing with such an unknown like the Ether. She had no idea what forces she'd be pushing away, and had no way of knowing if anything would push back.

Then there were the karmic consequences. Would working with the Ether be the darker side of magic?

"I am glad to know that there is a witch in the area with enough skill to attempt such a spell," Emmit said as though making casual conversation.

"How do you know how skilled I am?" Mira asked. "I mean, I'm sure Tyler could do something like this as well."

"You could say that it is part of my nature to see what someone may be capable of," Emmit said. "Tyler might possess the ability, but…"

"What?" Mira prompted when Emmit didn't continue.

"You have a firmness of mind and more importantly, my trust."

Trust. She had no idea what she had done to make him think that he could rely on her so much. This type of spell would take a great deal of trust.

On both sides.

"Do you agree to work the spell?" Emmit asked.

Mira drummed her fingers on the arm of her chair. Witches may have lost the ability to go into the Ether, but they had not lost the knowledge to work with it. They learn the Ether for two reasons. One, to assist supernaturals. For example, many seers go mad from seeing into the Ether. Witches can help them close the Ether away so the seer can keep their sanity. Secondly, it's a part of history and something happened on the other side. So, witches learn and wait.

She was fascinated with the prospect. Maybe too fascinated.

"I need to think about this overnight," Mira said.

"That is understandable." A hint of a smile broke through. "It has been a long day and I don't want you to feel pressured into a decision."

"I appreciate that," Mira said.

"May I call upon you tomorrow?"

"I'll be at the shop all day, until around six thirty. After that, I'll probably be here."

"I shall take my leave," Emmit said, standing. "I appreciate your time in this matter."

Mira walked Emmit to the door, Alchemy and Oracle flanking her on either side. "Good night."

For a moment, Emmit looked like he was going to say something, but then he appeared to stiffen his resolve. He nodded and left.

Alchemy and Oracle remained in place, staring at the door as though they could see Emmit on the other side. Mira tried to pet Alchemy, but he dropped his head, never taking his eyes off the door. Oracle did the same.

The Ether. The thought had Mira's imagination running wild. The spell for Emmit fell into the 'helping supernaturals' column, even though she still had no idea what the Harkers really were.

She didn't make a conscious decision to help with the spell, but the next day, she found herself thinking of exact ingredients. She even jotted down a few cryptic notes for herself before work.

Once at work, Mira let her employees handle customers while she took inventory of what she had in the store. That helped shake out a few more ideas for the spell.

When Brian Benton walked in, Mira sighed and put the spell out of her mind. Dealing with Brian needed her concentration.

"Ms. Owens," Brian said, all smiles. "I am so happy to run into you. Did you review my proposal?"

"I did," Mira said, wondering if vaguely flipping through it counted, "and I'm afraid the answer is still no. I'm sure you'll understand that the lease we have now in this location suits our needs."

Brian's smile was gone instantly. "I am sorry to hear that. You will be hearing from my lawyers shortly."

"Okay," Mira said. "My lawyer will be happy to review what they have to say."

Brian chuckled cruelly. "I'm sure your legal representation is *adequate*."

"I'm sure it is, too," Mira said cheerfully, knowing that Della would point her in the right direction.

He was taken off guard by her quick acceptance of the situation. "You'll be hearing from my attorney."

Mira kept an eye on him as he stormed out of the store.

"That man is more dangerous than you might suspect."

Mira startled at Emmit's voice. He was standing only a few feet from her with his eyes on the door. If he noticed her alarm at his appearance, he didn't show it.

"You startled me," Mira said carefully, looking at his stormy gray eyes. "Don't worry about Brian. He's just upset because I won't let go of my lease."

"He holds your lease?" Emmit asked.

"I helped his dad out when he still owned the property, so I have a really good deal. One that he can't terminate."

Emmit finally took his eyes off the door. "I hope that your day is going well." He sounded stiff and formal, which Mira hadn't expected.

"It's already getting better," Mira said.

Emmit's face broke into a soft smile and Mira's heart began to race. She watched the gray of his eyes melt to green.

They stared at each other, and something else began to stir in Mira. An intense attraction that she hadn't felt in a long time began to bubble up and she relished the feeling.

Mira saw the way he looked at her and knew he had similar thoughts. The air around them was charged with it.

Then Emmit looked away, breaking their contact. She watched him take a deep breath and step back, putting physical distance between them.

But why?

The atmosphere dissolved when he took that step back.

Maybe it was because she hadn't given him an answer.

"I'm sorry to interrupt your work," Emmit said formally.

"It's no trouble," Mira said, trying to stay optimistic.

"I was in the area and thought I would step in for a moment."

"I'm glad you did—" The bell on the front door rang, and by habit, Mira looked up. Ian and Detective Flint were paying her a visit as well. Frowning, Mira turned her attention back to Emmit. "This isn't going to be my day."

"Do not be concerned if your answer is no," Emmit said.

She thought she could detect a note of sadness in his voice, but his face was unreadable.

"What?" Mira asked. Then she shook her head and smiled. "Sorry. That wasn't directed at you."

Emmit followed her gaze to the detectives as they approached.

"Mira, we're sorry to bother you," Ian said, looking and sounding far from sorry. "And I don't know if I caught your name," Ian said to Emmit.

Emmit ignored him and turned back to Mira.

"Would you like for me to stay, Mira?"

"It's better if we talk to Miss Owens in private," Detective Flint said.

Once again, Emmit ignored them and waited for an answer.

"Thank you for the offer," Mira said, keeping her focus on Emmit, "but you don't need to stay."

"Are you certain?" Emmit pressed.

She gave him a weak smile. "No, but I'm sure it's better." She cleared her throat and thought fast. "But the answer to your other question is yes."

"Thank you," Emmit said without hesitation. Once again, he watched the detectives.

"Get in touch with me later?" Mira suggested.

"I'll do that." Emmit appeared to be focusing his attention on Detective Flint. His eyes narrowed in on the man, and for a moment, Mira was worried he was about to say something. Then he nodded curtly at them and stalked past, leaving the air almost cold in his wake.

"There is something wrong with that guy," Ian said to Emmit's back.

Both detectives watched him go.

"Sorry to interrupt," Ian said shortly, once Emmit was out the door.

"Would you like some coffee or tea?" Mira asked.

"Miss Owens," Detective Flint started.

"It's Mira," she interrupted. "We seem to be seeing each other more often, so we should be on a first name basis."

He cleared his throat and started again. "Mira, we'd like to ask you a few questions."

"I can't imagine you'd be here if you didn't." Mira resigned herself to the fact that Detective Flint wasn't going anywhere.

"If you'd rather, we could do this somewhere else," Detective Flint replied.

"Let's go to my office," Mira said. She led the way before anyone could suggest otherwise.

CHAPTER 10

MIRA WOULD BE THE FIRST to admit that her office wasn't meant for three people, but at the moment, she didn't care if the detectives were uncomfortable.

"What can I do for you?" Mira asked, sitting behind her desk and gesturing for the detectives to take a seat.

"We received your file this morning," Detective Flint said.

Mira nodded, but Detective Flint appeared to be waiting for something else.

"Was there a question in there?" Mira asked.

"The FBI has you listed as a consultant on the occult."

She nodded again, but seeing both detectives still watching her, she added, "Yes, I have consulted."

"Why the occult?" Detective Flint asked.

Confused, Mira looked from one man to the other, trying to understand their intentions. "What do you mean, why the occult?"

"Why do you know about it?" Detective Flint asked. "Why are you the expert?"

"I'm the expert because I studied it," Mira said.

Ian rolled his eyes and started looking around the office, obviously aggravated.

"Look, there was a need and I filled it." She tried not to get upset, but was having a hard time. "I studied various religions, historical practices, and case studies while I was in school."

"So," Detective Flint said, "if you wanted to create a scene that looks occult, what would you do?"

Mira rubbed her forehead. "I know I've mentioned this before, but there are a thousand different things that are considered occult. Can you get to the point of what you're looking for?"

Once that was out there, she wished she could take it back. She hadn't intended to be so direct, but the day had already been going on too long, even though it was still morning.

Detective Flint didn't look put out, but he studied her briefly before continuing. "Obviously, we can't use you as an official consultant on this case."

"Do you need one?" Mira asked. "And why not me?"

"I have a picture." Detective Flint appeared to be determined to ignore her questions. "If you were to be used as an expert, tell me what you see here."

He pulled some papers out of an inside coat pocket and handed them over. Mira noticed him give Ian a coarse look before she began studying color-copied photos.

The pictures demanded rapt attention. "What is this?" Mira asked poring over the details.

"You mean you don't know?" Detective Flint asked.

"Honestly?" Mira flipped the page to the next. "This is a huge mishmash of stuff."

"Such as?" Detective Flint prodded.

"Here you have the pentagram," Mira said, concentrating on one photo. "It's a sign of protection, but no one using it for protection would use spray paint to make one. Too many chemicals. There's a smudge stick to cleanse the area of evil, but over here is an upside-down cross and a skull with horns that suggested devil worship."

"You seem to know a lot about it," Ian muttered.

"Look up the term expert," Mira said dismissively without looking up. "Some of this is religious. The other items don't make sense either. The knife looks brass, which is used in many different mythos. It stands for gold, fire, and energy, and it is used for healing and prosperity. But this over here—I can't be certain without seeing its contents, but it looks like a Voodoo curse bag. They just don't mix."

"Anything else?" Detective Flint asked.

Mira looked up and saw that he was scribbling furiously on a notebook, and Ian had his arms crossed and looked like he wished he were anywhere but here.

Ignoring Ian, she flipped the page to another picture. "This looks Wiccan, but—"

"As in witchcraft?" Ian asked.

Mira frowned and looked at him. "It depends on how you are defining witchcraft, I suppose." She shook her head, trying to rid herself of Ian's attitude. "Anyway... some of this stuff doesn't mean anything at all."

"Say that again?" Detective Flint said.

"It's like someone watched a B movie with some sort of fake sacrifice and copied it. Is that blood on the smudge stick?"

"Which is the smudge stick?" Detective Flint asked, leaning forward.

"This could be one," Mira pointed at a bundle that appeared to be herbs. "It was probably meant to be one, anyway. I can't tell what it's made of by a picture, and the knife, it looks like there's blood on the knife. You mentioned sacrifices before. Was there an animal around or something? Santeria still uses animal sacrifice, but so do your older belief systems."

"Who uses human sacrifices?" Detective Flint asked.

"Well, the Aztecs used to..." Mira stopped and stared at Detective Flint. Her veins felt like they were filling with ice.

What was she looking at?

Mira leaned back in her seat. She wanted to ask, but she didn't want an answer. Not really.

"Several different cultures used to use sacrifices," she said in a quieter, less direct tone. "Is this..." She cleared her throat and tried again. "Was this..."

She couldn't get the words out.

"You've been a big help, Miss Owens," Detective Flint said, taking the pictures. He almost sounded remorseful. "If you could, we'd like you to come down to the station for a further interview."

"What?" Mira asked, trying to shake the feeling that she had just seen her friend's blood splashed across a crime scene. She was starting to feel numb.

"Not now," Ian said.

"Right," Detective Flint said. "If you could call and make an appointment, that would work best." He took out a card and slid it over. "Um, thank you for your time."

It was obvious that even he thought it was a bad way to end things.

"Right," Mira said, trying to pull herself together. "Sorry," she forced herself to say. "You caught me off guard."

Detective Flint nodded, looking more confident. "Let us know if you think of anything else."

Mira nodded. "And I'll call later to make that appointment."

"Thank you for your time."

Mira stood as they did and shook Detective Flint's hand. They left the office, Ian following Detective Flint out. Mira dropped down into her chair and took a few deep breaths. If she was going to lose it like this, working with the police wasn't going to work.

Detective Flint and Ian were talking in the kitchen, but she ignored them. There was nothing in there that she was worried about them seeing.

Had she made a mistake volunteering to work with the police?

No, she made it through during college; she would make it through this.

"You okay?" Ian was leaning against the doorframe, watching her. He didn't look happy, but he did show signs of concern.

"Yeah," Mira said, "I wasn't expecting…"

Ian nodded. "There's a lot of that going around."

Mira sighed. "I guess so."

"You were right, you know," Ian said.

Confused Mira tried to think over what she had told Detective Flint. "About the pictures?"

Ian looked behind him to make sure they were alone. "I wasn't able to tell my partner anything about last night."

"It has to be that way," Mira said, trying not to sound like she was pleading to make him understand. "You see that, right?"

"What I see is that it ties my hands in more ways than one."

"I'm sorry about that, but it's the best we could do."

Ian looked back out into the kitchen again. "I have to go and catch up to Gabe, but we need to discuss this further."

"Sure," Mira said, "I can be home after four."

He gave a curt nod and walked out.

Mira put her elbows on her desk and leaned forward to rub her temples. Everything would be so much easier if Ian would accept the situation. Maybe tonight he would.

"Huh," Mira muttered to herself. "Not going to happen."

She went out front and helped with the customers, all the while wondering how to get Ian more comfortable with the idea of the supernatural community.

Without spelling him further.

It wasn't until she received a text from her sister that she came up with an idea, though it was a long shot. She invited her sister to come over after the kids were out of school.

With that handled, she tackled the problem of how she was going to survive the next few days. Bliss was the first thing that popped into her head, but it was easy to dismiss the idea.

Well... easier than it could have been.

Contentment and Comfort were out. People were dying, and Mira did not intend to let the situation feel tranquil. She toyed with the idea of Clarity. That might be better for Ian. Maybe she'd bring it up.

On her way home, she came up with the solution. Fortitude. It wasn't something that she'd made in ages, but it was a simple spell. Everything needed for it could be found in her own kitchen.

At home, she had all the ingredients pulled out when there was a knock at the door. Oracle and Alchemy meowed and excitedly herded Mira to the entrance.

As soon as the door was open, Mira's niece, Megan, burst through and wrapped her arms around Mira's legs.

"Aunt Mira!" she squealed.

Her nephew and sister came in at a more respectable pace.

"Thanks for coming by," Mira said after Megan disentangled herself and ran off. "Come on in. Can I get you anything?"

"What are you making?" Megan called from the other room. "Can I help?"

Robin looked alarmed. "Don't touch anything! We've talked about that!"

"I'm only looking!" Megan called as her mother made a beeline for the kitchen.

"How's it going, Mark?" Mira asked her nephew while she picked up Megan's coat that had been discarded on the floor.

"It's okay," Mark said.

Mira smiled. "That's good." The more excited her niece was, the calmer her nephew seemed to become. Maybe it was an effort to balance things out.

Mark glanced to the kitchen.

"Toss your coat on the couch," Mira said. "Let's see if your mom will let us cook something up."

Mark grinned and hurried into the other room.

Megan had already lost interest in the ingredients on the table. Alchemy and Oracle were demanding attention and she was more than happy to oblige.

"What are you making?" Robin asked, looking carefully over everything.

"Fortitude," Mira said. "Low dose." Catching her sister's eye, Mira silently asked if the kids could help.

Robin gave a slight nod. "What do you guys think? Want to help Aunt Mira with her spell?"

"Yes!" Megan responded, and she jumped up off the floor.

"Yeah," Mark said, much more low-key than his sister.

Megan, concentrating very hard, went to work with a mortar and pestle under her mother's watchful eye.

Mark, being older and calmer, got to read the spell and measure out ingredients.

When the doorbell rang, Mira's heart started to beat faster and she looked at her sister. This had to work, right?

"I've got this," Robin said, waving Mira to the door.

Mira had to take a deep, steadying breath before opening the door. Ian stood on the deck, looking even more disgruntled than he had earlier in the day.

"Do you have—" he started.

"Shhh," Mira cut him off.

Frowning, Ian came inside and remained silent.

"Why don't you join us in the kitchen?" Mira led the way, not waiting for a response.

Ian hesitated at the kitchen entrance.

Mark noticed Ian and took his hands off the ingredients, looking worried.

Megan didn't even seem to notice. "I can't get this pod to crush." She had the most determined look on her face.

"It's okay, Mark," Mira said. "You can talk around Ian."

Mark looked at his mother for confirmation before turning back to what he was doing, giving sideways glances at Ian from time to time.

"Why won't you crush?" Megan said, her face scrunched up.

"Want me to help?" Mira asked.

"No," Megan said, "this is my job. What does this spell do, anyway?"

Mark cast a nervous glance at his sister and then Ian.

"It's called Fortitude," Mira said.

"What's that?" Megan asked.

"It's kind of like courage," Mark said.

"I thought there was a spell for courage," Megan said, looking accusingly at everyone around her.

"This is a certain type of courage," Mira said.

"Oh," Megan said, seemingly satisfied. "It's narrowed the… the…" She struggled and stared at the ceiling.

"Narrowed the focus of the spell," Robin supplied.

"Right." Megan took notice of Ian. "Who are you?"

Mira mentally crossed her fingers but didn't answer, forcing Ian to say something.

"I'm Detective Ian Burke," he said.

"You're a police officer?" Mark asked.

"I am in law enforcement," Ian replied.

Once that was out, Mira's niece and nephew started peppering him with questions. "Do you catch bad guys?"

"Do you carry a gun?"

"Can I see your badge?"

Kids around the country probably asked police officers and detectives the same questions, which is exactly what Mira wanted. She wanted Ian to see that they were normal people. They just happened to also be witches.

Then came the other questions.

"Are you friends with Aunt Mira?" Mark asked.

Ian glanced at Mira. "I am. We went to college together."

"Are you a witch?" Megan asked.

"Megan," Robin's voice warned. "We've talked about this."

"Oh, right." Megan said. "Sorry, Mom. Hey, can you help me crush this?"

Megan forced the mortar and pestle into Ian's hands. He looked at a loss for what to do.

"You just take this and grind the ever loving—"

"Megan!" Robin yelled in that 'we're going to talk about this later' kind of way that all mothers seem to know.

Megan frowned and crossed her arms. "That's what Grandma says."

"Well, you don't," Robin said.

"Fine," Megan said. "I'll show you what to do."

Within the next ten minutes, Ian became a master of the

mortar and pestle and then the kids began to clean up.

"I'm glad you could stop by," Mira said to Robin.

"I'm glad I could help," Robin said. "It was nice to meet you, Ian." Robin shook his hand and spent the next five minutes wrangling the kids, mostly Megan, into their coats. After hugging Mira, Megan hugged Ian's leg and then ran out the door as though embarrassed.

Once Mira had waved them off, she closed the door and looked at her visitor.

"Can I get you anything?" Mira asked.

"No," Ian said. He looked much calmer than he had when he first entered the apartment.

"Good," Mira said, flopping down on a chair, "I'm pooped. I don't know how my sister does it."

"That was a low blow," Ian said.

CHAPTER 11

"WHAT?" MIRA ASKED, FEELING LIKE she'd missed something.

"Gabe's my partner and I couldn't tell him, my captain, or anyone else about last night."

Mira sighed.

"I was waiting until tonight to tell you exactly what I thought about that, but you played the kids card."

Finally getting it, Mira laughed. "And I should have waited until you could vent?"

"It only seemed fair." Ian dropped into a chair. "I'm sorry about last night. No, not sorry, but I should have at least been sober."

"Sober would have been nice, but at least Emmit was there to cool things down."

"I needed to ask you about that," Ian said. "Your niece reminded me when she asked if I was a witch. Why is that something that people don't ask? Why hide it? From each other, I mean."

Mira shrugged. "A few hundred years ago you'd be hard pressed to find any witch that would admit what they were. Even to each other. It wasn't that long ago that we were burned at the stake."

Ian's eyes widened. It was obviously a new insight for him.

"It's been like that throughout history," Mira continued.

"Werewolves were hunted down and slaughtered. Druids were nearly wiped out. Vampires were dragged out into the sun." She thought about that a bit. "Well, okay. The vampires were pretty out of control at the time."

Looking stunned, Ian shook his head. "I never thought about it that way."

"We're people, like anyone else. People get slaughtered for their beliefs and for who they are all the time. The Christians were once hunted, and even in recent history, the Jewish population was decimated by Hitler."

Ian looked thoughtful. "It's a lot to take in."

Mira nodded. "Normally, we wouldn't introduce someone into the community like this, but in this case, we didn't seem to have a lot of options."

"I've been thinking about that too. Do you think it's one of you that's been doing this?"

Mira crossed her arms and looked at him. "It's not us and you, or us against you. Like I said, we're all just people."

"Sorry, but do you think it's a... supernatural?" he asked, taking the name for a spin.

"I'm not sure," Mira said. "I don't know anyone that would kill people. I can't imagine anyone wanting to hurt Sally."

"What can you tell me about Sally and the others?"

"Sally was human, but she was also clairvoyant," Mira said, wishing she had already taken the Fortitude. "She could touch something and know about a person."

"That explains a lot. Sally got on the bad side of a lot of people."

Mira's eyes narrowed. "What do you mean?"

Ian held up a hand. "Can we wait on the case? I'm still having a hard time wrapping my head around all of this. Tell me about who I saw last night. Is that even okay to ask?"

Mira relaxed and smiled. "They agreed to show you what they can do, so it's okay to ask. I think it started with Della. What did you see?"

He grimaced. "Sparks popped out of her eyes and they glowed fiery red. Her hair went all wild, like it was stuck in the wind, but it was a calm night. Also it looked... darker around her, like a storm was gathering over her head."

"Illusions," Mira said. "They take a lot less energy than something physical."

Ian looked puzzled.

"Della is a sorcerer and makes things happen. Magic. They conjure something from nothing. They just need a few symbols to unlock the spell. Sometimes it's real; sometimes it's only an illusion."

"How is that different from a witch? You are a witch, right?" he asked.

"Yes. I'm a witch as well as the rest of my family. As you saw tonight, we make potions and spend time with spells."

"Who was the guy I saw next?" Ian asked.

"That would be Tyler. He's also a witch."

"So he planned what he did ahead of time?"

"Not exactly. He planned specific spells ahead of time, but not for something like this. He could only work with the ones he had available, since there wasn't time to create anything new."

"So sorcerers are more powerful than witches?" Ian asked.

Mira tried not to roll her eyes, reminding herself that he knew nothing. "It's not that simple. Della can make something from nothing, but it saps her strength. She can draw symbols on the air and make one big display, like she did last night, but she pays a price for it. She probably slept half the day away. If she had created something physical, she might have had to sleep for more than a day to regain her strength and she'd be hard pressed to do any more magic for a few days longer. With some prep time, Tyler or I could cast spells and pass out potions for days on end without it affecting us, but we have to have the prep time. The more rushed we are, the more of our own energy we have to throw into the spell and we can't pull something from nothing."

Ian nodded, but he looked like he was having trouble absorbing everything. "And the last person. Was that... who was that?"

"That was Noah. He's a werewolf, as you may have guessed. Helen was also a werewolf."

Ian sighed. "That's another mystery solved."

Mira wasn't sure what he meant but didn't ask. Ian looked like a heavy weight was weighing him down.

"What can you tell me about Dennis Simmons?" Ian asked.

"The name isn't familiar," Mira said.

Ian frowned. "What about Yvonne Childs?"

Mira shook her head.

"Karen Green?"

"The name sounds familiar, but I don't know who she is."

"So the other victims weren't supernatural, um... people?"

"It's hard to say," Mira said. "No one has mentioned them, but that doesn't mean they weren't supernaturals."

"Wouldn't you know?" Ian asked, looking confused again.

"It's a big city and easy to hide in. I can ask around, though—if that's okay, I mean. How does this work? Am I allowed to talk to others about those names?"

Ian sighed. "How am I supposed to know how this works? As far as I can tell, it doesn't."

Mira's temper rose. "Can I ask people if they knew the others or not?"

"Go ahead," Ian said. "Ask your people to be discreet if they can." He sounded dismissive, which only aggravated Mira more.

"I'm pretty sure that supernaturals can keep a secret," Mira said.

Looking tired, Ian rubbed his hands over his face and then leaned back in his chair. "Of course they can."

"We need a plan," Mira said.

"I'm going to have to talk to people. People who knew Sally, Helen, and the others if you find anyone who's familiar with them. Can you get me a list?"

"I can take you around to talk to people," Mira said.

"You're not joining me on this," Ian said.

"Then no one's going to talk to you," Mira said.

"This is obstruction. You know that, right?"

"You throw that around a lot."

"That's because you keep doing it." Ian looked like he was trying to rein in his own temper.

Mira drummed her fingers on the arm of the chair. "Look at this from our point of view. No one knows who you are. They aren't going to talk to you unless someone they know is there." Plus, Mira could check the spell for loopholes, but she wasn't going to mention that.

"How is that going to look?" Ian asked.

"It's going to look like you're taking an expert along to talk with people. It's probably pretty obvious that I'm not fond of your partner," Mira said.

"You seemed to get along today," Ian mumbled.

"He wasn't jumping down my throat today," Mira said.

"Gabe isn't a bad guy. He knows you're keeping things from him, though."

"Doesn't everyone?" Mira asked.

Ian sighed, but didn't say anything.

"Don't you two work apart sometimes?" Mira asked.

"It's the only way to get stuff done," Ian said.

"What's the problem, then?"

"You're…" Ian shook his head. "It's not the way things work."

"I don't know if it will work bringing your partner along with us," Mira said.

"It won't." Ian sounded resigned. "We'll have to make this," he motioned to Mira and himself, "work. Somehow."

The 'somehow' made it less likely to have a stellar start, but Mira didn't want to make things worse by saying it. She began having second thoughts, though. Could the supernaturals have investigated on their own?

Probably not.

"It'll be fine," Ian said. "We can do this."

Mira nodded, but didn't feel any better about the situation.

"So," Ian said after a few moments of silence, "Fortitude?"

"What?" Mira look confused, but she caught up fast. "Oh, yeah."

"What's that one going to do to me?"

"Nothing," Mira said. "You're a detective—trained for this kind of thing. The spell is for me."

"But you're a witch," Ian said.

"Which means what, exactly?"

"I don't know. You're magical or something. What do you have to worry about?"

She gave Ian a pitying look. "Someone is killing off people in my community. I'm only a person, remember?"

"So you cast spells on yourself and not just on other people?"

"Yes," Mira said. "If I can help in some way or if someone asks, then I'll spell other people, but otherwise, I steer clear."

"So spelling me was you helping?" There was a weak smile on his face, and Mira didn't hear any accusation in his tone.

"I hope so," Mira said.

"I'm curious. What keeps a witch or sorcerers, or any other kind of... person... what keeps them from doing whatever they want to people? Why aren't you just forcing people to do what you want? Like confess to the crime?" Ian sounded excited about the last prospect.

"It's complicated, but in short, we can't go around spelling people any way we want. There are consequences to what we do."

Ian looked troubled. "Consequences?"

"Forcing someone to do something they don't want to do can have big repercussions, especially if they fight the spell. Even casting when the person knows it's being cast can have backlash."

"For the person being spelled?"

"No, unless that was the intention of the spell. It doesn't matter what the spelled person does. Whatever happens, if it's because of the spell, the caster pays the price."

"How do you get around it?"

"You don't," Mira said. "You can't."

"But you did something to me and nothing happened."

"Like I said, it's a simplistic explanation. The results aren't immediate. You could say that the universe stores things up. When it's ready, it'll let it go."

Someone knocked on the door, which was a welcome relief to Mira.

"Coming," she called.

"Wait," Ian said as she went to the door.

"It's been a long night," Mira said, hand on the doorknob. "For both of us."

"I want to know what's going to happen." Ian stood up, looking cross again.

Mira shook her head and opened the door. Her bad mood disappeared when she saw Emmit.

"Hi," Mira said, "I'm glad you came by. Come on in."

"Did I arrive at a bad time?" Emmit asked when he spotted Ian.

"Yes," Ian snapped.

"No," Mira said, ignoring Ian.

"Fine," Ian said. "I'll be here at seven a.m. tomorrow. I can bring you to the station to take a look at a few more things. Gabe won't object to that."

Emmit watched, plain faced, while Ian put on his coat.

Ian watched him just as closely. "I'll have to ask you a few questions, too."

"Let me know when and I'll be sure to make myself available," Emmit said, and then a hint of a smile appeared. "Or I can call on you anytime you'd like."

"I'll be sure to let you know," Ian said, glowering. "I'll see you tomorrow, Mira." He hesitated. "Unless you'd like me to stay."

"Like I said, it's been a long day." Mira said. "I'll see you in the morning."

With one last glare at Emmit, Ian left the apartment.

"Forgive my intrusion," Emmit said as soon as Mira had returned from seeing Ian out, "but are you sure you want to work with that man?"

Alchemy and Oracle came out from wherever they had hidden themselves and sat next to Mira.

"Sure. I don't get along well with his partner," Mira said. Oracle dodged the scratch behind the ears that Mira attempted, but Alchemy was more amenable.

"But you get on well with Detective Burke?" Emmit asked.

"You caught him at a bad time. He's trying to learn a lot all at once."

Emmit didn't look convinced.

"Have a seat," Mira said, changing the subject. "Can I get you anything?"

"No, thank you," Emmit said.

Mira noted that he didn't take off his coat when he sat down.

She smiled at him in the hopes of putting him at ease. "I'm glad you came by."

"I will only be here for a short time," Emmit said. "I have another engagement this evening."

Mira couldn't help but wonder what Emmit did at night, or during the day for that matter.

"Well, it's good you stopped by, anyway. I have a few questions for you."

Emmit didn't react, but there was a difference in the atmosphere. It was as though the weight of the air began to bear down on the room.

"I will answer if I can," Emmit said.

Mira took a deep breath, because it felt as though something sat on her chest. "First off, are you allergic to anything?"

"You are asking about allergies?" Emmit asked, sounding as though he were unconvinced.

"Yes," Mira said. "Some supernaturals are very sensitive to certain ingredients or even specific aspects of spells. I don't want to make you sick."

"That is... thoughtful," Emmit said carefully. "I have no known allergies."

"Okay. Is there anything regarding your... nature... that I may need to know about ahead of time?"

Oracle issued a low growl that rumbled up and out.

Mira kept an eye on the cat, but continued when Emmit didn't say anything. "For example, I wouldn't do a spell that strictly used the energy of fire with Noah around. It might cause more agitation than he can handle."

"I can't say anyone has asked me that type of question before," Emmit said.

When he didn't add anything else and Oracle had gone quiet, Mira felt the need to fill the silence. "I think people are fascinated by the Harker name. It could be that they don't feel comfortable asking."

"I'm not sure fascinated is the right word," Emmit mused.

Mira grinned. "Maybe not."

"Yet, you don't seem to mind requesting details," Emmit said. "And last night you told me to 'chill out,' I think was the phrase."

Mira couldn't help but laugh. There was something about his tone that she couldn't place, but hearing him say chill out in his distinct British accent was something she'd remember for a long time to come.

"I probably wouldn't have asked it quite like that if not for the spell," Mira said. "But I'd like to think that I would find this out on my own as we get to know each other."

"Perhaps," Emmit said.

"You don't think so?" Mira asked, puzzled by his response.

"It's not in my... nature, as you say, to let people get to know me."

"Well," Mira said, trying not to feel rejected, "this will be a new experience for you, then."

"We haven't discussed what you want in return for this endeavor," Emmit said.

"What do you mean?" Mira asked.

"Remuneration," Emmit said. "Payment."

"Oh. Of course," Mira said, feeling like she was slow on the uptake. "I don't know the cost of materials yet. I'll let you know when I have a better idea of what the spell will be."

"And your time?" Emmit asked.

"I don't charge friends for spells."

"This is a big undertaking, and we've only known each other a short time. I really must insist—"

"I don't charge friends for spells," Mira said, more adamant. She winced at her own tone and tried to lighten it. "It's not like I've ever charged Tyler for a spell, and he's never charged me. It's not the way things are done."

"I thought you and Tyler were... very close," Emmit said, using that same careful tone.

"Tyler and I aren't seeing each other, if that's what you're suggesting. We're friends."

The heavy atmosphere started to lift, but Mira still found it hard to breathe. It took her a moment to realize it was because she was holding her breath, waiting for a response from Emmit.

"Is your spell with Detective Burke working well?" Emmit asked, changing the subject.

Mira let out the breath. "The spell has settled in, but as you can tell, he isn't too happy about it."

"If you find yourself in need of assistance with him, please call on me."

"Thank you. I'm sure he'll come around."

"Do you have protection of some sort?" Emmit asked.

Mira blinked, wondering how she should take the question. She was pretty sure Emmit's thoughts weren't surging toward the bedroom.

Although, she most likely wouldn't mind if his thoughts wandered in that direction at some point.

"To protect me from Ian?" she ventured.

"If necessary. There is, in fact, a killer in our midst."

"Oh," An odd sadness fluttered by when she realized the direction he was thinking. "I have a ward."

"That you created?"

"No. It was created for me." Mira wasn't sure how much Emmit really knew about wards, but the best ones were created by someone else that wanted to keep you safe.

"The fact that you will be working with the police is bound to attract attention. If possible, I think that you should wear your ward for the duration."

"That's not a bad idea. I'll get it out tonight."

Emmit seemed satisfied. "I really must be going."

"Will I see you tomorrow?" Mira asked.

"I would love to, but Tyler and I have some business to attend to tomorrow."

"The day after?"

Emmit gave her a small smile. "I will ensure that I'm available."

CHAPTER 12

MIRA WASN'T SURE IF IAN was trying to make things difficult on her by picking her up at seven am, but it looked like he was only hurting himself. Usually she opened the store sometime before seven, and she was relieved to hand off that responsibility to a trusted employee.

Aside from a few yawns and a begrudging 'good morning,' Ian didn't have much to say on the way to the office. Once there, his partner proved to be a morning person, much like Mira.

Ian and Detective Flint had a small conference room set up with files to go through. This morning, however, Mira was mentally prepared to go through the photos. She studied the pictures she had already reviewed and added more detail, picking up where she left off last time.

The next set of pictures showed a scene covered in graffiti of strange symbols. It took Mira a while to wade through, but she pointed out the discrepancies in what she saw. She recognized some of the Germanic runes and Druidic runes, at least enough to discern their origin. She had no idea what any of them meant. There were Celtic symbols thrown in the mix, along with other markings. One or two symbols she thought looked like Native American pictographs.

Detective Flint was being personable to the point that Mira was asked to use his name, Gabriel. Not Gabe, like Ian used, but it was a step in the right direction. He was excited that they had a direction to turn to, even though they had more research ahead of them.

Once Ian was fully awake, he took notes and asked questions right alongside of his partner.

The third set of pictures was truly strange.

"It's like they were trying to be eldritch, but had no real knowledge of the occult."

"They have the spirit board and a crystal ball," Gabriel said.

"Exactly, it's like something a teenager would throw together at a slumber party. The spirit board is store bought and the crystal ball looks like it's glass."

"Aren't they usually glass?" Ian asked.

"If they needed something that large, glass would be the least expensive. Someone who uses this stuff regularly would prefer to spend the same amount on something smaller, but made out of crystal. Depending on the vein of occult belief a person follows, they may even prefer something that isn't completely clear."

"What's the difference?" Gabriel asked.

"Something about the cracks confusing spirits." Mira rubbed her temples and studied the pictures further. "A crystal ball that large would be expensive. Was there a bag or wrapping for the tarot cards?"

"There was a velvet table cloth, but it looked way too large for a simple deck of cards," Gabriel said.

They discussed the scene a little longer before turning to a much simpler set of pictures.

"What is this?" Mira asked.

"There were only a few items that appeared significant. These pictures were taken here, not from a crime scene," Detective Flint said.

That didn't add up for Mira. "You didn't get pictures of the scene?"

"We do have pictures of the scene," Gabriel said. He glanced at Ian before continuing. "But these are what you'll work with."

"Are you sure you would know everything that could be important?" Mira asked.

"No," Gabriel said.

"Just work from these for now," Ian said.

"Okay. You have a stick, a stack of bullets, and a cross, in addition to what looks a glass bottle half filled with clear liquid. I don't think there's anything here that you all can't guess for yourselves."

"The bullets are silver and the liquid is water. Medical-grade water, but it's still only water," Ian said.

"And I think we'd consider the stick as a stake," Gabriel said. "As in, a stake through the heart will kill a vampire."

"A stake in the heart would kill almost anything," Mira muttered.

"Almost?" Ian said, looking quizzical.

Mira flashed a glare in his direction before turning back to the pictures. "Are the bullets really silver?"

"They are," Gabriel said.

"Where do you even get something like that?" Mira asked. *And why?* Mira kept that thought to herself. Werewolves don't have an issue with silver specifically. Everyone in the supernatural community knew that, unless they lived under a rock. A silver bullet was like the wooden stake—it would kill just about anyone.

"The lab believes they were homemade," Gabriel said.

"So whoever did this had someone make them?" Mira asked, staring at the close up of a bullet

"If the perp hired someone to make them, he didn't hire a professional," Ian said. "According to the lab, they were poorly made. They'd fire, but not well."

"I don't know what that means," Mira said, rubbing her temples again.

Ian gave quick overview of muzzle flash burns and bullet impacts. He also mentioned the fact that silver bullets were less accurate, even if they were well made, which meant to hit someone in the heart, the killer would have to be close.

"Did they teach you about silver bullets in your Criminal Justice courses?" Mira asked.

Ian blushed, "Ah, no. Actually, it came from an episode of MythBusters. Gabriel brought up a clip on his phone."

"MythBusters? Who knew," Mira said, dropping the picture.

"Is there anything else you can tell us from these items?" Gabriel asked.

You mean, like the fact that it's all fake? Instead, Mira said, "There's nothing else I can tell you."

"You're sure?" Gabriel asked.

"I'm sure," Mira said.

"Nothing about the bullets?" Gabriel asked, focusing hard on Mira.

"Nope." Mira tried to hide her irritation.

Gabriel began to glare. "The stake?"

"No." She vaguely wondered what type of wood it was made of, but it didn't really matter. She wondered briefly if she should give Lance a heads up.

"The water?" Gabriel's agitation was rising.

"I assume you were supposed to think it's holy water," Mira said.

"There's nothing else you know about any of these items?" Gabriel asked again.

Mira rubbed her temples. There was so much she wanted to say, or even to yell, but she held her tongue.

"Why don't we take a break?" Ian suggested.

"I think we've done all we can, anyway." Gabriel stood. "Thank you for your help in this matter." Each word was stilted, as though he were reading the words and having a hard time with them.

Mira was glad when he left the room.

"He's under a lot of stress," Ian said.

"So are you." Mira shook her head, deciding she didn't want to have that conversation. "What is the plan for the day?"

"Wait here," Ian said, "let me talk with Gabe."

Mira was just starting to get comfortable again when Ian returned.

"Let's go," he said.

"What about your partner?" Mira asked, while following Ian back out to his car.

"He's going to run down a few leads on his own. I let him know that you offered to introduce me to other subject matter experts."

Mira grinned. "Is that what we're calling it?"

"For now."

Once they were safely ensconced in Ian's car, Mira felt free to talk a little more openly.

"I've never done anything like this," Ian said, "obviously. Who am I meeting today?"

"Well, Sally was human, so she was close to other humans. I thought we'd start there," Mira said. She gave Ian an address for their first stop.

"I thought she was a supernatural," Ian said.

"She was, but she was also human."

Ian looked uncomfortable. "You're saying that you're not human?"

"It's more complicated than human or not. Some humans, like Sally and some of the other people we'll meet today, have abilities. As I mentioned, Sally was clairvoyant. There aren't races of people that are clairvoyants. It's a trait."

"So, as a witch, you're human, but a different race?"

"Again, it's not as easy as that." Mira struggled with a way to explain things to Ian. "It's almost like we're on a different wave length. Witches and humans look alike, but the energy around us is different."

"I think I understand," Ian said, looking as confused as ever.

"It'll become clearer with time," Mira suggested, trying to sound more confident than she felt.

"Who are we seeing first?"

"I thought we'd start with the people who knew Sally best. Barney is first on the list. He's a seer."

"Should I know what that is?" Ian asked after a few moments.

"Seers can stare into the veil between the Ether and our world. From there, they pull out the future."

Ian sighed. "The Ether?" he asked.

"It's not important," Mira replied, trying to pull back the flow of information. "But you often see seers staring off into space. When they do that, they're looking into the future."

"They see the actual future?"

Mira shrugged. "They see *a* future. Most seers go off their rockers or need medication to survive. From what I understand, they see what might happen. They aren't always right, and they don't always know when or where the visions are supposed to take place. Mom really knows more about it than me. She had a friend when she was younger that was a seer."

"So they see things that may or may not come true, either here or somewhere else? That sounds—" Ian broke off, taking a moment to pick his words. "It's awful to say, but it sounds like he's schizophrenic."

Mira nodded in agreement. "Barney stays at home mostly. I'm not sure what he does for a living. He may be on disability or something."

"Can he tell which visions will definitely happen, and which are only probable?" Ian asked.

"I think you need an Oracle for that," Mira said. "And as far as I know, we don't have any."

"Okay," Ian said, "Barney knew Sally, but did he know any of the others?"

"I'm sure he knew Helen, at least in passing. I'm not sure about the others, since I don't know them myself."

"How do I know that you aren't handpicking people for me to meet?" Ian asked.

Mira hadn't expected that change in thought, so it took her a moment to answer. "I am. I'm introducing you to the ones that Sally knew. Starting with the humans."

"How do I know that you're not hiding someone from me?" Ian said.

"We want to find out who did this," Mira said. "That's the whole reason you were brought in, so you could find out who did this. We aren't detectives."

"Okay. Fair enough. Since you aren't a detective, though, how do you know you're taking me to the right places?"

"I'm hoping you can find that out by talking to people. Isn't that how you normally do things?"

"Yes, but there's too much here that I don't know. What are the politics like? Who hates who? How do you all know each other? What goes on in your lives that I, as a normal human, wouldn't know about or guess?"

"I see your point," Mira said. "I'll answer what questions I can."

"If you don't mind, can you also let me know if I'm doing anything wrong? Discreetly, that is. There are questions I'm going to have to ask, even if it's considered bad mannered or whatever."

Mira grinned. "No problem."

Ian pulled up to an apartment complex. The street looked like one they wouldn't want to drive down at night. They were at the edge of the city where it began to spill out into suburbs.

"There's one more thing," Ian said.

He turned off the car and Mira waited, expectantly.

"Yes?" she said.

"There are things you're going to learn about Sally."

Cold was already starting to spread through the car now that it wasn't pumping out heat.

"Okay," Mira said carefully.

"The others, too, but Sally was your friend." Ian frowned and looked around the neighborhood. "There are things about her that I don't think you know. That I *hope* you didn't know and keep from us."

"You're making me nervous," Mira said. "I'm sure Sally wasn't perfect, but I'm also sure that whatever she did couldn't have been too bad."

Ian said nothing.

An unsettled feeling began to rise up in Mira. "What—"

"Tell me what I should expect from Barney," Ian said.

Mira pursed her lips together. "Just go slow with him and let me introduce you." She wondered if she should push to find out about Sally, but did she really want to know?

Maybe it was better to remember her the way Mira had known her.

She got out of the car and waited for Ian to do the same. Putting her hand to her chest, she felt the metal of the pentagram necklace she was wearing. It was lying against her skin, close to her heart, to make it more affective.

Ian looked around, eyeing the windows suspiciously before combing the landscape. It's true it wasn't the best neighborhood, but Mira had no idea what it was Ian had expected to see.

Inside the building, their eyes had to adjust to the dimmer light. Smells lingered in the communal hallway. The patchouli scent was thick enough that it almost covered the scent of rotten eggs and... coffee?

An odd mixture, but then, you get that in some buildings.

Mira led the way and knocked on Barney's door.

There was no answer. Knocking hard a second time, she heard movement inside.

Ian moved to knock, but Mira held her finger up, silently asking him to wait. After almost a minute, she knocked again.

"Barney, it's Mira," she called. "Mira Owens."

Someone muttered behind the closed door, but it was just low enough that even if Mira strained, she couldn't quite make out the words.

"I've brought someone with me," Mira said once the locks started clicking.

The door opened a few inches before a chain caught it. Barney looked out, and then closed the door again and slid off the chain.

When you think seer, you think little old man, but Barney was almost the exact opposite. He was tall—more than a head taller than Mira and a few inches taller than Ian was—and skinny.

The interesting part was that, although he was around thirty, he looked like he was in his fifties.

There's a reason people think seers are old men. They age fast. They live the average human life, barring any accidents, but they reach their wise old ages early and stay there.

"Knew he'd want to start with me," Barney said. "Come on into the living room."

"I didn't see you the other night," Mira said. "I was worried you wouldn't know."

"John filled me in and everyone always wants to see the seer first." He didn't seem put off by their presence. Instead, he stood tall and sounded proud. "They want to know what we know and see what we see."

The entire apartment was neat and clean.

"This is Detective Burke," Mira said. "He'd like to ask you a few things."

Ian did his cop thing and asked a bunch of questions. First, about Sally, although he said nothing that Mira didn't already know, and then about the others.

"I knew Helen, of course," Barney said. "Everyone knew Helen and Sally. And Karen, well, it's been a long time since I've seen her."

"You knew her?" Mira asked.

"She moved to the city years ago," Barney said. "Caught wind of us and joined us one night."

"Us?" Ian asked.

"The community," Barney said. "She came to a gathering, not a full-blown conclave mind, but a gathering. She left early and didn't come back."

"Conclave?" Ian asked.

"I'll explain the terminology later," Mira whispered. "I don't remember her," she said to Barney. "Why did she leave early?"

"She was older," Barney said. "Lived a bit too much in the past, I think. She didn't take well to some of the others that were around."

"Any of them in particular?" Ian asked.

"Well, there's Lance, of course. Most people have an issue with him, at least at first. Karen was a banshee, though. We have a lot of witches in the area, and witches and banshees go together like fire and water."

"A banshee? What do banshees do?"

Barney frowned and looked at Mira.

"Wrong question," Mira said under her breath.

Ian looked uncomfortable.

Mira, worried he was going to ask the same question in a different way, asked a few questions of her own. "Have you seen Karen since then?" Remembering who she was talking to, she added, "either physically or otherwise?"

"No," Barney said.

Mira was about to ask something else, when Barney's eyes appeared to become unfocused. Beside her, Ian shifted and started to say something. Mira put her hand on his knee, gripping slightly, cutting off what he was about to say.

Being a witch this close to Barney, Mira could feel a cool wisp of the Ether as it pooled around him. She imagined movement in the Ether—witches from the past that hadn't come back. She shivered, and then relaxed her hand when the air began to stir and the ethereal atmosphere evaporated.

Then she noticed her hand, still on Ian's knee, and drew away. She could feel her face turn red and resolutely did not look at Ian.

Although he was back in the here and now, Barney looked thoughtful.

Mira cleared her throat.

"Sorry," Barney said, focusing in on them again, "you were saying?"

"The other names weren't familiar to you?" Mira asked.

"No," Barney said, and then he hesitated.

"You're certain?" Mira asked. "It looked like you remembered something."

"I'm certain, but…" Barney glanced at Ian, who was watching the exchange. "It's not likely, but I may have written something down."

"A journal?" Mira asked. There was no way she'd mention her journal to others and was surprised that anyone else would.

"Come with me," Barney said.

Mira stood up, but Ian lingered behind, hesitant.

"Both of you are welcome," Barney said without turning around.

CHAPTER 13

BARNEY LED MIRA AND IAN into a small bedroom that had been converted into an office. Stacks of cardboard filing boxes lined the walls. Barney took a notebook off his desk and flipped through it, taking a moment to jot down a note. He then opened a box and began inspecting others.

Mira peeked into the box he'd opened and saw it was filled with the notebooks. The notebooks were all the same brand, color, and type.

"I keep it all," Barney said, while digging through the box and inspecting notebooks. "The past ten years are in this room."

"That's a lot of journaling," Mira said.

"When I was a kid, my parents took me to a doctor. He wasn't sure what to do with me, but said it would be a good idea to write it all out. The visions, I mean. Get them out of my head. He was right, too. Between this, and now that I'm older, the occasional spelled tea from Tyler or your shop, I get by."

Ian looked at Mira, and she could see the questions starting to swim around his mind. When she was sure Barney wasn't looking at them, she shook her head slightly, hoping to cut off any questions in front of Barney.

"Take a look if you'd like," Barney said without looking up. He waved to the other boxes in the room. "Try not to mix them up."

Mira lifted the cardboard lid off one of the boxes, hesitant to jump in and look through Barney's personal journals. There were markings on the lid. She lifted out one of the notebooks and found similar markings on the cover. They were a mixture of letters, numbers, and symbols.

"What are these?" Ian asked, motioning to the lid where he examined similar writing.

"Filing system." Barney said. "Only I know the code. I'm not stingy with what I know, though. Some seers hide it, but not me. I put it out there."

Barney dropped a notebook and opened up his laptop. He went straight to a site called *Postsfromtheether.com*. Mira and Ian looked over his shoulder while he scrolled through some recent entries.

Barney was a blogger.

"I don't put everything up." Barney said. "I learned early on that no one wants to hear that you stared at a light bulb for twenty minutes before it went out. Only big things go up here."

Twenty minutes with the Ether pulled around him sounded like a nightmare to a witch.

Barney was kind of a recluse, a very nice one, but solitary all the same. Even at meetings, he seemed distant. Because of that, Mira had never expected so much computer aptitude. She was impressed.

"How far back do you want to look?" Barney asked, moving around his boxes.

Ian took a moment to respond. "I'm not quite sure how this works. What you do, I mean. Knowing anything you may have, uh, seen from the past three months or so, would be a good place to start."

"There are four or five notebooks that may be of use, then," Barney said, handing two to Ian before moving to another box.

Mira mused that, however he filed his notebooks, they weren't necessarily in chronological order.

"That's a lot of notebooks," Ian said, flipping through a few pages of Barney's neat handwriting. "Would it be possible to take them with me?"

Looking unsettled, Barney began to stammer. "I, um, I, uh, I don't know."

Ian glanced at Mira with a worried look in his eye, unsure if he'd asked the wrong thing again.

"It wouldn't be for long," Mira jumped in. "Maybe Ian could get them copied or something?"

"I could get them back to you tomorrow," Ian added.

"Tomorrow?" Barney looked a little calmer. "Tomorrow. Right. That— that might be okay. Tomorrow morning?"

"If the copies aren't done, I'll bring them back anyway," Ian said.

Mira hoped that Ian was being truthful. Did cops lie to get what they needed? For Barney's sake, she hoped he would have them back.

"Let me see." Barney went to the notebook on his desk and flipped to a blank page. He made a few notes before looking the notebook over, checking his filing marks, and setting the book aside.

Barney moved to the closet and opened it. Inside were other boxes, different from the ones that littered the room. When Mira got a look inside, she could see that they were filled with the same notebook.

There must have been ten more boxes of empty journals hidden away inside.

Her interest in the unused books didn't go unnoticed.

"They discontinued the first notebooks I used," Barney said. "I couldn't let that happen again."

"It looks like you have enough to last a long while, then," Mira said, some nervousness leaking into her voice.

"Definitely," Barney said. "My parents keep the rest."

Mira only nodded and hoped even more intensely that Ian would have the notebooks back when he said they would.

Barney set up his new notebook, and once he was satisfied, he handed that one, along with four others, over to Ian.

Feeling the cool atmosphere of the Ether return, Mira took a step outside the room and watched Barney once again gaze into the unknown. Ian watched her, but stayed where he was, looking unsure if he should move or not. This time, it lasted longer and the pool of Ether was thicker. Mira ended up stepping farther back, sensing unseen movement.

"Excuse me," Barney said when he focused back in on the present. He blinked and looked around. "Is there anything else I can do for you?"

"You've been a great help," Ian said. "I'll be back tomorrow morning."

"Thank you," Barney said. "I'll see you out."

"Thank you for everything, Barney," Mira said. "Is there... do you have everything you need? I can bring more tea by if you'd like."

Barney beamed. "Tyler dropped some off this morning. If he hadn't been in such a rush, you would have seen him leaving."

"Well, let either of us know when you want more," Mira said.

Mira and Ian bundled up and thanked Barney again.

Once outside, Mira was thankful for the naturally cold air. It might scour the skin when the wind blows, but it also stripped away lingering sensations of the Ether.

Seeing Barney had given her an idea, though. The tea that Barney sometimes used blocked a seer's power. Since that involved the Ether, it might help her with the balance spell for Emmit. Inspiration and ideas jumbled together in her head to the point that she hadn't heard Ian.

"What?" Mira asked.

He looked at her, and she could see the concern, but he appeared to be struggling with it.

Looking away, Ian flipped through one of the notebooks. "These might help."

"Maybe," Mira said. She'd have to think about the spell later. "Barney said he didn't remember anything, though."

"Yes, but you mentioned that he doesn't always know what it is he's seeing." Ian shrugged and handed the notebooks over to

Mira. "They aren't real evidence. We'll take them down to Copy Shop and get copies made."

"A store? Don't you have a copy machine at the station?"

Ian blushed a bit. "There's always someone getting something copied. Plus, I don't think I want other officers reading through this. Word might get around."

Mira wasn't certain if it was the binding spell, or if Ian was uncomfortable about something strange getting around the office. Peering close at Ian as he drove across town, she saw that the spell had settled in quite well, but some areas still existed where Ian rebelled. Hopefully he wouldn't push too hard. The harder the struggle, the worse the results could be. Still, she wasn't too concerned, yet. In a few days, if the spell weren't permanent, then she would worry.

"About the question with the banshee," Ian said, "where did I go wrong?"

It took her a moment to remember. "You asked him what a banshee does."

"And?" Ian asked.

"Well, what do humans do?"

"What do you mean?"

"What skills or traits do they have?" Mira asked, trying to press the point.

"That's different," Ian said. "We don't have anything we're known for. There's nothing collectively as a group that sets us apart."

"Really? Barney's a seer. He's human."

"But that's not a common trait."

"For supernaturals, it's kind of the same way. If you look at a book, it will say something about a banshee's scream. At least I think that's a banshee. Anyway, there may have been one or two banshees in history that screamed and killed someone. Unless you are a banshee, you can't really say what it is that they do."

Ian appeared to mull that around a bit, but wasn't ready to give up. "What about witches? You're known for spells, right? That's a trait you all have."

"No," Mira said. "For you to say that is an assumption. Not every witch does magic. In fact, there are some witches that couldn't do magic if they wanted to."

"Werewolves?" Ian said.

"They don't all shift. One person is different from another, same as humans."

"Wouldn't a non-shifting werewolf be just a human?" Ian looked confused.

"No. It's not turning into a wolf that makes them a werewolf. Yes, most of them change, but not all."

"But if most of them do, couldn't you just say that most of them do? I mean, it's a pretty defining trait."

"Supernaturals learned long ago not to lump everyone together. It's why so many people got killed in the past. When people hunted werewolves, a lot of wolves and humans died as well. Same with witches. Most of the people killed weren't supernaturals."

"Okay, how about a seer? You could tell me what a seer does, right?"

"Yes, but only because they are one subset of human. And only because witches work with seers a lot."

"I was going to ask about that, too. The tea?"

"Seers see what they do by peering into the Ether. Witches can help minimize that—give them a break from the visions."

"He seems to do okay with them," Ian said, nodding toward the notebooks. "He even shares them."

"Would you want to see something else all the time? Not knowing when it would come or how long it would stay? Then not knowing if it was true or not? It's enough to drive a person crazy."

"Good point," Ian said.

If Mira went into Copy Shop and asked for something to be ready by the next morning, she'd probably be laughed out of the building. When Ian flashed his badge, he was assured that the notebooks would be copied and that all their work remained confidential. They even offered scanning services. Mira was thoroughly impressed, until she discovered scanning was just one extra button to press and Ian had to buy a memory stick. Copying service didn't come cheap, but it came quick.

"Tell me about John Parnell," Ian said once they returned to the car.

"He's an insurance agent," Mira said. "Sally and I used to talk with him quite a bit. I think he's pretty close to William and Tyler as well."

"And he's the psychic?" Ian asked.

"He is a psychic, yes."

"I bet he does well in the insurance industry."

"He does," Mira said, "but not for the reasons you're thinking."

"I suppose you supply him with the same tea Barney gets," Ian said.

"No. Barney stares into the Ether and sees random futures. John predicts the future, although sometimes he lives in the future as well. Most of the time, though, it's his future."

"He lives in the future?" Ian asked.

"Sort of. Sometimes John runs a little faster than those around him do. If he does that, just keep asking questions and he'll meet up with you again."

"I'm not going to pretend I understood any of that."

"I'm not an expert in seers or psychics." Mira realized she was confusing Ian worse than he had been. "Treat him like you would anyone else."

The agency John worked for was downtown. A fast elevator took them up to the thirtieth floor, where the doors opened to a smiling receptionist. Ian looked ready to flash his badge until Mira nudged in front of him and asked if John was available.

"My sister used to work here," Mira told Ian while the receptionist contacted John. "Well, not here exactly. There's a cubicle farm on the floor below. She worked there."

"Used to?" Ian asked.

"She hated missing so much time with the kids while commuting."

Ian only nodded and looked around.

"You two can go back, John is in his office," the receptionist said.

"Thank you," Mira said. She received instructions to get to John's office. "What's up?" Mira asked when Ian remained quiet on the way to the office.

"You know I'll want to talk to your sister, right?" Ian asked.

Mira shrugged. "Fine by me. I know she's not involved."

"You're certain of that?" Ian asked.

"Yep. She's the good one."

Ian grinned and lowered his voice. "Good witch bad witch?"

She chuckled. "Something like that. There's a reason you found *me* on file and not her."

"Now that you mention it, there weren't many details about why you started to work for the authorities."

"There's his office," Mira said, ignoring the implied question. "Ready?"

"Sure thing."

John met them at the door, wringing his hands. "Good afternoon. Please, take a seat." He shut the door behind them before settling in behind his desk. "What can I do for you?"

Mira smiled, hoping to calm his nerves. "This is Detective Ian Burke. We're making the rounds."

"And this is the one that knows…" John asked, trailing off.

"Everything," Mira said, "yes."

"And your, uh, spell. It's working?" John asked.

"Yes," Mira said, taking another deep look at Ian and the spell. She tried not to be insulted by the question. John was only human, after all. "You're safe to answer any question and he won't be able to repeat anything about a supernatural aspect."

Ian twisted in his seat, looking agitated by the reminder.

"I've been working here for the past nine years," John said. "I'm an actuarial manager."

"Thank you," Ian said. "I was just going to ask that."

"Sally and I had only known each other for around two years or so," John said.

"Um, okay," Ian said, twisting again.

John glanced at Mira. "I'm not sure if I should answer that."

"Well," Ian said, "since I haven't asked anything, I can understand."

John gave Mira a panicked look.

Mira put a hand on Ian's arm to stop the agitated detective from going any further. "What were the first three questions you were going to ask?"

"How long he's been working here and what he does, how long he knew Sally, and…" Ian trailed off, frowning.

"Things got off track." Mira bit her lip and looked at John. He was living in a future that hadn't quite happened the way it was supposed to. "Go ahead and ask those questions. It'll be easier to catch up."

"I don't know what you mean," Ian said.

"Thank you," John said.

"Ask the questions and leave him a bit of time for the answers." Seeing Ian was going to argue, Mira added. "Trust me."

"Fine," Ian said. "John, how long have you been working here and what is your job title?" He paused. "When did you meet Sally? Do you know if Sally had any enemies?"

"Those were rather abrupt questions," Mira said as she watched John move from future to present. "You can move onto the next question in a moment."

"But he didn't answer—"

"He answered everything you asked," Mira said under her breath.

John looked uncomfortable, but didn't say anything. To Mira, though, it looked as if he had joined them in the present, and she motioned for Ian to continue.

"Do you know anyone that had a grudge against Sally or Helen?" Ian asked.

John looked to Mira, back down at his hands, and then back up at her again. "Sally was at a meeting a little over a month ago. I can look up the date if you need it, but I remember her being at a meeting. Sally said something to Emmit during the meeting. Afterward, she went up to him. She seemed to be arguing with him." John shook his head. "That's not quite right. Sally was upset with Emmit, but Emmit looked normal. Normal for him, anyway. He said a few words and left. I'm not sure what they talked about."

Ian took a few notes. "Can you look up that date?"

"Sure," John said. He woke up his computer and started clicking around.

Sally and Emmit, Mira thought. *Why would Sally be upset with Emmit? Emmit rarely spoke with anyone, aside from Tyler, that is. And now her.*

John gave Ian the date of the meeting and mentioned that there were more people at the meeting because it was a holiday for some of the group. Supernaturals loved celebrating with other supernaturals. It was the only place they could really be themselves.

"Was Martin there?" Ian asked.

John shook his head and started wringing his hands again. "It's rare for non-supernaturals to attend. An exception would not be made for someone Sally had only known for a few months."

"Do you know if anyone might have had a grudge against Helen?" Ian asked.

"I didn't know her that well," John said.

"Had you ever seen Helen with Emmit?" Ian asked.

Why focus on Emmit? Mira tried not to grind her teeth in frustration.

"I saw them talking one night," John said. "Briefly. I don't know why, but it looked like they only said a few words."

"Did either of them look upset?"

"Emmit doesn't look upset," John said. "He doesn't look anything. Helen looked fine."

"Is there anything else you can think of?" Ian asked.

John cleared his throat and looked at Mira again. "I, uh, found out what Sally was doing."

Not knowing where this was going, Mira said nothing, but she was suddenly glad of the Fortitude running through her system.

Ian shifted. "Mira, would you mind waiting in the hall?"

"I would," Mira said.

She almost felt bad for Ian. He looked as though he had no idea what to do with that response.

"It looks as though John would be more comfortable with you outside at this point," Ian said.

There wasn't much conviction behind the words, but Mira relented. "It was good to see you, John." She shot a glare at Ian. "I'll be in the hall."

When she was out of the office, she paced.

CHAPTER 14

MIRA WASN'T SURE IF IAN could read the atmosphere, or if he was just tired from having so much new stuff thrown at him. Either way, he didn't have much to say after they left the towering skyscrapers of downtown.

Trying to put Sally out of her mind, Mira thought about the spell she was putting together for Emmit. She had started gathering cryptic notes in her notebook as new ideas came to her.

The car stopped and Mira looked around. "Where are we?" She hadn't even thought about introducing Ian to anyone else.

"It's getting late," Ian said, "and we missed lunch. I thought we'd stop for dinner."

With the fortitude flowing through her, Mira hadn't noticed that she was hungry. With any spell, little side effects could occur that you had to look out for. They were natural parts of the spell, but you had to be careful and pay attention to make sure that you knew everything the spell was doing to you.

Which made her think about the spell she had put on Ian.

"Food is a wonderful idea," Mira said.

On their way inside, Mira checked the spell. The spots where Ian struggled against it looked aggravated again, as though he was wrestling with the pressure of not saying anything. Those areas hadn't spread, though.

Internal struggle?

It was hard to say, but she knew she needed to keep an eye on it. In the meantime, she'd have to make sure there were no other little side effects that would start to show themselves.

"Have you been here before?" Ian asked. He was obviously at home in the place, nodding to a member of staff as he found his way to a booth.

"I think so, but it's been a long time," Mira said.

A waiter dropped off menus and brought them drinks. Ian ignored the menu and chatted with the man while Mira examined the selections. After they ordered, Mira noticed that Ian had shredded his straw wrapper and was watching her.

"What's up?" she asked.

"I need to know about your relationship with Emmit." Ian looked uncomfortable, but forged on. "If you two are close, I need to know up front."

So, he was starting with Emmit. Mira looked around, noting that it was too early for dinner and too late for lunch, so there weren't many diners and none near them.

"There's not much to tell, really," Mira said. "We hadn't even spoken until a few nights ago."

"He's been at your house several times in the past few days and John said he doesn't talk with very many people. Most of the other people he's spoken with are dead."

Mira tried not to take offense on Emmit's behalf, but Ian made that difficult. "You think that because you've only asked about Sally and Helen. John barely knows Emmit."

"But you do?"

"We're friends," Mira said. "We've had a few conversations. He's been to my shop; he's spoken with my sister and Della. He's spoken with you." Mira tried to emphasize that fact.

"Only once," Ian said, "which is still a little fuzzy."

"Imagine that," Mira said, rolling her eyes.

"What I do remember is that there seemed to be something wrong with him."

"The only thing wrong with him was that he was trying to deal with you," Mira snapped.

Ian changed tactics. "John mentioned that Emmit knew Tyler. You've mentioned him a few times, too."

"That's not a question," Mira said.

"Can you introduce us?" Ian asked.

Mira shrugged, but before she could say anything, someone came up to their booth.

"Mimi," Ian said with a smile, "come sit down with us." Ian slid over to give her space.

Not that she needed much of it. Mimi looked like she was seeing the early sixties. She was a skinny little waif of a woman and wore the sweetest smile—like a mixture between your best friend and your grandmother.

"I think I'll take the time to do just that," Mimi said, settling in next to Ian. "Who's your date?" she winked at Mira.

"Mimi, this is Mira Owens. Mira, this is Mimi Cantrel, owner of *Harman's*. And," he added to Mimi, "I'm not on a date."

"Nice to meet you, Mira," she said, reaching out to shake Mira's hand. Mimi had a firm handshake.

"It's nice to meet you," Mira replied. "You have a nice restaurant."

"Thank you, Dear." She nudged Ian. "Why haven't you asked this lovely young lady on a date?"

"Uh, Mira is helping me out with a case. She owns the *Essence of Tea* downtown."

"Well, that's no excuse for not asking her out. Can't wait on things like that," Mimi said to Ian before turning to Mira. "The *Essence of Tea*, I know that place. You have some wonderful tea blends. And fantastic pastries."

Mira's face turned crimson, both from the compliment and from what she had said to Ian. "Thank you, Mimi. I have a business partner that does the baking."

That led Mimi straight into business talk. Mira could see how she remained successful, despite all the chain restaurants around. When the food came, Mimi made arrangements to call and set up a taste testing at Mira's shop with the prospect of *Essence of*

Tea supplying her desserts. It was a fantastic idea, one that Mira had never considered before, and she let Mimi know that she would fill in her partner right away.

Mimi had brought a great disruption with her. Over dinner, Mira and Ian kept their conversation light. When the check came, Mira started to pull out her purse, but Ian shook his head.

"What?" Mira asked.

He wordlessly slid over the bill.

It had already been paid with a note from Mimi. She told Ian that she'd see him on his next date. He left cash for the tip.

Mira felt lighter than she had when they'd stopped. "That's a nice place. How'd you and Mimi meet?"

"She's a friend of my mom," he said. "She watched me a bunch when I was growing up."

"She's really nice," Mira said, getting into the car. "Did you want to visit anyone else tonight?"

"Actually," Ian said, losing his smile, "we still need to talk."

Inwardly, Mira groaned. More questions. "Want to talk at my place?"

"Sure," Ian said. "Do you think you can arrange a time for me to meet with Tyler?"

Obviously, he wasn't going to wait until they got to the apartment. "Okay. When would you like to see him?"

"As soon as I can. I have a feeling tomorrow is going to be pretty busy. Tonight, if possible."

"I think he has plans," Mira said. She wasn't about to bring Emmit's name into the conversation again. "I'll call, though."

Mira tried Tyler on his cell and at home, leaving a message in both places. Finally, she texted, knowing full well that Tyler would answer a text before he would a call.

"I'll let you know what he says," Mira said. "You've met a few people today. Was there anyone else I mentioned that you want to see tomorrow?"

"Is there someone in charge?" Ian asked.

"In charge of what?"

"Everything. All the supernaturals. I mean, you all have rules and stuff, so who's in charge of it all?" Ian asked.

She tried not to laugh. "No one is in charge. Not in the way you think, anyway." She told him about the council and the regular meetings. She told him about the gatherings of supernaturals and she had just started in on more specific details when they arrived at her apartment.

"Can I come to one of these council meetings?" Ian asked.

"I'm not sure," Mira said evenly. "Like John said, it's rare that humans even know about them, much less attend."

"There has to be a better way of talking with everyone," Ian said. "There's still too much I don't understand."

Mira hurried up the cold stairs and into the apartment, Ian tromping behind.

"I can ask," Mira said. "But the next meeting isn't for two weeks."

"That's too long to wait," Ian said.

"I know this is a lot to take in," Mira said, greeting Alchemy and Oracle before taking off her coat. "And there's no way to become an expert overnight."

"Right," Ian said. He looked dejected.

"Come into the kitchen. I'll make us some tea."

"Got anything extra to go into it?"

"I have alcohol if you want something stronger." After seeing him drunk the other night, she wasn't sure if it was the best idea, but she offered anyway.

Ian shrugged off his jacket. "I was thinking something with a more magical kick."

"Really?" Mira asked, eyebrows raised.

Ian sighed. "I don't know. Maybe…"

"Maybe what?"

"The spell you used on me. Can you use that on Gabe?"

"Oh." Mira sat down at the table next to Ian and tried to formulate her response in a way he would understand. "What I did—with the spell, I mean—it was kind of a desperate measure."

"And I'm glad you did." Ian seemed to take note of the incredulous look on her face. "No, really, I am. I've learned more about the world in the last few days than I ever thought possible. I can see why you hide, and this case needed someone to look at these connections."

"I'm glad you feel that way." She wasn't convinced, though it was a nice thing for him to say.

"But the thing is, it's always better to have two sets of eyes on this stuff, and there's a lot here. Too much for one detective to cover and not enough time to go through everything."

"I get that," Mira said, trying to sound reassuring. "And no one is expecting miracles here."

"So you're saying no," Ian said.

"I bound you without your permission. There are consequences to that. To do it twice—"

"Right," Ian said. "Just think about it. Please."

Mira felt at a loss. "Okay. There's other stuff to cover, though, right? I mean, there's a whole non-supernatural side to things."

"Yeah. We need to talk about that, too." Ian leaned forward. "If we move forward—"

"If?" Mira asked. She felt like she was floating out to sea. She put her hand on the pentagram hidden beneath her shirt, as though hoping for strength from it.

"If," Ian repeated. "I'm not sure what I can tell Gabe about what I learned today, so I'll be working on something in the morning. But if you and I continue, you might hear some things."

"About Sally," Mira said, looking down. "That's why you sent me out of the room so you could talk with John."

"Yes," Ian said. He was trying to sound matter of fact, but Mira noted some hesitancy in his voice.

"What did she do?" Mira asked, still unsure if she really wanted to know. She needed to know, though.

"Sally was blackmailing people," Ian said. "We aren't sure how many yet, but there have been quite a few."

People don't really do that, do they? Mira kept that thought to herself. She wanted to ask if he was sure and how he knew, but she couldn't bring herself to ask that either. Not after seeing John's nervousness before Mira was forced to leave the interview.

She'd be denying the truth. Somehow, she knew that.

When Mira said nothing, Ian tried to fill the gap. "From what I've learned about Sally, I think she was using her clairvoyance to find out things about people to extort money from them." Ian waited for a moment before going on. "Even when I found out about her powers, I figured there wouldn't be many people. But it sounded like she was blackmailing supernaturals as well as other people around her."

"She wouldn't threaten to out a supernatural," Mira said without thinking. It was a knee jerk reaction and she knew it.

Apparently, Ian knew it as well. "Everyone has things to hide. She wouldn't have to threaten to expose their supernatural secrets. Only what they've done. She'd been extorting money from people for quite a while."

Mira only nodded in a dull way.

"You can see why I might need to bring someone else in on this now, right? About her powers, I mean," Ian said.

What could she say to that? It sounded as though Ian was having to climb a mountain on his own, with no support. However, Gabriel, who could spot lies and press hard in just the right spot, would struggle like hell against the spell. She was confident enough to know her spell would hold, but she knew the price would be higher.

"You'll think about it?" Ian asked.

Mira sighed. "I'll think about it."

CHAPTER 15

MIRA SPENT MOST OF THE evening with Alchemy on her lap reading *Postsfromtheether.com*. She spent hours looking for anything that might be related to the murders. As she expected, she found nothing. Some of the predictions were interesting, but nothing that would help them track a killer.

The next morning, snow greeted the city. With Ian spending the early part of the day doing other things, Mira was determined to make up for missing so much work. Fortitude was doing some heavy lifting as the roads got worse and snow steadily built up on her way to the city.

The usual early bustle of city noises was muffled and she found that she was enjoying the walk from her car to the store. The street was virtually empty, the snow hadn't yet been trod upon, and it hadn't had time to get dingy. She held her gloved hand out to catch snowflakes, and then looked up as she watched the flakes dance through the air.

Her legs slid out from under her, and Mira landed on her back with a muffled thud.

Crap. She stared at the sky while sensing for any injuries before she got back up. Besides the pain radiating from her backside, she was relatively unscathed. Making her way slowly to her feet, she vowed to be more careful.

It didn't take her long to get the store up and running, but with the snow, customers were few and far between. A few tenacious employees from neighboring businesses stopped in to pick up something to warm them up, and some serious shoppers made their way in.

While fixing coffee, Mira managed to break a coffee carafe. It was made of metal, but she somehow managed to drop it in just the right way for it to crack. After spilling two drinks, one on a customer—for which Mira apologized profusely—she excused herself from the floor and went to the kitchen.

Deciding that the lack of sleep was making her more clumsy than usual, she filled up on coffee and cleaned the kitchen. Every surface was scrubbed as if she were doing penance for ruining the customer's morning. The oven had some particularly stubborn spots that Mira attacked with a single-minded ferocity.

"Good morning, Miss Owens!"

Mira jumped and banged her head on the oven. Rubbing the aching spot, she looked up into the last face she wanted to see.

"Mr. Benton," she said, trying to curb her frustration. "I'm surprised to see you here today. And back here."

"I'm doing a quick inspection," he said in an overly cheery voice.

She sighed before she could stop herself.

"Don't worry, this won't take long. Can you point out your smoke detectors?"

"Sure." She motioned to the two in the back, not trusting his cheerfulness for one moment. "There, there, and another up front."

"I need to check your cold storage as well."

It was such an odd question that Mira showed him without knowing why she was doing it. "The city did a health safety check last month, if that's what you're checking for."

"I need to take a few measurements," he said, ignoring Mira.

"Okay," she crossed her arms, "what's this for?"

"I'm checking up on Dad's records. I'll be out of the way in no time."

Mira was tempted to leave him alone. It had been a bad morning and spending more than a minute with her landlord usually only made things worth.

However, she didn't trust him.

He took out a fancy electronic tape measure and jotted down a few notes. Occasionally, he would hum to himself. She let him into the offices to measure, but she was ready to put her foot down if he wanted to do anything in the store itself. She'd be seriously ticked off if he started bothering the few customers she had.

Her cell phone rang and Mira hesitated, not wanting to answer it with Mr. Benton lurking around. Ian's name flashed across her screen. There was no way she could talk to him with her landlord around, so she silenced the phone.

A few minutes later, the phone rang again.

"I'll get out of your way," Mr. Benton said. "Have a good day and stay safe out there. The roads are bad."

Her mouth almost dropped open. Mira mumbled what she hoped was an appropriate reply and answered the phone.

"Hello," she said, watching the man leave the store.

"It's me." Ian sounded brisk. "I wanted to see if your friend ever got back to you."

"Tyler, you mean?" Mira asked. Mr. Benton had been smiling the whole time. He was up to something, she was sure of it.

"Yes," Ian said.

"No, I haven't heard from him. I'll let you know when I do, though."

"Are you available?" Ian asked.

"I'm at work, but I can get free," Mira said.

"I should be out front in ten minutes."

He didn't wait for a reply. Mira let her staff know that she was once again leaving. She felt bad having to leave her partner another note. Luckily, as a fellow witch, her partner knew what was going on.

She was getting coffee ready to go when she realized that she had spent her morning scrubbing the kitchen—and she looked like it. Mira tried to tell herself that it didn't matter, but she dropped what she was doing and ran to clean herself up as best she could.

It didn't matter, right? She had spelled Ian without him knowing and appeared to be frustrating him at every turn. He was nice and seriously cute. Even if there was nothing between them, Mira figured it didn't hurt to look your best.

When Mira hurried back to the front of the store she saw that Ian was waiting for her. Ana had two piping hot drinks ready to go, and she waved Mira out the door.

The day had gone bad so far. Really bad. So Mira took her time across the sidewalk. The sun was out, and although it was no longer snowing, what had already fallen was being mercilessly thrown around. Thankfully, Mira made it to the car without incident and handed a cup of coffee to Ian.

"You look like you could really use this," Mira said, taking note of the dark circles under his eyes.

"Thanks," Ian said.

"I thought you were busy this morning. You took Barney's notebooks back, right?"

"He has the originals back." Ian was intent on the road. It had been plowed, but not well enough.

"Where are we going?" Mira asked.

"Your place. I have some questions for you and…" Ian sighed. "And the case files. I need you to take a look at a few things."

"No problem." Mira's cell phone rang, so she checked the caller ID.

Her mother. Well, she had been expecting a call from her, but there was no way she'd take the call in front of Ian.

Mira silenced the phone. "Aren't you working with your partner today?"

"We worked together this morning," Ian said. His hands gripped the steering wheel as though it were a life preserver. "Gabe is running something down, but we're interviewing a suspect this afternoon."

"That's good, isn't it?" Mira asked. "If you have a likely suspect, what am I doing?"

"Making connections," Ian said. They moved onto a well-treated road and Ian relaxed his grip, though Mira thought he still looked tense.

"What kind of connections?"

"Between the victims and everyone that might have known them."

"Isn't that what we've been doing?" Mira asked.

"We're not moving fast enough. I need you to call every supernatural that knew Sally and Helen and ask if the other names are familiar. We need to find what links them together."

"What happened?" Mira asked.

"What do you mean?"

"What happened to spur this on? You look upset, and you're suddenly rushing through this."

"When we talk to this suspect, we need to know more. We have to know who he knows."

"Who is it?" Mira asked.

"I can't tell you." Ian said.

"What? Why not?"

"I'm not discussing it with you. Anything that I might say could bias the results."

"It might make things go quicker."

"No." His voice was stern enough to be emphatic.

"Okay," Mira said. An eerie feeling began to settle in her stomach.

Nearing her neighborhood, the roads became considerably clearer.

"I didn't think the roads would be this good," Ian mumbled.

"A plus side for living in an area of high salaries, old money, and crushing amounts of debt hidden in the closet with all the skeletons."

"I could see how that has its upsides," Ian said derisively. "You have a neighborhood watch, right?"

"I never really thought about that," Mira said. "There hasn't been any trouble around here, though."

"No one will be out in this mess, at least."

"We are," Mira grinned.

"Well, you'll be at home for the rest of the day anyway," Ian said, pulling into the driveway. "Is Della around?"

"I doubt it. She'll be at work."

He nodded and looked around the white wonderland. "Let's get inside."

Cold air engulfed them. Mira clutched at the handrail, worried her feet would slide out from under her again. Once inside, she shivered and caught her breath, which the frigid air had taken away.

"I can't stay long," Ian said. "Where can we work?"

"The kitchen table is probably best." Mira hung her coat and reluctantly peeled off her gloves.

Alchemy and Oracle didn't seem inclined to get any closer to the cold air their human had let in, but once the pair was in the kitchen, the cats wrapped themselves around Mira's legs until she gave them an affectionate scratch behind the ears. Ian had apparently passed some sort of unwritten test among the cats. They rubbed against him until he relented and petted them. Some of Ian's tension dissipated as Alchemy purred his appreciation.

"What are we doing first?" Mira asked.

"These are case files," Ian said. "If anyone asks, you've never seen them." He sat them on the table and put his hand protectively on top of the stack. "I need to know now if you'd rather not see these. There are—" he floundered, "-there are pictures in here you haven't seen, and some of them are pretty graphic."

Was she ready for that? "Are you showing me pictures of my friends after... well, after what happened?"

"God no," Ian said. "You don't need to see that. They are pictures before any, um, cleanup was done."

Blood. She could handle that, right? At least with the Fortitude still holding strong.

"What am I looking for?" Mira asked.

"Anything that we might have missed before. We think we showed everything important, but we could be wrong. There was stuff that we purposefully left out as well, though."

"I'll do what I can," Mira said.

Ian looked reluctant when he slid the stack of files over.

The first folder held pictures that Mira had already seen. She studied each of them anyway in case there was something that had been overlooked.

She wasn't expecting what she found in the second file. "Good lord. This place is a mess."

There was some blood, but the dominant parts of the scene were broken furniture, cabinet doors falling off their hinges, and some with what appeared to be random junk thrown around everywhere.

The next few pictures had familiar items. Bullets that shined silver, a glass bottle of water, and a wooden stake. They had been placed together.

"This is Helen's house, isn't it?" Mira asked, trying to keep her mind focused on the objects.

"I can't tell you that," Ian said with a hint of apprehension.

"It's the only thing that makes sense. Out of all of them, she was the only werewolf." Mira flipped to the next photo. "None of it means anything. A few werewolves have a silver allergy, but it's no more likely to kill them than anyone else." She flipped the photo over, trying to make sense of what she was seeing. There was blood, but she was forcing her mind away from that. A snake? She flipped to the next picture and found a closer photo. "Rope?"

Ian said nothing.

Rope that had been lying in the blood. Mira felt her blood pressure drop and she paled significantly. She flipped through the rest of the pictures, concentrating on the ones that that didn't paint a chilly picture of what might have happened in that room.

It was no good. She closed the file and pushed it away, immediately grabbing the next to find something else to focus on.

"Why don't we take a break?" Ian said.

Mira didn't bother to respond.

Ian took the files that she was done with, and then tried to grab the one she was holding.

Mira tugged it back. "You didn't show me these before."

"No."

These weren't gruesome. Once again, they bordered on the bizarre.

"Is that a turtle shell?" Mira asked.

"Not everything has been fully processed. We're still waiting for confirmation on most of the items. It appears to be a turtle shell, but it could be a plaster replica."

"Still processing?" Mira said. "You'd think they'd put a rush on this stuff."

"There is," Ian said, sighing. "There's been a lot to process."

"Real or not, all of this adds up to nothing. Someone is staging a scene." Mira couldn't help but shudder. "But the scenes themselves don't mean anything. Is that an actual cauldron?"

"We think it's cast iron."

"As I'm sure you know by now, witches don't actually use cauldrons."

"Not for anything?" Ian asked.

Mira forced a chuckle. "Halloween decorations? It would take forever to clean and take care of, if you really used one. Stainless steel, or occasionally copper pans work best."

"The candles?"

"Well... Okay. They aren't necessary, but some witches still use them. Everything around us has energy, and some witches prefer to have the power of raw fire around them instead of electricity."

"How is it different?"

She searched for the right words. "It's like the difference between snow and rain... no, that's not right... Like vanilla ice cream and chocolate. They're still both ice cream, but they have different flavors."

"I think I get it."

Mira flipped through the last file. "There are a lot of interviews here."

"Those aren't half of them." Ian looked tired when he stared listlessly at the paper. "You don't need to go through those."

"Did you have other suspects?" She turned the pages without really reading anything

"There was another person Sally worked with, Tom Anderson. He was upset that Sally always sold more cars than anyone else did. She'd stolen several customers from him." He leaned over and thumbed through the file.

His hand rested on her arm. Mira thought it could be her imagination, but he seemed to hesitate before removing it.

Ian cleared his throat. "That's what we got when we talked to Tom."

Mira flipped through the notes. The man sounded pissed off by the end of the interview. He said Sally was somehow cheating.

"He could be right," Mira said after speedreading through the interview. "Sally could have used her clairvoyance to get to know buyers on a whole other level. She could probably say exactly what they wanted to hear."

"When we interviewed him again, he knew nothing about anyone else, and we can't place them together."

"I've never heard of him," Mira said, closing the file. "Who else do you have?"

"I really shouldn't be talking about this." Ian glanced at his watch. "I should go."

"Do you want to leave these here for me to go through again?"

"No!" It came out in a forceful rush. "I mean, no. You've already been a big help," he said in a more normal tone,

"If it helps, the cauldron couldn't have been cheap, and I doubt there are too many of them out there."

"Thanks. Are you staying here for the rest of the day?" Ian asked.

"I think I'm stuck here," Mira said. "My car is in the city."

"Oh yeah," Ian said. "Sorry about that. The roads are probably still pretty rough, anyway. You'll make those calls for me?"

CHAPTER 16

PIECING TOGETHER THE HIDDEN PARTS of Sally's life felt like it tore a hole in Mira's soul. How had she never noticed that her friend was blackmailing people?

When she began to contact other supernaturals on Ian's behalf, a few people had said nice things about her friend. One had refused to say anything, two people were reluctant, but talked after Mira explained what was going on, and another cussed Mira out and hung up on her.

She had better luck when she started with the other names. A few remembered Karen Green. She felt like she had hit the jackpot when someone recognized the name Yvonne Childs. The only thing they knew was that she was supernatural and kept to herself, but at least someone knew her.

It wasn't until she got around to calling the elders and felt as if she had been rung through a wringer that she found someone who knew Dennis Simmons. Turns out, according to Noah, Lance knew him.

Ms. Vears knew most of the people on the list, and she could draw a line between Sally and Karen. It turns out they had only known each other a few months. She didn't know what their relationship was, but she was certain that Karen hadn't liked Sally or her boyfriend, Martin.

Mira knew that Lance held the key to at least one of the names, but still, she had put off calling him until she had exhausted other options. Although she would never admit it, the vampire made her nervous.

Lance knew them all. He hadn't met Yvonne, but had known of her. Dennis was a muse. *Who knew muses even existed?*

There was no way that the vampire had killed everyone. Remembering the amount of blood found at what she was sure was Helen's house proved that the vampire couldn't have done it.

It was such a waste of food.

Ian called when she was talking with Lance, which gave her a good excuse to get off the line. Something about talking with a man who was centuries old made her feel exposed.

"How did your interview go?" Mira asked.

"Not great. I think Gabe disagrees," Ian said.

"How so?"

"I'm not sure. He's already gone for the day. Do you have anything for me?"

It didn't take long for Mira to distill what had taken her hours to discover.

"You haven't mentioned Lance before," Ian said. "Do you trust him?"

"I don't think he'd have any reason to lie," Mira said.

"Well, if this information is good, I'll owe him dinner."

Mira felt her nose curl up. "I should mention," she said, lowering her voice despite the fact that they were on the phone, "that Lance is a vampire."

Ian chuckled. "Scratch dinner, then. Listen, I need to move on this."

"Move on what, exactly?"

"This makes someone's statement contradictory. I need to do some research. Thanks, Mira. Can I call you tomorrow?"

She couldn't help but smile. "I'll be around."

Once Ian hung up, Mira took a long look outside. The world was covered in white. It looked like the wind had stopped blowing. The sun was also out, making it look almost inviting. A quick dash out into the snow?

Checking the temperature, Mira chucked the idea. A shower and some time spent on Emmit's spell was what she needed.

She dressed carefully after her shower, making sure she looked nice, but trying not to look like she had gone to too much trouble.

When she moved to the kitchen, notebook in hand to finalize the spell, she saw that Oracle was standing at the front door, watching it intently. Mira had just settled down at the kitchen table when there was a knock. She glanced at the time, pleasantly surprised that Emmit would show up so early.

In the dead of winter, night came early. The sun was setting, turning the cold day even more frigid when she opened the door.

It wasn't Emmit.

"Gabriel?" Mira's confusion was written across her face. "Is something wrong?"

"Good evening, Miss Owens."

Crap, they were back to Miss Owens.

"Would you mind stepping outside for a few minutes?"

"What? It's freezing out there." Movement behind the detective caught her eye. There was a police officer behind him, waiting on the stairs.

"We have a warrant to search the premises," Gabriel said.

"Oh." Mira's mood dropped in record time.

"Are you currently alone in your home?" he asked.

"Yeah," Mira said. She felt completely dejected. It wasn't even an hour ago that she had spoken to Ian. He had said nothing. She opened the door wider to let them in.

"We need you to step outside," Gabriel said.

"Seriously?"

"Yes," he said.

"Let me get my coat," Mira mumbled.

"One moment," Gabriel said, stepping inside. "I need to see your coat."

Mira rolled her eyes and shook her head, but she still pointed to the coat rack. "The blue one."

He checked the pockets and handed over the coat.

Mira bundled up with gloves and a hat, shot Gabriel a dirty look, and then stomped outside. She heard Gabriel give instructions to the officers.

The last thing she wanted to do was watch from the door as they searched, so she started down the stairs. The thought of them pawing through her stuff infuriated her. How could Ian not tell her? And where was he?

Hiding, no doubt.

Fuming, she forgot the bad karma that had started swirling around her. Her feet flew out from under her, and she bounced down the last quarter of the stairs.

Snatching at the rail only twisted her around. She landed on her back, sinking into the snow around her.

"Jesus, Mira!" Gabriel swore and hurried down the stairs, taking much more care than Mira had.

Once again, she found herself staring up at the sky. Shivering, she forced herself to sit up before he reached her.

"Are you okay?" he asked, offering her his hand.

She held up her finger in the universal 'give me a moment' gesture, wishing she were brave enough to use a different finger to mean something altogether different.

She leaned forward and gingerly touched the side of her head. Under her fingers pain radiated, which dampened her anger. Looking up caused outrage to brew again when she saw that the door was still open.

"I have cats," she snapped. "Go close the door."

When Gabriel left her alone, she took the moment to pull herself together. She shakily stood up and looked at the big house. There was a light on.

The first thing she should have done was call Della. Gabriel deserved whatever the lawyer dished up.

"They're inside," Gabriel said.

"Which is where I'm going," Mira said.

"We need another minute before you can go back in."

"No, you don't. I have no clue why you're doing this, but I'm wet, my head is killing me, and I'm freezing to death."

He sighed. "Are you hurt?"

"No," Mira snapped.

"Shit," Gabriel said. "Is it bad?"

Mira rolled her eyes. "I'll let you know when I thaw out." She had no idea what his lie detector abilities would do with that.

"Fine," he said, stepping away from the staircase and waving her up. "But you sit where I say until the place is cleared."

On the way up, she was much more careful where she put her feet. Inside, the temperature wasn't too much better, since the door had been left open.

"Wait here," Gabriel said.

"I need my cell phone," she said.

"You can call Ian after."

Mira felt the heat behind his words.

"Actually, I'm calling my landlord," Mira said.

"Fine. Wait here."

Gabriel went to an officer that was searching Mira's bookshelf and redirected the man's attention. Once the officer had searched the couch, she was implanted there with her cell phone.

"Della, you'll never guess what's happening over here," Mira said moodily while watching an officer show a stack of books to Gabriel. "I've been served with a search warrant."

"What?" Della's voice carried, causing the officer and Gabriel to look up. "Did you read it?"

Mira felt like she had been called out by her teacher. "No." She twisted in her seat.

"I'll be right there."

Mira hung up her phone and grinned. "Detective, Della Yates is on her way over."

It looked like a number of angry responses went through Gabriel's mind before he settled on something simple. "Why?"

"Why not? It's her place."

He rubbed his forehead as though pained more than Mira, and went back to work.

Rubbing her hands vigorously over her arms wasn't helping Mira get any warmer. The wet cold had seeped through to her bones.

When Della banged on the door, Gabriel looked at Mira, who purposefully gave him the sweetest smile she could manage.

When he answered the door, Della had her hand out.

"Your warrant?" Her voice was sharp.

Gabriel only shrugged and handed it over.

Mira watched as she read over the document, taking note that her friend started smirking early on.

"Detective Flint?" Della moved over to Mira and then handed the papers back to Gabriel. "I'd like to draw your attention to a section of this document. You have permission to search her property which, in this case, is her car."

Gabriel frowned. "Which I'm sure you know will also cover space in which she leases."

"Which adds the store," Della looked at Mira, who nodded in confirmation. "She doesn't have a lease here."

"You, of all people, didn't make her sign a lease." Gabriel looked like he was seriously losing his cool.

"No."

"It won't take long to get the warrant updated," Gabriel said.

Della shrugged before sitting next to Mira. "This is up to you, Mira. It won't take long to update, like he said, but you could always make them wait."

Mira gently prodded the knot that was forming on her head. Mentally, she went over every item it was possible for them to find. Ian had taken the police files back. The books that were blatantly spell books were coveted away. Her spell ingredients were also impossible to leave in the open. Many of the hidden items were poisonous, illegal, or just plain gross.

"They may as well search the place, then." It was said resentfully, but she just wanted this over with.

Gabriel eyed her suspiciously. "I'll need you to sign something for that."

"Sure," she said.

Della's phone rang. "I need to take this, but I will be overseeing this farce."

Telling herself repeatedly that Ian hadn't known about what Gabriel was doing, didn't really convince her. He'd have to have been blind not to see what his partner was doing. There would have been paperwork, gossip, or something. Ian had to have known.

Gabriel stayed where he was, watching Mira as though analyzing her.

"What?" Mira glared at him.

He said nothing, but didn't look away.

Mira rolled her eyes and crossed her arms, rubbing them once again to get warm.

"I'll be right back," he mumbled.

When he went into her bedroom, she tried not to let her lip curl up. Thinking about him rummaging through her things made her want to kick them all out.

Thankfully, Mira figured he wasn't in there long enough to go through anything. Imagining what they might have found in her bedroom made her blush, and she had to bite back the urge to tell him off.

He was chatting with one of the officers that came out with him. They went to the other officer in the room and put their heads together, talking too low for Mira to hear.

The man who had been going through the living room pointed to a few things on her desk. Gabriel nodded, and before long, he was shaking their hands and ushering them out the door.

"It's over?" Mira asked, feeling confused.

"No," he said gruffly, "and I want to know what you're playing at."

"Excuse me?" Mira couldn't believe the man's nerve. "I'm not playing at anything. This is on you. I don't even know what the hell you're doing here."

He ignored this statement and went back to her desk. "What are these books about?" he asked.

Mira crossed her arms. "Need help with the big words?"

"Just answer the question," he said.

Glancing in the kitchen, she saw Della watching. The lawyer's eyes were narrowed at Gabriel, but she left them alone and stayed on the phone.

"They're exactly what they say they are," Mira said. "They're books on the occult throughout history." He looked like he was going to ask another question, so she hurried on. "Which shouldn't exactly surprise you. Did you think I was making up everything I told you?"

His lips pursed, and he shuffled through some papers. "What about these?"

She was prepared to be as obstinate as possible at this point. "I don't know what you're looking at. I'm guessing paper."

He snatched one of them up and brought it over.

One of the notes that had been left for her. She gently rubbed her head again, wishing once again that the mess would be over.

They were interrupted by a knock at the door.

"Great," Mira mumbled, "it's a party." Louder, she shouted. "Come in!"

She almost groaned when Emmit opened the door. Having him see her like this was an embarrassment.

"Good evening," Emmit said after taking in the situation. "Am I interrupting?"

"No—" Mira said.

"Yes—" Gabriel said at the same time.

They glared at each other.

Emmit raised an eyebrow before taking off his coat and joining them. There was a curious look on Emmit's face when he moved toward Gabriel.

Although, moving seemed quite the wrong word. It was as though he were easing himself closer to Gabriel, so as not to startle.

"I saw police officers leaving," Emmit said, not taking his eyes off Gabriel. "I trust I am finding you both well?"

The detective didn't look like he knew what to do about Emmit, so he turned back to Mira. He looked at the paper in his hands, as though needing to be reminded about what he was doing.

"The note, Miss Owens?"

"What about it?" Mira asked.

"We didn't find any notes at the scene, but that doesn't mean one wasn't left. Did you write this?"

"What?" Mira was shocked at the accusation. "What are you talking about?"

"Did you write the letter?" Gabriel asked.

Emmit strolled over and looked at what Gabriel held out.

"No, they were left for me."

Gabriel eyed her critically. "Did you leave anything like this for any of the victims?"

"Are you kidding me?" Mira looked at Gabriel as though he were an idiot.

Emmit was reading the letter and Gabriel gave him a sideways glance, but didn't stop him.

"This isn't a joke, Miss Owens," Gabriel said. "Please answer the question."

She glowered at him. "No."

Mira could feel a stirring of the energy in the room and looked at Emmit. His face had gone blank, but his eyes looked pinched around the edges. He snatched the letter out of Gabriel's hand and reread it before he settled his eyes back on Mira.

They were both looking down at her, which she didn't like.

It was unfair, Mira thought, that her own anger wasn't warming her up. "What is your problem? Both of you." She wanted to make sure Emmit understood that he was included in her ire.

"Are there more of these?" Emmit asked.

"On the desk," Gabriel answered for her.

"What exactly are you accusing her of?" Emmit asked, going

to the desk. "There is an accusation in there somewhere."

"I need to know if the letters are related to the case," Gabriel said, trying to keep his voice even.

"Then why don't you ask the question you want the answer to," Emmit said.

Oracle padded into the room and jumped up onto Mira's lap. He rubbed against her in an unaccustomed and reassuring kind of way. She gave the cat a pat before he settled down on the cushion beside her and watched the two men.

"Do you know who wrote the letters?" Gabriel asked.

"No," Mira said, automatically.

His eyes narrowed.

CHAPTER 17

MIRA LET OUT A DISGUSTED huff of air. "I don't *know* who sent them. I *assume,* however, that it is my landlord from the shop. He wants me out of the space."

Emmit came back over and sat down beside her, opposite the cat, with two letters in his hand. "Did you see him leave them?"

"No."

"And you didn't tell anyone about the letters?" Gabriel asked.

"No. Why would I?" She rubbed the side of her head again and winced. "They're just stupid letters."

Emmit sat the papers aside and turned toward her. He put his hand on her chin to move her head and examined what was surely becoming a bruise.

The gesture felt very intimate to Mira and some of her agitation slipped away. She watched his eyes grow darker in color. He was eyeing the side of her head. Instead of his look turning softer with concern, as she had expected, the look hardened.

He put a hand on her cheek and his brows furrowed, and then he took her hand and rubbed them briefly in his to warm them up.

A high-pitched growl came from Oracle. The atmosphere in the room changed and Mira started to feel buffeted by manic energy.

Emmit turned his attention to Gabriel. "What happened?" His voice was like molten lava, smooth, almost silky, but with enough power behind it to burn a person to ash.

Without her pentagram pressed against her, Mira was certain that the energy could have broken her. To her surprise, however, Gabriel hardly seemed affected.

She felt an answering call of energy ripple away from Gabriel, which no human she met could have managed. Mira's skin felt like it was being stung by fire and ice. Emmit's energy merely built around them undirected and with no focus. Whatever was happening around Gabriel, it was in direct response to Emmit.

Della walked out of the kitchen. "What's going on?"

Their concentration broke.

It was over in the blink of an eye. The build-up of power evaporated, and both men looked as though nothing had happened.

Oracle stopped growling and jumped off the couch. He wrapped himself around Gabriel's legs, purring. The detective absentmindedly bent down and scratched Oracle behind the ears.

Della looked at Mira with a raised eyebrow, but Mira shrugged and put her hand on her chest, pressing the pentagram reassuringly.

"Since the warrant is invalid, we aren't taking anything from the apartment." He looked pointedly at Mira, and then nodded to the letters. "Unless you want to report anything."

"No," Mira said.

"This isn't an end to anything," Gabriel continued, but without any anger or malice behind the words. "Right now, you are still a suspect. You should stay away from Ian until this is over. I don't want my partner dragged through the mud by gossip."

"That's uncalled for," Emmit said.

"And maybe you should check up on your partner before you say that," Della suggested with a smirk, sliding her phone away.

"I'm just telling you what's best for him," Gabriel said.

"Maybe you'd know what was best for him if you answered your phone," Della said. "I'm guessing that you avoided Ian's calls while you were here? Bad move."

In response, Gabriel whipped out his phone and stepped away, listening to his voice mail. Apparently, Ian had called a lot, so it took him a while. While Gabriel listened to Ian, Della filled Mira and Emmit in.

"Ian brought in Martin. Turns out, he has a connection to Helen as well," Della whispered as they both watched Gabriel's face. "Ian's interrogating him again now. Doesn't look good for Gabriel, since he's here harassing his partner's girlfriend, leaving Ian alone to deal with a possible killer."

"His girlfriend?" Mira choked out, trying to keep her voice low and avoid looking at Emmit.

"Well," Della said, "that's the way it looks, doesn't it? He's spending a lot of time with you. You and I know what's going on, but the guys at the station? Trust me; they're thinking girlfriend and jealous partner."

Mira turned scarlet.

"I have to go," Gabriel said, still attached to his phone. "Mira," he said stiffly, "thank you for your cooperation tonight."

Before Mira could think of a response, he was gone.

"Cooperation," Della mocked, "yeah, he's going to spin this to save face with Ian."

"Let him," Mira said, trying to sound unconcerned. "Maybe he'll chill out some if I don't rat him out."

Della shrugged. "Need any help cleaning up? Or," she raised an eyebrow suggestively, "do you have other plans?"

"I'm good," Mira said, trying to hurry her friend before she became any more embarrassed. "Thank you for coming by, though."

Della winked and saw herself out.

Mira was unsure of what to say when she and Emmit were alone.

After a few moments, Emmit once again took one of her hands and rubbed it between his. "You're freezing."

"Yeah. Wet clothes." Mira said.

"If you would point the way to the ingredients, I could make us some tea to give you a chance to warm up," Emmit said.

"That sounds wonderful," Mira said.

Before she could stand, though, he gently turned her chin again.

"Are you okay?" he asked.

Mira smiled, trying to be reassuring. "I slipped on some ice. I'll be fine."

He traced his fingers lightly over the spot where she had hit her head and butterflies began to stir in Mira, making her feel lighter.

Emmit nodded and stood up. Mira already missed the feeling of his hands.

"Where may I find your kettle?" Emmit asked, seeming to take a step back.

Mira wondered vaguely if he was bringing up a wall of formality around himself. "I'll show you." She stood, but hesitated. "Is Gabriel a supernatural?"

"Interesting information bubbles up from the past. Once upon a time, a witch knew who was who, and what was what," Emmit said.

Mira stared at him blankly, not certain if that was an insult and trying not to take it as one. "Was that a no?"

Emmit smiled, the formality seeming to bend. He seemed to be drawing closer without moving. "You should get warm."

Would it be worth it to ask again? To press for an answer? She dismissed the idea and showed Emmit where to find everything.

Once she was ensconced in her bedroom, Mira was torn between wanting to stand under a hot shower for the rest of eternity and rushing back out to spend the time she could with Emmit.

The need to get warm won, and she split the difference, taking a hot shower, but keeping it short. She put on cute shirt, which needed, unfortunately, to be covered with a heavy sweater. Hopefully, the apartment would warm up enough to lose layers as the evening progressed. Blushing furiously, she thought about the number of layers she'd like to lose with Emmit. Putting the thought out of her head was difficult.

When her face returned to a fairly normal shade—she could, after all, blame the pinkness on the hot shower—she joined Emmit.

"Sorry that took so long," she said.

The tea was waiting for her. She took a seat at the table next to Emmit and made a face when she saw that he had the letters with him.

"These," Emmit said, moving the letters to the side, "could be considered death threats."

"I don't think they're anything that dramatic," Mira said, concentrating on the tea.

"When I went to your shop, I ran into this man, didn't I?"

It seemed like eons ago to Mira. "Yeah. He was on his way out."

"Are you certain it's him?" Emmit asked.

Mira shrugged. "I guess I'm not certain, but who else?"

Emmit didn't say anything.

Using his momentary silence to her advantage, Mira opened her notebook. "I think I'm done creating your spell. I need to double check some of the measurements, but I should be able to cast it tomorrow."

"So soon?" Emmit asked.

"Yeah," Mira said, "I visited Barney and it gave me the idea to model your spell off the seer's potion."

Emmit smiled. "I wouldn't have thought of that."

"It was just the start. I brought in the physical Balance potion. I had to add a few other things to counteract the reactions from some of the ingredients. Ingredients that work in the Ether and the physical don't mix well together."

"This is brilliant work, Mira."

She blushed. "I'd still like to go over a few things. But, except for the items from you, I think I have everything we need."

"I hadn't expected it this quickly," Emmit said, looking thoughtful.

Mira had no idea if he considered it was a good thing or a bad thing that the spell was almost ready. "If you'd rather wait, we can. Or... if you'd like someone else to go over it..." The idea made her stomach clench.

"No, of course not." He gave her a small smile. "On both accounts. I have some additional requests, however. For the actual performance of the spell."

She tried not to frown. The performance of the spell was usually up to the witch. "I'm not sure I know what you mean."

"As you are aware, this is a unique situation. I'd like for there to be a double circle."

"Oh." She relaxed a little. "I thought we'd perform it here, so that won't be a problem. Below us actually, downstairs, not in the actual apartment. It's not a physical Balance spell, but I still think it would be performed better in closer contact with the ground. Della has let me put in a permanent circle, but I can add another circle inside."

"With me in one inner circle and you in the other?"

Mira tried not to read too much into the suggestion. "I can do that." That was usually only done when the witch needed to be protected from the effects of the spell or to protect one aspect of a spell from another. It seemed like overkill.

It also appeared that Emmit wasn't done. He looked like he wanted to say more, but wasn't sure how to go about it.

"Out with it," Mira said at last.

He raised an eyebrow at her, but seemed to notice her smile. "It's a matter of defensive magic. I know that witches keep several spells ready to go. Ones that they don't have to spend much time casting or ones they've already cast, but not yet released."

"You know a lot about witches," Mira said.

"I have known a few."

"It's true. Witches are known to keep a few spells handy. What about them?"

"Tomorrow, it may be wise to have something prepared. Not only for defense, but I'd like you to consider offensive options as well."

"Because of the spell?" She was tempted to ask what it was he expected to happen. Although, would he even tell her?

Emmit's eyes fell on the letters. "For that and…" he nudged the letters, "and anything else that you may face. I wish that the police task hadn't fallen to you."

Mira hadn't thought it was too bad until tonight. "Are you available tomorrow? Maybe around noon?"

"I'll make sure that I am."

Mira heard the wind howl outside. It was enough to make her feel cold all over again.

"How's your head?" Emmit asked.

"Sore," Mira admitted. Her heart melted seeing the tenderness in his expression. "But I'll be fine. More importantly, I'm warm."

There was a thump in the living room and Oracle meowed. Mira couldn't see the cat, but knew the sound well. Oracle had jumped onto the windowsill.

Emmit looked toward the sound. "I'm glad to hear that."

Mira followed his gaze, though she saw nothing but the wall. Oracle meowed again, and as though the cat were calling for her, she went into the living room. Oracle accepted the attention Mira gave him before she pushed back the curtain.

It was a bleak and cold landscape. The limbs shifted as the wind rushed by and the lights flickered but stayed on.

Mira turned and found Emmit standing close behind her. She hadn't heard him follow her.

"You've had a long day. I should go for the evening."

"You don't have to," Mira said.

"You'd like me to stay?" Emmit asked.

She hadn't really thought about her words before the offer had popped out of her mouth, but he was right, she wanted him to stay.

He moved closer to her.

"If you'd like to," she said, struggling to make her voice normal.

"Are you nervous to be alone?" Emmit asked.

"No."

"But you'd like me to stay?"

"If you want to," she repeated.

He was close enough that she could feel the warmth radiating from him. She looked up into his eyes and watched the green turn darker. A tingling feeling of anticipation started to spread. Something she hadn't felt in what seemed like ages.

Emmit started to reach out, but seemed to think better of it. "Not tonight. It's not... I shouldn't stay tonight."

He didn't move away, though, which made Mira hopeful. "It's not what?" she asked.

"Not a good idea."

"Why not?" Mira asked, her eyes still locked with his.

"My control isn't what it should be."

The words made Mira more inclined to get him to stay. She tried to remember when the last time was that she had been with someone.

"And that's a bad thing?" Mira asked.

"It is," Emmit said with all sincerity.

"It doesn't look like a great night for driving." It was a last ditch effort.

He smiled. "I have a car service waiting for me."

She nodded, finally breaking eye contact and wishing she hadn't. Emmit's face changed subtly, and he ran his fingers softly over the side of her injured head.

"I'm fine," Mira reminded him.

"Of course," Emmit said, putting some distance between them.

"Do you want more tea or anything before you go?" Mira asked.

"Thank you, but no." Emmit went to retrieve his coat.

"You know everything you need to bring tomorrow?" Mira asked.

"I'll be ready," Emmit said. "Is there anything else you'll need?"

"No."

Emmit looked out the window while putting on his coat. "The weather does seem to be turning worse again. If you need anything," he pulled a card from his pocket, "call this company and let them know I sent you to them."

Mira took the card. "Reinfield Concierge Services? I haven't heard of them."

"They can arrange almost anything."

"Including a car service that will go out in this weather?" Mira asked with a smile.

Emmit grinned slightly. "Even that."

Mira walked Emmit to the door. "I'll see you around noon?"

"You will."

She was hoping he would move closer to her again, but he seemed to keep a measured distance away.

"Good night," Emmit said before disappearing into the cold night.

CHAPTER 18

THE IDEA OF HOLDING OFFENSIVE spells close at hand didn't sit well with Mira. At least not now with the negativity building around her on its own. There had to be a better way.

Maybe it wasn't about keeping a spell ready.

While Mira readied the spell the following morning, she went through and discarded several ideas. Frustration over her indecision started to mount. When she found herself getting cranky, she decided on a different tactic.

Clarity was what popped into her mind first. The Clarity spell would mix well with the Fortitude and she hoped it would make her next course of action clear to her.

Then something else nudged its way in.

On her own, Mira wouldn't have thought of offensive spells. She hadn't even planned any defensive spells that one might find necessary when tracking a murderer.

Then there was Gabriel. One minute he was asking for information and the next, he considered her guilty of something. Not murder, maybe, but he obviously thought she had done something.

What would Emmit, Gabriel, or Ian do in her shoes? Better yet, Della? If Della had been placed in Mira's situation, what would she do?

Perspective.

Much more potent and powerful than Clarity, Perspective would put her in the heads of those around her. She would see what choices they would make and become more intimate with their points of view.

It might really help with Ian as well. If she knew why he kept struggling against the spell so much, she might be able to ease his concerns.

That alone was worth Perspective. Tumbling down a few stairs could turn into something a lot worse if she wasn't careful.

Content in the fact that she was heading in the right direction, Mira prepared for the other spell as well. It would take her longer to cast since she hadn't done any prep work, but it would be worth it in the end.

By the time Emmit arrived, she was calmer and felt confident.

A gust of cold air wrapped its way inside the house when she ushered him in.

"Did it snow more?" Mira asked, taking a glance outside before shutting the door.

"Yes, but the roads are much better. How are you feeling this morning?" Emmit asked. He sounded more formal and rigid than he had the night before.

"Much better," Mira assured him. "Do want some tea or coffee, or do you want to jump straight into the spell?"

"Moving forward sounds like the best plan," Emmit said, appearing to distance himself from her. "I appreciate your assistance in the matter, as well as your discretion."

"I've enjoyed it. It's not every day that I get to stretch my witchy abilities." Mira cleared her throat, not wanting to give Emmit a disclaimer that should come with a new spell, but knowing she had to. "We're going to need to measure the effects of the spell in order to fine tune it in the future. Overall, more work may need to be done."

"It is possible, I would assume, that the opposite could be true. That this spell could be exactly what is needed and work in short order," he said.

"It's possible. The spell will be using your blood, which automatically tunes it to what's needed to bring you into balance. We'll also have to see how long it lasts without needing to be renewed. However, it combines two spells that last for extended periods of time—from months to years. So time may not be an issue. It's hard to say without knowing more details of what is being balanced by the spell." Mira watched Emmit closely for a moment, trying to see if he would share any further. It wasn't necessary for her to know in order to make the spell work, but she could make the spell more effective if he gave more details.

Emmit apparently did not feel the same way. "I am sure that the time will be sufficient for now."

"I'm only giving you fair warning. Everything could be perfect."

"Do you feel it possible that something could go wrong?" Emmit asked.

"No, I mean—" Mira hesitated, "it is a possibility, but I sincerely doubt anything could go wrong with what we're doing. But, since I don't have all the details and I'm not overly familiar with the Ether, it's also a possibility that adjustments may need to be made."

"Understood," Emmit said.

Mira didn't understand why he seemed so standoffish. Maybe she shouldn't have asked him to stay last night. Maybe she had tried to jump into something that wasn't really there.

"Do you think you'll need this spell in the future?" Mira asked, grabbing her notebook.

Emmit's eyes tightened, but his voice remained neutral. "It's hard to know what the future may hold."

Mira stood there and drummed two fingers against her notebook. Something was wrong and she didn't know what it was.

"Is there anything else?" Emmit asked.

Maybe it was none of her business. "No," she said, ripping a page out and dropping her notebook on the table. "You know basically everything that we're doing in this spell—the ingredients, anyway." She tried not to sound aggravated when she said the words, but she wasn't sure she succeeded. "I thought it possible that you may need this again in the future, since the two spells I'm modeling it after have to be renewed."

"I can see how you would come to that conclusion," Emmit said.

She wanted to say, 'whatever,' but managed not to. "Well, I wrote everything out," she handed him the paper, "in case you need it again and I'm not available. Or if you'd rather not have me perform the spell again." She couldn't help but put in the last quip. It wasn't his fault if she had misread things, but she didn't like the distance he was placing between them.

Emmit raised an eyebrow at her. "You are sharing a spell, freely, outside of your family or coven?"

He understood that, at least. It wasn't something a witch did regularly. In fact, Mira hadn't shared a new spell with anyone outside her family and Tyler since college.

"I am," Mira said stiffly.

Emmit stared blankly at the paper, but said nothing.

"Let's get downstairs," Mira said. "I turned on the heat, so you may not need your coat, but you should probably take it just in case."

Emmit gently grabbed her arm when she strode past. "Mira…"

She stopped, but didn't want to admit that she wanted his hand on her arm. His face was unreadable.

"This... thank you," he said, still looking at the page. "I hope you will always see me as worthy of this."

That erased some of her ire, but Mira had no idea how to respond, so she just nodded. "Come on. There's an inside staircase we can use."

The stairs spilled out into an empty garage bay. It was interesting to see Emmit look over the space, and then walk around the invisible circle in the floor. Wordlessly, he passed over a small white paper bag. Mira lined the items up on a workbench before dumping them, one at a time, into a small crucible. A thin vial of blood was the last to be added.

There was no mistaking the fact that Emmit was watching her closely.

"Do you want me to burn these or would you like to take them?" Mira asked while she placed the bottle and little plastic pouches back in the paper bag.

"I'll take them," Emmit said.

He hadn't rushed, Mira noted, which was a good sign showing that he wasn't overly worried about the items. It was understandable that he wanted them back. Witches can do some horrible things to a person, especially when the witch has their blood.

Nodding, Mira handed the bag back and stirred the spell ingredients with a small glass rod. When she was done, she passed him the crucible.

"Hold that until I give you the go ahead," Mira said. She pulled a long length of braided silk from the workbench. "You know where the circle is, but I want to make sure you can see the boundaries, since you won't be able to leave."

Once Emmit moved to the center, Mira let one end of the silk dangle to the ground. When it hit the circle, it stuck to it as though magnetized. She walked around Emmit and dropped the end of the silk, which fell neatly into place.

"Are you ready?" Mira asked.

Emmit looked at the braided string and cringed. He clearly didn't like the idea of being held by anyone's power. Not that Mira blamed him. When she was young, her sister had held her in a circle once. It had pissed her off to no end, even though Robin had been grounded from all spells and potions for a month when their mother found out.

Usually you set yourself up in a circle, not the other way around.

"The spell won't take long," Mira reassured him.

He gave her a weak smile. "I'm ready."

She brought the power to life, and then walked to another larger circle. Once both boundries were awake, she looked over the crackling fire of magic, checking for points of weakness. Emmit was looking as well, but since he wasn't a witch, Mira wasn't sure if he could see the power or only sense it.

When she was satisfied that energy surrounded them securely, she nodded to Emmit. "Go ahead and take the potion."

While he was distracted, she took the opportunity to wipe her sweaty palms on her jeans. It might have been the fact that most of Mira's ancestors had disappeared into the Ether, or maybe it was because her mother had warned against it so thoroughly. Either way, the Ethereal Plane creeped her out as much as it fascinated her.

This was as close to the Ether as she was likely ever to get and she wasn't exactly sure what to expect.

When Emmit had finished choking down the potion, he stowed the bottle in his pocket and watched Mira intently.

Once she started the spell, Mira fell into her own power and lost track of everything except the magic and Emmit.

Her power reached through the inner protections, through Emmit, and then straight into a cold wash of Ether.

A guttural noise from Emmit started low and grew into a growl.

Forcing power through, Mira felt a heaviness drawing on Emmit from the Ether. It left her with a better understanding of the need for the potion. There was more of Emmit being drawn into the Ether than there was keeping him in this world.

Not his body, but everything else. His power, his energy, his soul—everything that made him Emmit, was stretched thin.

Once she reached the end of the line, the end of Emmit's power leaking into the other world, it felt as though a cold hand was wrapping itself tightly around him.

He went quiet.

Mira repeatedly had to tell herself that no one was reaching for her. She ordered her imagination to take the blame for the sensation as she began to draw back, dragging the power of Emmit with her, leaving a dam on the energy in their wake.

Heat started pouring from the inner circle. Mira wasn't sure if it came from the Ether or Emmit, but he started breathing hard and his eyes turned dark.

Calling on the blood from the spell, Mira wove Emmit's own energy, forcing the Ether back. It was tempting, oh so tempting, to cut off the Ether that remained. Despite the heat, she felt a chill as she imagined a dark shadow grasping from the other side.

Balance was what he was asking for, so that is what she did. The Ether still weighed heavier against him, so she drew further back.

Emmit violently threw himself against the barrier. She fed more energy into the circles and concentrated on the balance. Once again, he slammed himself against his invisible prison.

Then she found it. Pulling Emmit's energy to a central point, she began probing. He dropped to the ground, but Mira kept going, testing the magic, ensuring it would hold. With blood fueling the spell, it didn't need much time to settle. It was only when she was satisfied that she began to reel herself back in.

Mira found that she was shaky when she let go of the spell, but that realization fled her mind when she saw Emmit on the ground, seemingly asleep.

"Emmit?" Mira called. When he didn't stir, Mira knelt down next to him. Remembering the feeling of something lurking in the Ether, she kept the inner circle charged. "Emmit?"

Eyes snapped open.

Mira let out a breath she had been holding. "Are you okay?"

Emmit sat up and rolled his shoulders, then looked around the workspace. Mira wasn't sure if he was looking at his shell of magic or at the garage itself.

Knowing that magic could have drastic effects she waited for him, letting him take whatever time he needed to get himself in order. She looked him over, though, and everything appeared to be normal.

Emmit let out a sigh and then stood in a rapid movement. "It worked."

Still feeling unsteady, especially after seeing Emmit move so quickly, Mira made her way to her feet more slowly.

A smile broke out on Emmit's face. "It worked!"

Mira wanted to catch his excitement, but was still leery. "I'm glad to hear that." She studied his face, focusing on his eyes. The green turned darker and golden flecks stood out in contrast. He looked like Emmit. More animated, maybe, but it was him.

Smiling, she dropped the protection.

As soon as the shimmering field dropped away, Emmit laughed and pulled Mira into a hug that lifted her off her feet. When he sat her down, he kissed her. There was an alarming amount of heat, and for a moment, Mira felt like fire was pouring into her veins. In a flash, the heat melted away and became a mixture of longing and passion.

When Emmit stepped away, he looked as surprised as Mira felt. "I'm sorry," he started.

Mira didn't give him a chance to finish the thought before she pulled him into a kiss of her own. At first, Emmit was hesitant, but then the kiss became more intimate and they clung together.

For a few minutes, the rest of the world didn't exist. A new, fluttering heat spread through Mira and she wanted to lose herself in the moment.

But her mind didn't work that way. Not when magic was involved. Reluctantly, she broke the kiss.

Emmit put a little space between them. When Mira caught her breath, she saw that he was smiling as intently as she was.

Before silence could permeate the space, Mira turned her attention to the spell. She stowed the silk braid in her pocket and started to clean up.

They watched each other from the distance that Emmit had placed between them.

"Did it work like you expected?" Mira asked, more for something to say than anything else.

"Better than I expected." Emmit's voice sounded less formal. Less exacting. The adorable British accent was still predominate, however, which Mira loved.

"I'm glad to hear that," she said, running a critical eye over the area. Very few people would think there was anything here but an empty garage. Once she was satisfied, she turned back to Emmit. "Let's go back upstairs."

The shaky feeling left over from the spell was starting to fade. Worries about side effects started to mount.

What if the kiss was a side effect?

Emmit declined a drink, but Mira got a bottle of water to busy herself while she tried to think of how to word her questions.

"How are you feeling?" Mira asked.

"Amazing," Emmit said without hesitation.

"Are you experiencing... anything unexpected?" She fumbled over the words, still not sure exactly what to say.

"Nothing," Emmit said.

"You should pay special attention to what you do for the next few days."

"How so?"

"It's good to monitor the spell. I mean, casting the spell had some pretty major reactions. Spending the next few days studying side effects might be a good idea."

"Is there anything you have in mind that I should look out for?"

Mira shook her head. "Just don't do anything rash. Make sure you think things through. That sort of thing."

"You're the witch," Emmit said, grinning broadly. "I'll take your advice to heart."

"You'll let me know if anything seems... odd?"

"You will be the first to know."

"What are you doing for the rest of the day?" Mira asked.

"There are a few different matters that I am supposed to attend to today." He brightened again. "Unless, of course, you'd like to make plans."

There was a hint of a question in his last statement. "There are a few things I need to do today," Mira said.

Emmit shifted. "I understand." He glanced at the clock. "I should go."

"Are you free tomorrow?" Mira asked.

Mira hadn't noticed that he had grown tense until she saw him relax.

"I'll clear the day," he said, standing.

"You don't have to rush off," Mira said, mirroring his movement.

He moved closer. "I'd like to stay, but I really do have some things I should attend to."

"No problem."

Emmit wrapped his coat around himself and Mira was once again struck by how animated he appeared.

At the door, she felt the need to confirm. "You'll come over tomorrow?" *That didn't sound needy, did it? Hmmm, she'd have to analyze that later on.*

He turned and took her hand as though it was something he did every day. "I'm looking forward to it already."

She squeezed his hand and dropped it, reaching to open the door for him.

Only a hint of sunlight made it inside before Emmit reached out and pushed it closed. When she turned, his lips found hers again. He leaned into her, pushing her into the door. They lost themselves in the moment.

When he gently pulled away, she let out a contented sigh.

Wow! Every goodbye from Emmit should be like that. Every greeting as well.

After he left, Mira reveled in the experience a little longer before she narrowed her focus on the next spell.

CHAPTER 19

FORGETTING THE KISS WASN'T AS easy as she thought it would be. A part of her wanted to linger on the memory of his lips and remembering how his body had pressed into hers. The passion that he brought out was something that she was sorely missing in her life.

Perspective was waiting for her, though, and the measurements needed to be precise. Portions of the potion required heat, while others had to be cold.

It wasn't as difficult as her previous spell, but there was a bit more ceremony to it. She needed the circle, but was satisfied with the one in her apartment.

Inside the circle, she set down items that helped tie her to the perspective she was searching for. A crystal Sally had given to her, werewolf hair—not one of Helen's, but she would make do—and a small bottle of distilled hemlock. The poison was symbolic of the damage that the killer had inflicted and could inflict in the future.

Once those items were in place, Mira readied herself. She was saved a trip downstairs when she realized she still had the silk cord that she had used to mark the circle during Emmit's spell. She wrapped it around herself three times and put a rock in her pocket as an anchor. Then she took a deep breath and stepped into the circle with the potion in hand.

The day wasn't getting any younger. The rock kept her grounded, and the protective power that the string had soaked up would ensure that the potion's influence wouldn't overwhelm her. Mira drank the potion and invoked the spell.

Heat, as though from a furnace, poured over her and she saw... herself.

It was an odd sensation, because it wasn't her, not quite. This version of her was younger and prettier than the person she saw in the mirror each day. Nevertheless, there was no mistaking that she was looking at herself and had pushed herself against the door, her door, with a haze of passion growing around her.

Emmit was thinking about her.

The thought slammed into her head and she tried to extract herself. Whatever Emmit was, he could sense magic even better than she could. The last thing she wanted Emmit to think was that she was spying on him. Knowing how secretive Emmit was, this felt treacherous.

Since her mind had been on Emmit all afternoon, it was difficult to drag her thoughts away. It wasn't real... it was Perspective.

Mira gripped the rock in her pocket and thought of the other items around her. The burning desire faded fast, leaving her feeling chilled from the inside.

The werewolf hair. Mira switched perspectives.

An intense ache tore through her, leaving a gaping hole behind. The pack's grief was still new and raw. Even though this hair was only a representation of Helen's pack, it was strong enough to take Mira's breath away.

Taken off guard, she flipped once again through perspectives. Concentrating on Sally's crystal, Mira found other people thinking of her. Someone was thinking about holding hands with Sally. Of kissing her and watching her head out of the door on a run. There was such a feeling of finality that Mira was sure Martin was seeing Sally leave for the last time.

Quickly, she left that perspective, only to find one even worse. Sally was a little girl sitting on her dad's lap, reading a book. Mira cried out and jerked away.

Breathing hard, Mira gripped the rock, and worked to keep her thoughts her own. This killer had left so much heartache in his wake. So much anger and pain.

Right, Mira thought, she was going about this wrong. Switching gears, she closed her eyes again and gently stepped into the spell. This time, she thought of all three items together.

Surface thoughts fluttered past. It took Mira a moment to realize that there were investigators and reporters thinking about the murders.

There were also people worried about the deaths. Who would be next?

She concentrated on Gabriel. As one of the main detectives, he was probably preoccupied with the case. Even though she was trying as hard as she could to focus on him, she came up empty. She must have needed something with a closer connection to Gabriel in order to find him.

Maybe if she added the hemlock?

Taking a deep breath, Mira added the bottle to the others in her mind's eye. Her stomach clenched as she lurched into another mind.

It had to be done.

The mind was cold calculation. Thoughts of Tyler floated up.

It's almost over.

A few more to go.

The phone rang, breaking Mira's concentration. Blinking, she looked around the kitchen.

Was that Tyler, or was it someone thinking about Tyler? Mira still had a death grip on the rock. Once she made sure the braided silk was still wrapped securely around her, she dropped the circle.

The phone stopped ringing, which was good, because Mira didn't think she could stand yet.

Tyler, or someone thinking of him?

It had to be someone thinking about Tyler, right? He wouldn't hurt anyone.

That didn't make Mira feel any better. Whatever else that could be said about that perspective, it came from the mind of a killer.

She lurched to her feet and snatched up her cell phone. She texted Tyler.

Call me.

If it was Tyler she sensed, then was he about to kill someone? If it wasn't Tyler's mind she saw, did that mean the killer was going after Tyler?

Ian. He could help.

No answer. She sent Ian the same message she had left for Tyler.

Mira grabbed her purse and dug around for her car keys. It was only then that she remembered her car was in the city.

The car service.

Her mind was lurching instead of really thinking things through. She snatched up the business card Emmit had left and called the concierge service.

When the phone rang, she tried to steady her breath.

"You are calling from an unknown number. Please state your name."

"Um," Mira stumbled over her words, "I'm Mira Owens, a friend of Emmit Harker. He said I should call if I needed anything."

"What can we help you with today?" The voice was like honey, smooth and soothing.

"I need a ride. It's really important."

"Are you at your residence?"

"Yes," Mira said.

There was a short pause. "We have someone on their way."

"I—" Mira stopped. That didn't sound right.

"Is Mr. Harker with you?" the mellow voice asked.

"No, he's not."

"Would you like for us to give him a message?"

Mira bit her lip. "Um... no. No thank you."

"We should arrive within ten minutes. Is there anything else we can do for you?"

"Thank you, no."

The line disconnected. Mira looked at the phone. The strangeness of the call gave her something to focus on and began to calm her racing heart.

Should she chance calling Gabriel?

Strings of disconnected thoughts flowed around her.

It's done.

...her fault.

...almost over but...

...Helen...

Mira closed her eyes and reached again for the rock in her pocket. Trying to dislodge the thoughts was difficult when she kept trying to find out whose mind she was seeing.

A horn honked.

Without really thinking about it, Mira grabbed her coat and her purse and ran outside. A sleek black Escalade with darkened windows was parked in the driveway. Someone was holding the back door open for her.

Mira practically flew down the stairs. "Thank you," she said when she jumped into the vehicle.

The man got into the passenger seat, and the car began to move the moment the door was closed.

She had no idea who these people were. The thought flitted around.

And they're taking me somewhere, but I haven't told them where I need to go.

It was too strange to contemplate, so she told them where she was headed to settle her nerves.

"I'm sorry I'm in such a rush. Thank you for picking me up."

"It's our pleasure."

Mira stared out the window and tapped her fingers on her purse.

"Is this a situation in which you need further assistance?" the man in the front passenger seat asked without turning around.

"What?" Mira had almost missed what he said. "Oh, um... no. I just need..."

What? What did she need to do?

"I just need to reach someone," she finished.

The man nodded. They didn't ask anything else, and they didn't attempt to make conversation. What they did make was time. At least it seemed that way. They were pulling to a stop in front of the building faster than she ever could have if she had been driving.

"How much do I owe you?" Mira asked as the man got out of the vehicle and walked to the other side.

"We don't work that way," the driver said.

"I don't understand."

"Mr. Harker has you covered," he said.

The strangeness washed over her again. When the door opened, she thrust the thought aside.

"Thank you," she said, then jumped out of the vehicle and hurried into the building.

The moment Mira stepped inside she realized that she had never entered the building from the front. They had always taken her in through the garage.

She hurried up to a thick glass window and waited, bouncing on her feet with impatience, until she was noticed.

"I need to speak with Detectives Burke or Flint," she said.

"What is this visit regarding?"

Mira blinked at the man behind the glass. "I'm a consultant on an investigation. It's very important that I talk with them."

"I'll let someone know you're here," the man said.

When he didn't move, she glared at him and whipped out her phone, starting her string of calls over again. Each time she received no answer, her heart beat faster. Where was everyone?

There was that mind, that killer's mind that continued to lurk alongside her own. She should have concentrated on the spell longer. It was still moving through her, though. Maybe she could reestablish the connection.

Uncomfortable looking seats were in the foyer, which didn't look conducive to spell casting, but Mira decided it was worth a try.

"Mira?"

It was Gabriel. Of course it was. She couldn't have been lucky enough for it to be Ian.

"If you're here to file a complaint about yesterday—"

"Is Ian here?" Mira asked.

Gabriel looked like he had smelled something bad. "He's not."

"Fine. We need to talk," Mira said. "Now."

Gabriel shook his head, but said, "Fine, follow me." He nodded to the man behind the glass and led Mira into the station, where they climbed up several flights of stairs.

"Where's Ian," Mira asked when she couldn't stand the silence anymore. There were things she needed to discuss with the detectives and she was sure she wouldn't get far with Gabriel.

"Out," Gabriel said. "We do have a job to do."

"Who was arrested last night?" Mira asked, ignoring his disgruntled attitude.

"I'm not going to discuss an ongoing case with you," Gabriel said. "In here."

He led her into a small interview room.

"You know I'm going to find out from Della anyway," Mira said.

"Great, find out from her," he said, sitting down. "I'm assuming that this is about last night?"

"What about last night?" Mira said, trying to concentrate on Gabriel and not the perspective of someone else.

"The search? Your fall down the stairs? Any number of things."

She looked at him blankly. "You had a warrant. It's not like you forced your way in."

"I was doing my job," he stressed.

"Right," Mira said without a hint of sarcasm.

He sighed. "I could have been nicer about it. I figured that's why you were looking for Ian." He wasn't as gruff as he had been. There may have even been a trace of regret hidden in there.

She had really been counting on Ian being at the station. What could she say to Gabriel?

Well, she had to say something. "I'm looking for Ian because I think a friend of mine is in trouble and it might be connected to the case. And I know you don't like me, so I wanted to talk with him."

"What makes you say I don't like you?" Gabriel shook his head. "Never mind that. Tell me about your friend."

"His name is Tyler and I think—" What *did* she think? The name had weighed heavily in the mind of the killer, so he had to be thinking about Tyler, right? It couldn't be Tyler, right? "I think he has a connection to the other victims."

Gabriel frowned. "Wait here." He strode out of the room, not waiting for a response.

Mira tried to put her thoughts together, but she felt like her mind was being torn in two. Using Gabriel's absence to her advantage, she closed her eyes and let herself fall back into the spell. The hemlock and other items that had been in her circle danced in her thoughts.

Another witch. Witches can find proof.

Mira probed the mind, but whoever it was wasn't thinking about Tyler.

She distinctly felt that the person was male, and he was thinking about witches. *Which witch?*

"What about witches?"

She hadn't noticed Gabriel coming into the room, or that she had spoken out loud.

Mira shifted in her seat. "Nothing." Grappling with her own mind, she tried to push herself away from the spell.

Gabriel had a notebook with him. "Tell me about Tyler."

It took Mira a few moments to remember what she had said before. "I think he's connected to the other victims somehow."

"We haven't made any connection to all the victims," Gabriel said. He watched her closely.

"Maybe that connection is him."

"What does Tyler think about this?" Gabriel asked.

"I can't reach him," Mira said.

"Did you try visiting him?"

"No. Ian took me home yesterday. I didn't have my car."

Karen didn't have to die.

"Of course she didn't," Gabriel said.

Mira blanched. Was she talking?

"Um, can I get a glass of water?" Mira asked.

He looked at her for a few heartbeats before setting down his notebook. "I'll be right back."

As soon as he left the room, Mira was closing her eyes and frantically trying to push the spell away. She took out the rock and concentrated on grounding herself.

I can see that the witch has to wait.

She felt her lips move that time. Getting away from the spell wasn't working. There had to be another way out of this.

Her eyes landed on Gabriel's notebook and pen. Snatching the pen up, she realized that it might not even be his, but he had been holding it. It would have to do.

She concentrated on the pen.

Her mind shifted.

And she watched herself through Gabriel's perspective when he returned to the room.

He sat down across from Mira and she openly gaped at him. It was almost as though two Gabriels were there, superimposed on one another. One was the everyday Gabriel that she saw, and the other was like nothing she had ever seen. He shimmered.

"Are you ready to talk about Tyler?"

Mira was mesmerized. Gabriel alone was one of the most handsome men she had met, but this new Gabriel, the hidden one, was beautiful.

"Or maybe you'd like to talk about Karen," Gabriel said. "Or witches?"

The second Gabriel was also larger somehow. Bulkier, maybe.

"What do you have in your hand?" Gabriel asked.

She looked down and it was as if a spell was broken. Unfortunately, not the one she cast.

"Oh, sorry," she said, handing Gabriel the pen.

"I mean your other hand."

"Nothing," Mira said. She moved to put the rock back in her pocket.

"Mira." There was a warning in his voice.

"It's just a rock."

"Let me see."

She didn't move.

"If it's only a rock it's not going to hurt to show me," Gabriel said.

She shrugged and handed it over.

The room dimmed.

"Why are you carrying a rock?" Gabriel asked.

"No reason," Mira said. Her eyes flickered to the corners of the room and back. Impressions of a shadow darting by made her look again. "Did you see that?"

"I've seen a rock very similar to this recently," Gabriel said. He ignored her question and twisted the stone over in his hands.

Out of the corner of her eye, something moved close to the ground. Instinctively, she lifted her feet off the ground. "Is there something under the table?"

"There's nothing here, Mira." He was inspecting the rock as though he were trying to memorize every line.

Both Gabriels appeared to be talking. Mira stomach lurched and she closed her eyes. She couldn't look at Gabriel anymore.

"I came here about my friend," Mira said. "Nothing else. Please, give me the rock back."

"Where did you get this?" Gabriel asked.

"It's a rock, who cares."

"You need to tell me."

"It was a mistake to come here," Mira said, opening her eyes and trying not to look at the detective. "I'll go find Tyler." Taking a steadying breath, she put her feet on the ground.

That's when she saw the shadow standing in the corner. Trying to tell herself that shadows don't stand did her no good. This one clearly stood.

A dark shape moved, but she didn't take her eyes off the corner. The thing in the corner was much worse than anything she had seen.

"Have a seat," Gabriel said.

The dark misty form was starting to gel and come together. As it became darker, her fear grew.

"I need to go." It came out as barely a whisper.

Gabriel followed her gaze before looking back at her. "I need an answer. Where did you get this?"

She only shook her head and slowly stood, as though she were afraid the thing in the corner would charge her.

"I'm going," she said.

"I can't let you do that," Gabriel said. "Look, I'll get Ian here if you'd rather talk to him. I'll call Della or any other lawyer you might want to have with you, but I'm going to have to ask you to stay."

Mira heard the words, but she did not intend to listen to them. She began to ease away from the table.

Gabriel stood, and his doppelganger did the same a heartbeat behind.

Mira glanced behind her to the door. Something was standing there, still misty, but almost fully formed.

She hadn't noticed that she'd moved back until she bumped into Gabriel.

Mira whipped around and Gabriel grabbed her arm. The air started to grow heavy.

"What are you doing? Are you on something?" he asked. "Because that would explain a lot."

Mira was shaking from head to toe. "Don't you see them?" Her stomach was clenched so tightly that she was forced to take shallow breaths.

"There's nothing here." Gabriel said.

Mira felt a tug at her waist. The woven silk cord was being pulled away, but there was nothing grabbing it.

Nothing she could see.

"Let go," Mira said, twisting around and moving away.

"I'm worried you're going to hurt yourself," Gabriel said.

Pressure pushed at Mira from all sides. She had two Gabriels, superimposed onto each other, holding her arm.

She closed her eyes tightly against the atmosphere that strained to crush her. There was a pop and the weight lifted.

Mira no longer felt the pull at her waist.

CHAPTER 20

GABRIEL LET GO, RELEASING HER as though in slow motion.

The air felt strange, so Mira opened her eyes, then immediately wished she had kept them closed. There was a haze in the room, as though someone had started a fire down the hall.

If it were only the haze, she could have handled it, but the creatures that gathered around them, she had a problem coping with.

The dark thing in the corner stepped out. It vaguely resembled a person in that it had arms, legs, and a head, but that's where the similarities stopped. The skin of the creature was wrinkled and black, like leather that had been set on fire before being doused with water.

"What did you drug me with?" Gabriel asked. "I swear to god, Mira, if you drugged me I'm locking you up."

"Quiet, Gabriel," Mira snapped. She was grateful that she felt like herself again. There were no other people wading through her mind. Although, that was only a small comfort as the creature in front of them took another step forward.

"Quiet, my ass." Gabriel still sounded like himself. "What the hell is that thing? Oh shit. What the hell are *they*?"

Mira marveled at how he could still sound the same. She felt like she was having a meltdown, but Gabriel was in his normal state of being pissed off at her. She would have expected his attitude in her house, the office, the store, and anywhere else in their normal reality. It was surprising to hear that same aggravation when pulled into another world.

It was comforting in an odd sort of way. Seeing his everyday reaction helped keep Mira on an even keel.

There was a hissing noise that extinguished when the creature began to speak. "Bassstard son of a god, we have no quarrel. Leave here now."

"What the hell?" Gabriel asked.

Mira wondered the same thing. She thought the noise came from the creature in front of her, but it was difficult to be sure.

The hissing rose and the voice came again. "Hell is what waitsss in store for the Witch. Ssshe has meddled and ssshe is oursss."

Gabriel tensed behind Mira. She tried to step back to get both creatures in sight, but Gabriel was still at her back. It was clear these monsters weren't happy with her.

When she angled herself, she caught sight of the other thing in the room. It was light green in color and looked as though a weird mold was growing over it. It was just as hideous as the first.

Then she saw Gabriel from the corner of her eye. She gasped and tried to step away from him without getting closer to the others. There were no longer two Gabriels, but the Gabriel she knew was gone. In his place stood an angel.

He took her breath away. His skin was pearly, as if light were trapped inside. The size difference she had noted was now explained. Wings. Fully formed and as clear as could be. At first glance, she thought they were pure white. She couldn't help but look again. Toward the end of the feathers, the tips were light gray.

"Gabriel?" Mira's voice was filled with awe.

"What are they, Mira? What did you do?" Gabriel asked.

Turning her attention back to the two creatures, it dawned on her where they were.

"No," Mira said softly, "I didn't do this. I didn't take us here."

A gasping breath of a voice sounded from the creature closest to Gabriel. "You, witch, were brought here by usss. The cossst was great, but you meddled and you must pay." It took a step forward.

Gabriel lost his temper and reached instinctively for his gun, but his hand came back holding a sword. Out of the corner of her eye, Mira saw his puzzlement, but it didn't slow him down.

"I don't know who or what you are," Gabriel said, holding the sword out as though it were a loaded gun. He reached in his pocket and took out his ID. "But you are in the wrong place. You have ten seconds to start out that door."

The absurdity of what he was doing wasn't lost on Mira. The twisted creatures, however, didn't seem fazed.

Gabriel held out his badge. At least, Mira had thought it was his badge. When she saw him pull it from his pocket, she knew it was his ID and badge. Now they were gone, and he held a shield instead.

The angel didn't so much as blink with the change. As beautiful as Gabriel was before, his beauty was doubled with the gleam of the sword and shield. They'd appeared out of nowhere, but fit so perfectly with the angel that Gabriel had become that you could tell they belonged to him. Gabriel, the warrior angel.

"Basstard sson of a god. We have no quarrel with you," hissed the first creature again.

"And I don't have a quarrel with you," Gabriel said. "If you aren't going to leave, we're going to walk out of here."

He moved toward Mira. She hadn't realized that she had backed so far away from everyone else in the room. As he approached, she saw that he was breathing heavy.

Maybe he was freaking out.

"The witch stays with us," gasped the other creature.

"The witch stays with me," Gabriel said. "Mira, we need to head toward the door."

"It's in front of the door," she said quietly.

"Right." With his sword still pointed out, he wrapped an arm around Mira, putting his shield between them and the creatures. "Hold on to this."

Mira had no idea what Gabriel's plan was, but she grabbed the shield as best as she could. It was heavier than it looked. The two creatures each moved forward.

Gabriel and Mira both tensed when they moved.

"Get back!" Gabriel's voice came like an avalanche.

No human could have sounded like that. It was an order. A demand. Now Mira understood why they called him the son of a god. They could not stand against that voice. Squealing and hissing, they fled the room. Mira wouldn't have been surprised if they had fled the building, but that might have been asking too much.

The shield is what held Mira in place. She felt the demand, but it had slid over her and caused no more than a shiver down her spine.

They could hear shrieks fade away in the distance. Mira sank down in a chair, still trying to hold up the shield as Gabriel leaned against the table, sword still in hand. When she passed the shield back to him, Mira saw that he was shaking almost as much as she was.

Gabriel went over to the door and slammed it. The hand on his sword was white knuckled. Once he made sure the door was secure, he let himself fall into a chair. He did not relinquish his weapon or shield.

"Okay, I'm trying to stay real calm here, Mira." He wouldn't look at her. "But I need to know what you gave me."

Mira shook her head. "I didn't give you anything." She leaned her elbows on the table and rubbed her temples, but she kept her eyes open and on the door. Her heart raced as though she had run several miles and needed a break.

"This is bullshit," Gabriel replied.

"This is bullshit," Mira agreed, trying to keep the tremor from her voice, "but you know I'm not lying. I would have never have brought us here. Even if I knew how to do this, I wouldn't have done it. No one comes here."

He stared at the door, but looked as though he was looking at nothing. "Where do you think here is?" he asked.

"We've been moved into the Ether," Mira said. "The Ethereal Plane."

Gabriel sat unmoving while Mira tried to wrap her own mind around what she had said. They were in the Ether. When witches went into the Ether, they didn't come back.

Mira jumped when Gabriel stood up like a shot. "Those things are in the station. We have to make sure everyone is okay."

"There's no one else here," Mira said. "People don't go to the Ether."

"We're here. I'm checking." He stood at the door. "Are you staying here or coming with me?"

"Gee," Mira said sarcastically, "wait for my death alone in a room or go with the warrior angel. Which should I do?"

"Warrior angel?" Gabriel asked.

"Never mind," Mira said, getting up. "I'm going with you."

"Stay behind me, but you have to keep an eye out behind us. Don't let anything sneak up from behind."

Mira nodded and kept herself plastered to Gabriel's back as he led them through the second floor and then down to the first. She felt jittery trying to see every direction at once.

Out of the corner of Mira's eye, she caught sight of movement. When she jerked her head around, however, there was nothing there. Gabriel had the same twitching that told Mira that he must have been seeing movement as well. Maybe it was just the atmosphere of the place making them think something was lurking just out of sight.

It's probably the haze, Mira thought. It was a constant smoky reminder that they were not in their world. It didn't help Mira's nerves. Neither did Gabriel's voice, calling out to see if anyone was there. It kept Mira taut with tension, half hoping for someone to answer, while at the same time fearing what it might be that answered.

On the main floor, they worked their way steadily toward the entryway. Knowing that the front doors were glass, Mira thought that was a bad move, but she had nothing better to suggest. Nothing that Gabriel would accept, anyway.

At the door that Gabriel had led her through not an hour before, there was a scratching noise.

Gabriel's wings billowed out and stretched wide behind him, throwing Mira back. They stood as still as possible and listened to the noise. Something scraped along the door, wanting to come in.

When Gabriel moved forward, Mira bit her lip and scrambled back until she hit the wall. Every instinct she had screamed that opening that door was a bad idea. Instead of opening it, however, he clicked the lock.

The scratching grew more insistent and Gabriel backed away, holding his sword out in front of him. With her back to the wall, Mira slid down to sit on the floor. Gabriel backed up beside her, wings first. They watched in silence until the sound went away. Neither of them took their eyes off the door as Gabriel sank down to sit next to her.

"I don't feel like I've been drugged," he finally admitted. "This shit is weird. What's going on?"

Taking a deep breath, Mira started with the most obvious, "Did you know you were an angel?"

Gabriel rolled his eyes.

Mira gestured to his wings. It was as though he had never noticed them. He rubbed his hands over the feathers, inspecting them. Mira wanted to do the same, but it seemed intrusive.

Looking tense in the face, he stared hard at one of his wings. Trying to figure out what he was doing, Mira watched him. It wasn't until he raised one arm up and down that she realized he was trying to make the wing move or flap.

A hysterical little giggle escaped Mira, and she clapped a hand over her mouth.

He glowered at her.

CHAPTER 21

W HEN MIRA THOUGHT SHE COULD trust her voice, she swallowed hard and removed her hand. "I'm sorry you didn't know," she said, unsure of what you say to someone who just found out they were an angel.

"Yeah, well, if this is real, I think my parents have some explaining to do. Although," he added, "I'm still not convinced this *is* real. Start talking."

While letting the idea of being an angel sink in, Mira plunged on. She told him why she had showed up at the station. Before she was too far into the story, he went into cop mode. He started asking questions and pulling more details out of her. Mira managed to keep Emmit out of it. The spell she had performed that morning was none of his business, and she had made a promise to Emmit.

Gabriel was able to fill in some blanks for Mira as well. Everything she didn't remember saying from the Perspective spell. He said it didn't really sound like her voice, yet did in a way.

Whatever that means. When Mira got to the part of the two Gabriels, he held up a hand for her to stop. He rolled his head on his shoulders. Mira had to bite her lip to keep another bout of tense laughter from escaping when he hit his head on his wing.

She almost succeeded.

After glaring in her direction, Gabriel started inspecting his sword and shield and let Mira continue talking. She went up to the point where they had entered the Ether, and he stopped her again.

"Tell me about the Ether. What is this place?" Gabriel asked.

He wanted more information, but she wasn't sure what to tell him. "People don't come here. Witches, warlocks, alchemists, it doesn't matter. No one comes here. Seers look into the Ether to tell the future, but even looking at it tends to drive them mad."

"You said witches used to come here."

"Hundreds of years ago, we witches destroyed practically all of our knowledge on the Ether. We were almost extinct at that point. The Ether stopped being a safe road to travel."

"What do you mean, 'safe road to travel'?" Gabriel asked.

Mira let out a noise of frustration. "It's just a saying. There is an old nursery rhyme for witches warning against traveling the ethereal roads. Darkness lying in wait and things like that."

"Wait, what's the rhyme?" Gabriel asked.

Mira wracked her brain for a minute, but she was getting impatient. "I don't remember! I was kid. It was just a kid's saying."

He looked frustrated, but let the subject drop and picked another. "So these things. They say they brought us here. How do we get back?"

Mira slumped, feeling defeated. "There hasn't been a way out for my people in hundreds of years."

"Keep it together," Gabriel snapped. "We've gotta think of a way out of this. What about angels? Do angels have a way to get out of here?" He gestured at his wings as if she needed the reminder.

Mira looked at him as if he'd lost his mind. "Gabriel, angels aren't— I mean… you look like an angel. That, that thing called you the son of a god. But I've never met an angel." She stopped and thought for minute. "I've never heard of anyone meeting an angel."

Gabriel looked down at his lap.

"Look, Gabriel, I'm sorry. I'm just—I don't know everything.

And I don't know that many people." She thought for a moment. "Emmit might have known. I think he sensed something in you."

Gabriel snorted. "Great. My number two suspect. Number two, since you're number one."

"You can't still think that I did this," Mira said.

Gabriel shrugged. "Doesn't matter much here, does it?"

Mira looked around and started to shake again. She took a few deep breaths and really started to look around the room—taking in all the detail under the haze, focusing her mind away from the fact that she could die here in the Ether.

The building and doors looked solid, but the furniture blurred around the edges. Almost as if, it weren't quite there. Getting up, she glanced at the door, hoping not to rouse whatever wanted to get in. While walking over to a desk, she took in the lack of windows in the room. Her stomach was a nervous knot. She didn't want to reach out and touch the desk, but the more details the better. With one finger, she scrunched up her face and touched the surface. Although it was blurred around the edges, it was solid enough. When she took her hand back, she wiped her finger on her jeans.

She looked back at Gabriel. He was standing now, and his eyes were focused on her, his whole body tensed, as if ready to pounce or run. He was also glowing.

Where he glowed, the haze pulled away, as if the air itself was afraid to touch him.

"We need to make a plan," Gabriel said.

His skin was beautiful. Mira walked over to him, wanting to reach out and touch him, but he was far too pent up for her to try. They weren't exactly friends, and he had a sword in his hands.

"What's with you?" Gabriel asked. "We need to go back to the interrogation room and figure out our next move."

"Did you realize that you're glowing?" Mira asked.

Startled, Gabriel looked down at his skin, catching the tail end of the steady bright glow. He appeared less anxious while he watched the shine disappear.

He looked up at Mira. "I thought it was you. Well, your necklace and whatever the hell that thing is around your waist."

She held out her pentagram and turned it this way and that. A calmness stole over her while she had it wrapped in her hand. Carefully, she rearranged the necklace, making sure it touched skin, and examined the braided strand of silk. It, too, was glowing, though not as strongly as the necklace.

"Magic," Mira said. "Magic glows here."

The scratching noise started at the door again. Gabriel's sword swung up, ready to attack, but the thing didn't seem likely to make its way through.

"I think it can hear us," Mira whispered to Gabriel. "Let's go back, like you said, and figure out what to do next."

On the way back, they made a pit stop in the bathrooms. Gabriel was hesitant to go inside with her, but there was no way Mira was going to walk in and have something jump her.

She did a quick look around the room. The mirrors were gone. There were dark marks where they might have hung in the bathrooms out in the real world, but no other signs. Bracing herself, she checked a stall. No water in the toilet. Making one last-ditch effort, she turned on the water in the sink. There was nothing.

Gabriel was watching her intently, but instead of answering, Mira motioned him back out and led the way to the interrogation room.

"Want to tell me what that was about?" he asked when he had closed the door behind them.

"There are no reflective surfaces," Mira said. "No windows, no mirrors. There's not even any water."

"Does this tell us something?" He asked.

Mira shrugged. "Not by itself. Items with magic in them have some sort of effect on the world." She pulled at the knot in her silk string, and then hesitated. "Um, come put your hand on my shoulder. Just in case."

"In case of what?" He asked.

"Just—just in case," she said, motioning for him to come over.

He shifted his shield into the same hand as his sword and grabbed her shoulder. Taking a deep breath, she undid the knot and took off the string.

Nothing happened.

Mira slumped in her seat. "Sorry," she said. "I was hoping maybe the string was holding us here."

Gabriel shook his head and moved to the other side of the table.

Ignoring the slight, Mira started taking stock of what she had. Magic string, magic necklace, and clothes. Nothing else with her.

"What do you have on you?" she asked Gabriel.

Once again, he switched his shield to his sword hand, and then he started digging around in his pockets. He came up empty.

"I should have had a gun and my badge, but I ended up with these," he said. "But I also had keys, a wallet, you know, the usual stuff."

"Those things can't be light," Mira said, motioning to the shield. "Why don't you sit them down and rest? You may need your strength later."

Gabriel shrugged, but didn't let go. Instead, he looked over the shield.

"Will they disappear?" he asked.

"Good question. I'm not sure. If they do, I think they'll come back to you. They came to you pretty quickly when those creatures were here."

"When they came near I was thinking how I needed my gun," Gabriel said. He was quiet for a moment. "They feel good in my hands. Like they're a part of me."

"As long as they aren't wearing you out. Those monsters might not be willing to leave us alone."

"I'm good," he said.

She noticed that he rested the sword across his lap and his shield on his booted foot.

Standing up, Mira started walking around the room, trying to feel for a circle, or some trace of the magic that had pulled them through. She turned up empty. Tossing herself down in the chair again, she rubbed her temples. When she looked, she saw Gabriel watching her.

Before he could ask, Mira answered, "I was sensing for the magic that brought us here, but I can't find a trace."

"Are you sure it is magic?" Gabriel asked.

"What else could it be?"

"How should I know?"

She didn't have a reply.

For a while, they sat silently in the little room, each trapped in their own thoughts. Both glanced at the door from time to time, Mira's glances were a bit more nervous than Gabriel's was. Maybe the sword made him feel better. At the hint of any noise, Mira would freeze and listen intently.

The silence made Mira more unsettled, not less. It wasn't a break from what had happened. Instead, it was a constant running reminder that neither of them had any idea what to do. Mira couldn't handle the silence for long. It had felt like hours instead of minutes.

She drew the silk cord out of her pocket again. Staring at the dim glow, she wound it around and around her fingers, only to unravel it all again.

"I wonder why there are no reflective surfaces," Mira mused. Gabriel shrugged.

Mira didn't look up from the cord. "Magic from our world stands out here. The desks and stuff are here, and they're real, but they don't look solid."

"I'm not sure where you're going with this," Gabriel said.

"Is the magic here real or a reflection of the magic from our world?"

Gabriel rolled his eyes.

Heat rose to Mira's face and into her voice. "If we get to my house, we may be able to do something."

"I'm not sure I buy the witch thing."

"What?" Her voice was higher than she'd intended. At least she was trying. "You say that after sprouting feathers?"

Gabriel looked back, surprised once more by the fact that he had wings. Then his shoulders slumped, and he stared down at the sword across his lap.

Mira sighed. Now she felt sorry for him even though she really didn't want to. This was a lot to take in all at once.

"You know," Mira said after a while, "you're taking this much better than Ian. I told him about the supernatural and he ended up getting drunk after a few little displays. He hadn't been ripped out of his world or sprout wings."

Gabriel looked a bit better knowing how his partner had acted. "Is that why he's been working with you so much?"

"We needed someone for the case."

"We?"

"The supernatural community."

"Why didn't he tell me?" Gabriel asked.

Mira had a ghosted smile when she told Gabriel about the spell. That and she shared the rest of the story with him. Everything. In detail.

Well, everything except Emmit.

He looked more relaxed as she went on. "Why would the spell on Ian cause you to fall down the stairs?"

She looked around their little room and told him about the repercussions of spelling someone against their will. "The more they fight it, the worse things come back on the witch."

"It doesn't sound like Ian. Doing that to you, I mean."

"He didn't do it. I did it to myself when I cast the spell."

"But he keeps fighting it."

"He doesn't know what that will do."

"Then why tell me?" Gabriel asked.

Mira shrugged. "You're one of us. A supernatural." Then she winced. "And I'm really hoping that what I did didn't cause this."

He looked like he was going to say something, and then changed his mind.

"Anyway," Mira said, "you're taking it better than him."

"You should have told me as well." There was a sullen hint to his words.

"We were getting to that point. Ian really, really wanted me to."

"And you didn't because?"

"Witches that get in the habit of spelling people against their will, die." Mira tried to stress this. "You already didn't like me. I figured you'd fight the spell like mad."

"But I would have known you were telling the truth," Gabriel said.

She shook her head at him. "People don't always believe, even if they know it's true. Case in point." She gestured wide to the entire room around them.

He shrugged. "I could have been having an off day, and I told you before, I never didn't like you. It was the lies."

"Well, now you know why I lied," Mira said.

"Yeah, but when they came from you, it was like hearing nails on a chalkboard."

"Everyone lies. I would have thought you'd be used to it."

"For most people, I know when they lie, but it doesn't bother me. You? It's damn aggravating."

"Huh." She didn't know what to say to that. "Maybe it's a witch thing. And should an angel be saying damn?"

He chuckled, and she began to laugh with him. It didn't exactly break the tension, but every little distraction helped ease the stress a little more.

They lapsed into silence again and Mira thought about what magic she might have around the house.

"I'm not saying that going to my apartment will help us, but being here is definitely not getting us anywhere," she said.

Gabriel's smile faded away. "Maybe we should talk to whoever—whatever those things were."

"You want to talk to those things?" Mira's gaze darted to the door. "Easy for you to say, they said you could go. Who knows what they want to do to me."

"They want you for a reason," Gabriel said. "What did you do?"

"I don't think this is because I spelled Ian. If we were dragged here because of the spell, my chances of getting out are nil and I'll be lucky if I just die here."

"What are you talking about?" Gabriel asked.

"Any damage caused by the spell I cast on Ian falls back to me. I'm pretty sure getting you trapped here could be worse than a death sentence if it's related to the spell." Mira shivered at putting the thought into words. "Anyway, if we are forced to communicate with those things, then sure, we can have a chat, but I am going to go far out of my way to avoid that."

"What do you think you can do at your house?" Gabriel asked.

That was even harder to explain. "Sensing this magic," she shook the cord in her hand, "makes me think that other magic may fall into the Ether from our world. If any of it spills into this world, there may be a chance I can use it."

"This place could be easier to defend," he said, looking around.

"We can defend or try to find a way out," Mira said. "Defense is only going to work for so long. There's no water here for starters."

"Right," Gabriel said. "My car is in the garage. We can go out that way and avoid the front door."

Steering clear of whatever was scratching at the door was something she dearly wanted to do.

"We go straight to the car and steer clear of anything that may get in our way. If we have to talk, we talk. If we have to fight, stay behind me."

"Got it," Mira said. She hated the idea that she would have to step aside if it came to a fight. Why hadn't she listened to Emmit and prepared some offensive spells?

Once again, Gabriel took a white-knuckled grip on his gleaming sword and shield, and they made their way out of the room. Getting to the door was easy—it was straight down the hall. Gabriel tried to give her some hand signals as he stood next to the back door. Mira gave him her best *what the hell* look, and he rolled his eyes.

"Stand back to the left side of the door, look to the right and let me know if you see anything, or if we're clear." Through the whole exchange, he made the hand signals again.

They were still lost on Mira, but she knew what needed to be done.

Gabriel did a countdown from three on his fingers and kicked the door open. The darkness in the garage was thicker than they had anticipated. Mira tried to catch movements in the shadows, but found nothing.

"Clear to the right," she whispered.

Gabriel sprung out of the door. His skin blazed in light, and the haze and shadows fell away. They rushed out into the garage, pounding feet echoing in the empty, cavernous space.

Mira saw movement. She grabbed the back of Gabriel's shirt.

"To the right, to the right," she said, tugging on his shirt at the same time.

He swung around, but whatever had caused the movement was long gone.

They were so fast. Mira's hands started shaking, and she still clung to Gabriel's shirt, her hand twisting the material into a tight knot.

"We've got a problem," Gabriel said, stopping in his tracks.

"What? What is it?"

"The car is gone," Gabriel said. He strode forward a bit more, dragging her along with him. "Mira, let go. There are no cars. No cars anywhere."

CHAPTER 22

MIRA HAD BEEN CONCENTRATING SO hard on the creatures that the fact that the parking garage was empty hadn't registered.

No cars anywhere. Turning back to the station, she found the way blocked. Something, or possibly many somethings, if the shifting shadows were any indication, blocked the way. She clenched and unclenched her fists. How had she not picked up a weapon?

"Back inside?" she asked.

"Back inside," Gabriel agreed. "Put your hand on my back. Don't grab the shirt; just place your hand on my shoulder. As I move, you'll get an idea of where I'm going to move."

She found herself staring at a mass of feathers. "I can't reach your shoulder."

"You're not that short. I need to know where you are so I don't hit you on accident. My sword skills are non-existent."

"Right," Mira muttered. She put her hand on his wing, feeling feathers softer than cotton and smoother than silk.

"Good. Keep an eye behind us."

It was interesting that he thought she was holding his shoulder.

Gabriel moved forward, striding purposefully for the door. She felt him tense, but she hadn't expected him to stop in mid stride. Mira ran into his back and almost inhaled one of his feathers.

"Let us through," Gabriel said in a loud voice.

"The witch is ours," said a voice in front of them.

Mira tried to ignore the voice and concentrate on their surroundings.

"She has things to answer for in our world," Gabriel said. "We're going home."

"Her debt to you meansss nothing to usss," came another voice.

"Out of our way." Gabriel's voice didn't hold the forceful demand that it had earlier, but he was glowing brighter. It seemed the higher the emotions, the brighter he glowed.

Something darted forward.

"Left," Mira called to Gabriel.

He was already moving. In one swift turn, he lashed out with his sword. The blow struck home on a short creature that had too many eyes. It shrieked and collapsed. The smell of smoldering oil permeated the area.

Gabriel turned forward and swiped his sword. Another shriek.

Mira felt an urgent need to help, but she could do nothing except watch Gabriel's back. He couldn't see everywhere at once.

"It's still clear behind us," Mira said in a low voice.

"On the move," Gabriel said.

Before Mira could take in the meaning of his words, he was already moving around the limp form in front of him and toward the station. Their path was now clear. Things were still shifting out in the haze, but whatever was out there kept its distance.

Gabriel reached the door and pulled. Nothing happened. He pulled again.

Something surged forward, trying to take advantage of their delay.

"Behind us," Mira called.

Hoping she was dodging the right way, Mira moved aside while Gabriel turned, slashing the beast. It let out a wounded howl. The thing wasn't down, but it moved quickly away.

Mira let go of Gabriel and tugged at the door, trying to fight down the frantic feeling that was rising up. It didn't budge.

"Where's the key?" Mira asked.

"No keys here." Gabriel wasn't keeping his voice down. He looked amped with adrenaline from the fight. Breathing heavy, his head twitched from left to right, ready to lash out.

"Let's go to the front," Gabriel said.

"You locked the front door." Mira's mind frantically thought through her everyday spells, hoping there was something, anything, that she could use.

Gabriel pulled back his sword arm and raised his shield. He slammed into Mira and their fall was blocked by the door. Something thudded to the ground off his shield. Gabriel's weight on Mira disappeared while she staggered up and he lunged forward, swinging his sword as though he were a gladiator.

"Right," he said after another creature was dispatched. "We had a plan, let's stick to it. We're going to your house."

"Are you frigging kidding me?" Mira yelled over a new chorus of howls that echoed in the parking structure.

"We have to move," Gabriel said. "Staying here isn't going to help us. It's not safe. Besides, I think the smell might be attracting something that we don't want to deal with."

Mira looked at the motionless bodies on the ground. "My shop is closer." She didn't want to go any further than she had to with these things running around.

"Do you have everything you need there?" Gabriel asked.

"Hard to say." Mira thought over what she kept in her shop. Thankfully, her mail order business was thriving. "I'm not sure *what* we need. I'm not even sure anything can reach into this world."

"It has to be worth a shot," Gabriel said.

"Stick to the streets?" she asked.

"Unless you know more than you're saying, we have to play this by ear." Gabriel set off down the sloping structure and out onto the street.

There was no time for Mira to think this through. Cold sweat beaded on her forehead and it was all she could do to keep up with Gabriel.

Seeing a tremble in his wings did not help her frame of mind. Her eyes bulged, trying to take in everything at once. Was it night here? There was light of a sort, but everything around them seemed to absorb it.

Was it night in their world already? It had seemed like they had been trapped in this nightmare for days with their nerves stretched tight.

They hadn't gone more than a block when screeches and howls picked up in intensity.

The noise came from every direction, and each fresh sound made their heads jerk, expecting to see something running their way.

Compulsively, Mira looked behind and to the sides.

Gabriel slowed when they reached a cross street. Shadows darted around just out of sight. Mira stuck close as they rushed across the street.

Breathing hard, Mira caught sight of something approaching. "Behind us!" It came out much louder than she'd intended.

The creature was already gone when Gabriel turned.

He didn't say anything, but he did pick up their pace.

"To the right!" Mira yelled.

It was moving away when Gabriel turned, but he lashed out with his sword anyway.

The smell of burning oil fell away as they distanced themselves from the station. It was hot and the air felt denser and closer, as though the haze trapped their warmth against their skin.

It has also grown quiet.

Gabriel was keeping vigil up front. Mira could see his head checking from left to right and occasionally back. They were moving quickly, but Mira was beginning to feel the futility of what they were doing. There was no way she would be able to keep up the pace, and her store was miles away.

Gabriel swung at shadows of his own, almost as often as Mira called out others. They tried to stick close to buildings, but each door seemed to be inset from the wall. Each time they approached one, they'd have to slow down and carefully peek around the corner. Every moment in the hazy landscape seemed more terrifying than the last.

Howls and screams rose up once again. The beasts were closer. Mira began seeing them at each intersection, gathering and watching as Mira and Gabriel rushed by. Some dared to lurch forward, but they always fell back when the sword was raised.

"We turn left here," Gabriel said, looking around the corner.

"Wrong way," Mira said.

"There are fewer to the left, so we have to turn," Gabriel said.

Mira leaned back against the wall and tried to catch her breath. Her terror-filled mind was jumbled, and she needed a minute to pull herself together.

"What are you doing?" Gabriel turned. "We have to keep moving."

Mira shook her head, but kept her eyes moving ceaselessly, trying to take in every possible movement in the darkness.

"Look," Gabriel said, "if we turn left here, we can circle back around."

She shook her head again.

"Damn it, we have to keep moving!"

Gabriel looked like he wanted to drag Mira along or leave her.

It took Mira a few tries to find her voice again. "They're like animals, but they're smart." Her breathing was still rasping. "We can't go left just because it looks good."

"Talk while we move," Gabriel said.

"Fine. But move forward," Mira said.

Gabriel's face was pale. He was sweating, and now his nostrils were flaring and his eyes looked hard and cold. Finally, he nodded his head.

"I can't be sure," Mira said. "I don't know what these things are, but they seem smart. They talk and move like they are, anyway." She tried to take deeper, slower breaths. "When packs of people or animals hunt, they try to corner whatever they're hunting."

"You think they were herding us somewhere?" Gabriel scoffed.

The howling broke way into a snarl as one of the creatures jumped out. It had tufts of hair growing in patches over its body. The legs looked too thin and frail to support the rest of its bulk. Arms stretched far too long, but where the elbow should be, the arm broke into three long limbs.

It reached out, ignoring Gabriel, trying to grab Mira.

Gabriel was too quick. The arm of the thing, if it was an arm, was severed by Gabriel's sword.

The high-pitched keening noise that rang up from the creature was answered on all four sides. Then a chorus of voices took up the chant, "Give us the witch." It struck fear into Mira's heart and she froze, rooted to the spot.

Gabriel grabbed her arm. To Mira, it was as if he was talking through a tunnel. "Stick close behind me, we have to run."

Mira managed to nod in return. Fear was giving way to terror, which Gabriel must have noticed, because he hesitated.

"Give me that string," Gabriel said.

Hoots and whistles broke up the chant briefly, but it came back again, stronger than ever.

"The string," Gabriel snapped.

Mira fumbled in her pocket and wordlessly handed it over.

He wrapped it once around her arm and then to his belt.

The smell of burnt oil was thick in the air, which brought Mira's brain back from where it had fled.

"What are you doing?" she asked, covering her mouth.

"Making sure we don't get separated," Gabriel muttered. When he finished, he looked up and down the street. "Ready to go?"

They started at a jog to get away from the stench and find clean air.

Then they tried running. It had sounded like a wonderful idea. They'd shoot forward for a few yards only to be attacked by some hideous beast that jumped from the shadows. Sticking behind Gabriel was harder than Mira had imagined. Gabriel was breathing hard, but he swung his sword as if he had all the strength in the world. Mira knew that wasn't the case. He had to be as worn out as she was. This constant terror, the running, it couldn't only be Mira that felt tired to the bone. Right?

She knew she wasn't going to last much longer.

They trotted up to a wall that didn't exist in the real world. It was a little taller than Mira, but Gabriel could see the other side.

"Do you want to boost me over it?" Mira asked without much conviction.

"Not a good idea." He looked down its length each way.

"Maybe it could give us some extra time while those things have to get over it." *And give us a break*, Mira thought.

"It's covered with some sort of spikes," he said, "and little holes."

Hesitantly, Gabriel reached out a hand. As soon as it touched the wall, he yanked it back hard. Howls rose up behind them. Mira looked around, trying to catch sight of what might be following, and wondered how many and how far away they were.

She had backed up against the wall without realizing it. Gabriel grabbed her, almost dropping his shield in the process, and yanked her away. Mira stumbled and fell to the ground. She turned to yell at Gabriel, but saw that he visibly paled.

Gabriel took his sword and hacked at the wall. The long line of stone quivered. It started to bleed.

"Dear god," Mira whispered. Her mind couldn't grapple with that. *Does that make it a living wall or one of those things? Both?*

Gabriel pulled her to her feet with shaky hands. Wordlessly, they started to run, staying away from the wall, trying to find a way around.

They stopped short when confronted by a group of a dozen nightmare creatures. More monsters appeared out of the hazy darkness. They backed up a few paces.

"There's more behind us," Mira whispered, trying to keep the fear out of her voice.

Gabriel turned, putting their backs facing the wall, which Mira didn't think was much better.

"The witch is oursss." Something stepped forward. Others jostled themselves out of the way as it moved, looking in awe at the creature. It was the same beast that Mira and Gabriel had first encountered at the station.

"What did I do to you?" Mira called.

"You meddled." The other creature from the station stepped out. It, too, got the same reverent treatment from the others.

"What does that even mean?" she yelled.

"You sided with the Harkers," it said.

"Oh shit," Mira said under her breath. "Oh shit."

"Leave her!" it screeched.

"Not going to happen," Gabriel said.

"We will go through you if we must, bastard son of a god. You have lost your voice. You shall die if you stand in our way."

A flurry of twitches went around the group of gathered creatures. A few stepped back. None looked ready to fight Gabriel.

"Iss that your final decisssion?" the beast asked.

"It is," Gabriel said.

The creatures yelled and moved forward as though driven by invisible whips.

"Stay low and behind me," Gabriel said through gritted teeth.

Mira backed up, but not too far, fearing the wall.

This shouldn't be happening. This was her fault. She had somehow dragged Gabriel into this torment-filled world.

One of the creatures broke line and launched himself at Gabriel. Gabriel swung out and black blood was slung into the crowd of approaching beasts. The smell of burnt oil seemed to drive a few into a frenzy. Three more creatures leapt out. Gabriel was able to dispatch two, and the other didn't come close enough for Gabriel to hit. It snagged the first downed creature away.

Mira thought it must be clearing the fighting grounds, but then she heard the snapping of bone and chewing.

They were eating their dead.

Four more leapt at once, one heading straight for Mira. It clawed at her arm and tried to drag her away. Gabriel chopped off its arm and continued to the next animal. Something grabbed Mira's leg. She kicked out, making contact with what she thought was the thing's face. It screeched, but didn't let go.

Yanking hard, it managed to knock Mira off her feet.

Gabriel dispatched another, but they were coming too quickly. Mira yelled while she punched and kicked anything she could reach. The grip only bore down harder. She was dragged away from Gabriel, but she could see that there was nothing he could do.

The black beast with skin like leather appeared in front of her.

This was the last place that Mira wanted to die, but it looked like she wasn't going to be given a choice in the matter. She grabbed her pentagram; ready to say her goodbyes to the people she loved.

The moment her skin touched the metal, the ward activated.

The creature that was dragging her screamed and released her. He clutched a taloned hand, which smoked. Another creature rushed to take its place, but he struck an invisible wall. Parts of him burst into flame before he ran into the night, screeching.

Two creatures broke line to follow it. Mira's stomach churned at the thought that they were eating a cooked dinner tonight.

Clinging to the ward, Mira stood and unsteadily moved to Gabriel. He was sweaty and confused as the monsters started shrieking and falling away from him, even though they were untouched. The side of the living wall started smoldering when she walked too close. It quivered and moved back. Mira watched mutely as the entire length moved, quicker than she would have thought possible.

Gabriel looked at her, eyes wide.

"They can't come through it," Mira said weakly.

"But we can wait it out," hissed old leather-face. "Thiss world will eat through that flimssy magic, and we will be right here when it does."

The moldy-looking creature from the station moved forward as well. "You will pay for your crimes against us."

Gabriel was still in attack mode, but nothing advanced.

"You can sit here and wait all you want," Mira said. "We're getting out of here."

"You ssshall not be going far," hissed the monster. "You are bleeding and will be tracked. It's been a while sssince we've had a witch to eat."

Mira shivered. "You're not going to have this one." She wished she could have said that with more conviction.

"You have a ward that is ssshrinking and an angel that has lost hisss voice. What use are either against usss?" asked the molded creature.

"I can talk," Gabriel said, practically shaking with need to lash out.

"You sspoke once, but your voice is gone." The dense, black creature appeared almost smug.

"Look you—" Gabriel started.

"Gabriel, let's go," Mira said. "We've got to keep moving." If these creatures were right, Mira at least wanted to try to get to her store before the ward stopped working.

The wall behind them was gone, so they retreated that way. The two lead creatures gave them warped smiles, but didn't follow. Mira tugged on Gabriel's shield arm to keep him moving. A couple dozen yards later and she was leaning heavily on him to keep from falling over. The angel bore the extra weight without comment.

"We have to take a break," Mira said a few blocks later. "I really want to keep moving, but—" She felt worn down to the bone though she didn't want to say anything since Gabriel had done all the work. He looked like he could walk another mile without breaking stride. "Where are we?" Mira peered around, trying to determine where they were. She didn't want to think of how many miles lay between them and her store.

"This looks like Perry Road," Gabriel said.

"Let's swing right," she said. "I know where to go."

They went up a few streets to a white one-story house. To Mira, it felt like the building was singing softly, and the air around the place wasn't as thick.

Mira checked the front door. "A witch lives here. Maybe I can find something here to help us." It was Maggie's house. Good old Maggie. Mira wasn't sure what she had stored up, or if there even was a reflection of it in this world, but the place felt safe.

Mira used Gabriel as a crutch to hobble around back. The back door was unlocked. Once inside, they locked the door behind them.

Next to the door, Mira slid down the wall and sat on the floor. She was ready not to move again for a while.

"We need to check the house," Gabriel said.

Numb to the world, Mira nodded. Gabriel had already left.

Mira looked around from her spot on the floor, noting that there was no haze here. It was the closest semblance to their world she'd seen since arriving in the Ether.

Her eyes drooped. While Gabriel made his rounds, Mira blinked wearily until her eyes closed and she couldn't manage to open them again.

CHAPTER 23

A PAT ON MIRA'S FACE WOKE her up. She was ready to scold Oracle, but Gabriel's shining skin greeted her. Mira smiled and reached out to touch the shimmer that danced beneath his skin. With all that brightness inside, you would have expected him to look happy. Instead, he just looked pissed.

She wrinkled up her forehead in concentration, wondering why he was ticked off. When realization struck, Mira just wanted to close her eyes and go back to sleep.

"Oh no you don't," Gabriel said, not unkindly. He pulled her up off the floor. "You've got some talking to do."

"I just wanted a short nap," Mira grumbled, although she didn't actually remember making the decision to go to sleep.

"No sleep until we get out of here. I bandaged up your leg and arm, but I'm not sure how much blood you've lost. It might be good to not sleep until we get you to a hospital."

Mira looked down at her leg. Sure enough, Gabriel's shirt was wrapped around it, tied tight. Wondering how she hadn't noticed warrior angel without a shirt, she looked up at him. He had been wearing a shirt under that one.

Figures.

She was aware that her thinking was fuzzy. Everything was happening a little slower.

"What about you?" she asked.

"What about me?" Gabriel looked blank.

"Did you get hurt?"

"No."

The answer came too quickly for Mira's liking. "Let me double check."

It was an interesting inspection. He had a few scratches, but nothing major. Mira took time going over every inch of his wings.

"Don't you think I'd know if something was wrong?" Gabriel grumbled.

"We have no idea what a wing injury might look or feel like," Mira said. "Besides, I was holding onto your wing earlier and you thought I was grabbing onto your shoulder."

The feathers were soft. It was like a layer of down over thin steel. Mira ran her hands over thin bones, surprised that they didn't seem fragile.

She ran her fingers down until her hand neared Gabriel's back. That's when his wings twitched. It seemed involuntary, so she went through the motion again.

Gabriel stifled a laugh, and then gave her a stern look. "Don't do that."

It was good to hear him laugh, even if he wasn't happy about it. While she inspected his wings, Gabriel seemed to be studying the experience. Mira jumped when he made them expand wide behind him.

"Everything appears okay," Mira said. "At least as far as I can tell."

Her own body was bruised and bleeding. She inspected some of the larger areas where her skin was starting to turn purple. Thankfully, nothing was broken.

The only thing she wanted more than sleep was to get the hell out of the Ether.

"Let's start in the kitchen," Mira said.

"Start with what?" Gabriel asked. "You still haven't said what we're doing here."

"We're going to see if there's anything I can use to put together a spell."

There was a slight uplifting of Gabriel's eyes, but he squashed it fast. "Tell me what you're looking for and I'll search."

A wry smile spread across her face. "Witches have been hiding things from prying eyes for hundreds of years. An outsider may have a hard time finding anything."

"Don't put too much pressure on your leg." He offered her his hand and helped her into the kitchen.

Her leg ached ferociously, and the first few cabinets she found were empty. "Can you check the fridge and those cabinets over there?" She pointed behind Gabriel. When he turned, she leaned heavily against the counter.

"Those things out there," Gabriel said in a voice laden with forced calm, "they said I lost my voice. What do you think that means?"

"I think you suspect the answer to that, same as I do. In the station, you did something. You made a command with your voice." She half-heartedly pulled open a nearby drawer. "They think you've lost it. What they don't realize is that you just haven't found it."

"So you think I can do that again? Order someone to do something?"

Mira shrugged. "Seems plausible."

"Jump up and down!" Gabriel yelled, pointing at Mira.

"That's not funny, Gabriel, my leg hurts."

Going to a wall, Mira leaned against it and started sensing for magic. She wasn't that familiar with Maggie, but magic made itself known in this world. It was stronger and Mira felt sure she'd sense something.

"Say my name. Tell me what you are doing. Flap your arms."

Slowly, she walked around the room, inspecting for traces of magic while Gabriel tried to issue orders.

"Look, Gabriel, just yelling isn't going to do it. Think back to what you were feeling when you ordered them out of the station. Grab that feeling and then try. You have to really mean it." Mira hobbled to a stretch of cabinet on Maggie's island in the kitchen. "And be careful what you tell me to do, bird boy. I'm going to be pissed if you make me bark like a dog."

When Mira snuck a peek at Gabriel, it earned her a grin. Maybe he was loosening up a bit.

Gabriel closed his eyes. Mira could tell he was concentrating this time, so she turned and watched him. After a few moments, he opened his eyes, his skin gleamed white, and he pointed at her and said, "Confess."

Mira's eyes bulged and her mouth opened. Words flew out in confused strings.

She confessed.

Starting with the most recent and working its way back, Mira said everything she had stored away. Her suspicions, thoughts... everything.

"I was so relieved when we found this house. I didn't think I'd make it with my leg, but I tried to ignore it. Those things that talked to us creep me the hell out. You killed them as though you'd been using a sword your whole life. I was sure I was going to die during the fight. I thought you might be better off just letting me die when we were surrounded. You were smart to tie the cord around us. I really think that helped keep me alive, and kept me going. It was stupid that you forgot massive, feather-covered wings. You hate me, which makes me sad, but I understand why, sort of. It's my fault that we're here. They dragged me here and you got caught in the crossfire."

Out and out it came. It was like word vomit. Gabriel looked proud at first, but Mira was having a hard time getting a breath. Her eyes teared up, and she tried to pause long enough to take a breath, but the confessions kept coming.

Gabriel pointed at her again, and said, "Stop."

Good christ, she thought, *the idiot's going to make me stop breathing all together.*

All the feelings that she had kept buried when they came over to this world poured out. The feelings of uselessness, the feeling of awe when looking at Gabriel, the terror and fear, everything spilled out. She leaned heavily against the counter, trying to steady herself and grab another breath.

She was talking about their world now—the Perspective spell that had gone so wrong, the concern that her friend was a killer or going to be killed, and the fact that she was afraid she had screwed up by not telling Gabriel—it all came out.

On and on it came, like a valve she couldn't shut off. She panicked even more when she realized what was coming next. Emmit's spell, Emmit's thoughts. Her mind went into a frantic mode. Those were none of Gabriel's business.

Mira grabbed the ward around her neck and tried to concentrate, ignoring the words coming from her mouth. They would come without her thinking about them. Gabriel pointed at her and said something. Mira held her ward tight and prayed for protection against winged idiots. There was a buzzing noise in her ears, and then a white-hot needle slashed through her brain. Finally, there was nothing.

CHAPTER 24

MIRA JOLTED AWAKE WHEN SHE felt movement and realized Gabriel was carrying her out of the kitchen.

She didn't wait to see where he was taking her.

"Confess?" Mira yelled.

Gabriel was so taken off guard that he dropped her. She fell into a heap on to the floor before quickly untangling her limbs and forcing herself to her feet.

"Confess!" she yelled again. "Your dumb ass still thinks I committed those murders. Confess, you tell me. Confess what, you winged Neanderthal?"

She shoved past Gabriel, back to the kitchen, ignoring the pain in her leg and the newfound pain in her head. Her face flushed. What all had she told Gabriel? None of it was stuff she wanted him to know; she knew that.

Storming back to the island, she had to bite back the insults she wanted to sling at him. She was having trouble concentrating on her search.

When she was sure she had caught her breath, she turned back to him, glaring.

Gabriel's face was pale, his eyes were moist, and his skin ashen—far from glowing. It looked like he was in shock.

Mira crossed her arms. "You are such an ass." Being in shock didn't mean she was going to handle him with kid gloves. "If you tell a soul anything that I said, I will dig up the worst curse I can find for you, karma be damned. Are we understood?"

He blinked at her and said nothing until she rolled her eyes and turned her attention back to the cabinet. If he really was in shock, she had to find something he'd react to.

It took her a few minutes to find and open the secret compartment. Witches were good at hiding, but many of them used the same methods of concealing. If she hadn't been so monumentally ticked off, she could have worked faster.

Unlike the rest of the cabinets, this compartment was well stocked. She hadn't known what she was looking for until she found it. It wasn't a spell or potion. Just an ingredient. Something that smelled so foul, it was rumored to have been used to wake the dead.

Mira hobbled back to Gabriel and uncorked the bottle before shoving it under his nose.

He took a breath and gagged. Mira put the lid back on the bottle and waited, arms crossed, for Gabriel to get himself back together. Color flushed back into his cheeks and his wings ruffled.

"I dropped you," Gabriel said.

Rolling her eyes again, she returned to the magical stash. Once the bottle was put away, she dug through Maggie's supplies.

"That's not what I meant to say," Gabriel started. "What I meant to say was that I'm sorry. It was stupid. I didn't think it would work. I'm sorry."

It mollified Mira a bit.

"Are you okay?" he asked.

"I'm fine," she said stiffly. She stopped digging around in Maggie's supplies and turned to Gabriel. "Look, I'm practically worthless here." Her secrets were out; she might as well be honest. "For some unfathomable reason, you are the only protection we have here. You still thinking I'm a murderer is not filling me with confidence about my chances of survival."

"Really, Mira, I had no idea that was going to happen. I wouldn't leave you here even *if* I thought you were a murderer.

We'll get out of this. We're not sure what kind of power I have, but I swear I will do whatever I can to protect you."

A ghostly silver tendril slipped from around Gabriel's wrist. They watched as it quickly snaked its way to Mira. It was as insubstantial as air, but she stepped back as it neared her. The silvery gleam leapt forward, burying itself into her chest. She could feel a warm, tingly sensation as the cord settled into her.

The cord disappeared when she started to follow its trail back to Gabriel.

"Did you do that?" Gabriel asked.

"That wasn't me," she said.

"What was it?"

"I have no idea, but it's gone now," Mira said. "I'm ignoring it." She returned to digging around in Maggie's secret compartment.

"Agreed," Gabriel said. He was silent for a few moments. "I don't think you committed those murders."

Pausing long enough to throw him a dirty look, Mira pulled out a few items. "I was serious, Gabriel. You tell anyone anything that I said while under your influence and I'll curse you."

Gabriel gave her a half grin. "Honestly, you were talking so fast that I started to panic. I'm pretty sure I couldn't make heads or tails of what you said even if I tried."

Glaring at him, she couldn't tell if he was telling the truth or not. The stupid half grin wasn't helping any.

"What's all this?" he asked, changing the subject.

She wanted to yell or rant a bit more, but figured it was best if they just moved forward. Gabriel slid over a stool for each of them. They sat while Mira sorted through what they had. Some of the labels she could read clearly. The symbol for Relief, for instance, was almost universal. Some she uncorked and sniffed to try to figure out what they might be. One bottle gave her an uneasy feeling, and she capped it quickly and left it alone.

"Looks like we have some typical potions. Some of these will come in handy. We've got some Relief, Comfort, and Honesty," she said, naming the bottles that she could read. "This looks like

Foresight, but it doesn't quite smell right. This could be Luck, but I'm not really sure."

"Honesty? In a bottle? You know, I could use some of that," Gabriel said.

"Really, I would have thought you'd have heard enough honesty for one day," Mira snapped.

Gabriel's cheeks turned pink and he started poking around the secret compartment. "What's the rest of this?" he asked.

Slapping Gabriel's hand away, she pulled out the rest of the stuff. "Looks like the rest are ingredients."

"Ingredients for potions? What exactly do you do with the potions?" Gabriel asked.

"You do whatever you want with them. You drink them, or sell them, or share them with others."

"And these potions here—Relief, for instance. What does it do?" Gabriel asked.

"Relief helps alleviate pain, at least that's mostly how it's put together. Giving someone Honesty ensures the person is being truthful. You already know if they're truthful, but this makes them tell the truth, more or less. Comfort does just what it says."

"Sounds like drugs," said Gabriel.

"Some people take it like drugs," Mira said. "Drugs can heal or hurt, just depends on how you use them." As an afterthought she added, "Or abuse them."

"Anything here we can use to help us get out?" Gabriel asked.

"The fact that it's here at all tells us something. These are things from the real world that are reflected here."

A thud made them jump—something had crashed into the side of the house. They looked at each other and then around the room.

Another thud. Gabriel reached out, and his sword and shield materialized in his hands.

"Anything we can use now?" Gabriel asked.

Reviewing her ingredients, she tried to think through all the spells she knew. Protection would be most useful, but it wasn't an option. Maggie was missing way too many ingredients. Mira snagged a few items, just in case. "Nothing we can use now, but maybe when we get to my store."

"What about the Relief? Can you take that?" Gabriel asked. "For your head and leg?"

Surprised, Mira rubbed her head. "That might be a good idea."

Gabriel seemed to notice her injuries more than she had.

Without thinking it through, Mira drew the familiar symbols around the edge of the bottle. Each symbol flared and gleamed without dissipating. She glanced at Gabriel, but he seemed to be taking it in stride. She hesitated a few moments, but not wanting to show her unease, she closed her eyes and drank the potion.

The flavors burst in her mouth. The warmth of the potion slid down her throat. When it reached her stomach, it gathered and then jumped into the energy of her body and flowed to every corner, filling her. The areas where she had felt pain tingled and the discomfort evaporated.

Gabriel looked at her with concern.

She was gripping the counter and breathing heavily. Not wanting to let go of the feeling, she closed her eyes again and immersed herself in it. This was better than Bliss, better than any other potion she'd ever had. Mira was already making plans to track Maggie down and compare potion notes.

Something pounded on the roof and rolled off.

"I think we'll need to move quickly," Gabriel said. "How's your head?"

Mira nodded, forcing herself to stop thinking about the potion. "It's good. I'm good."

"Do we have a plan?" Gabriel asked.

"Yeah." Mira started to grin. "They think you've lost your voice. Let's prove them wrong."

"I don't want to screw this up," Gabriel said.

"We'll think it through first."

They spent a few minutes hashing out ways to make the creatures go away without causing her or Gabriel to be affected.

Just in case, they decided to bind themselves together again with Mira's thread. The silk was still glowing, although it seemed a bit dimmer than before. Mira tried not to think about Ether sucking the magic away. Putting her hand to the pentagram, she inspected it. It still glowed brightly, so she settled it back around her neck, making sure it touched skin.

"I'll open the door," Gabriel said. "Stand behind me and hold on tight around my waist."

They both moved to the door, pockets bulging with what they had pilfered from Maggie's place. Wrapping herself tightly against Gabriel's back, she could feel the muscles rippling. If she hadn't been scared out of mind, she mused, her body would be having quite the reaction.

Gabriel breathed deeply and shuddered. "Let's do this."

He opened the door.

From her vantage point, Mira couldn't see much. Her head was mostly buried in Gabriel's wing. There were glimpses of dark creatures stirring in the haze, their eyes flashing oddly in the low glow Gabriel radiated. Sometimes, far too many eyes grouped together.

Gabriel's wings spread out, blocking Mira's vision and throwing her off balance. She clung to him, refusing to fall.

"Creatures before us, fall back. Be gone and do not hinder our progress through this world."

Mira gripped tightly to Gabriel, fearing that she would be forced back by his words. Instead, screams and hisses broke out all around them, even to Mira's horror, from above. Inhuman sounds mixed with curses and words in other languages assaulted them from all sides.

Something streaked forward.

Gabriel repeated his words with more confidence and everything fell back. When the noise died, Mira peeled herself off Gabriel. Stuck to her sweat on her hand were a few of Gabriel's feathers. Even detached they glowed in the haze.

"That worked well," Gabriel said, sounding pleased with

himself. "It looks like a few of them are still in the shadows, but we'll keep an eye out. We may just make it through this."

"That was amazing," Mira said. "Um, I held on a little enthusiastically, though."

He looked at the feathers she held out and shrugged. "I didn't even notice."

"We shouldn't leave them in this place." Mira shoved them in her pocket. "And we shouldn't stick around here. Let's go."

They reached the street and the world lurched. An earthquake tore through town. Gabriel and Mira clung to each other's arm and rode the wave out. They stared at each other. Nothing like that had ever hit their city. Some silent decision was made and they ignored it. Gabriel kept his sword and shield together in one hand and held Mira's hand in the other.

Their short break had rejuvenated them some, but it was wearing off fast. Since nothing stood in their way, they were moving much more quickly than before.

Taunts came from the shadows through the haze. The ridicule reminded them that there was nowhere to hide. They scolded Mira for helping Emmit and for shifting the balance in the Harker's favor. Threats were made, and the creatures seem to take great relish in telling the pair how they would be tortured once the creatures got hold of them.

Through it all, Gabriel and Mira gripped each other's hand. Mira could feel a cold sweat coming from him as much as it came from herself, but she didn't dare take her eyes off her surroundings to look at Gabriel.

The trip to Mira's store was long, dark, and filled with hidden terrors.

It was a shock to see the buildings starting to tower up around them. The exteriors looked as though they were covered in soot and strange brown vegetation sprouted in odd places.

They saw that the windows were gone, replaced with brick, like all the others they had seen. It seemed as though windows and mirrors really didn't exist in this world. Instinctively, Mira patted her pockets for her key, not letting go of Gabriel to do so. Then she remembered that nothing non-magical had entered the world with her, unless one of them had been touching it.

The store had a soft glow and looked less dingy than others around it. Whatever magic that had fused into Mira's store was working to burn away the diseased effects of the Ether.

Mira almost cried out with relief when they reached the storefront. They looked around carefully for any shapes in the darkness.

There was hesitation when Gabriel reached for the doorknob. Mira let out a breath she'd been holding when the door swung open.

"I need my hand," Gabriel said, his voice low.

Reluctantly, Mira let go, missing the support almost as soon as it was gone.

Gabriel went room by room, checking under tables and in corners, trying to ensure they were alone. Mira trailed along behind, unwilling to take off the string that connected them until she was certain they wouldn't be forced to run away.

After making sure the back door was locked, Mira untied the silk. They silently sat in the kitchen, catching their breath while keeping their thoughts to themselves.

Mira was afraid to make the next move. The fear of finding out she could do nothing kept her frozen in her thoughts. Gabriel seemed to be going through something similar, but he was the one who finally broke the silence.

"What's next?" he asked. "The thought of sleeping in this place makes my skin crawl."

CHAPTER 25

MIRA DRAGGED HERSELF TO HER feet and began to move around the kitchen before stopping, suddenly shy about her secret hiding places. She was being hypocritical, she knew. Mira hadn't been reluctant about opening up Maggie's stash in front of Gabriel.

"Here's the thing," Mira said, "no one knows where I keep my supplies outside of my family. Even my best friends don't know. I need you to swear that you will not tell anyone my secrets."

"Sure, I promise."

She could tell by his tone of voice that he didn't care one way or the other. "Gabriel, this is important. There are spouses in our community that don't know where their partners keep everything. In the past, people have died and others have killed for a witch's secrets." That got Gabriel's attention. "Do you swear?"

He seemed to think over what she said before agreeing. "I swear that I won't tell anyone about your witchy secrets."

It was so subtle that she almost missed it. The silver cord that wrapped itself around them at Maggie's house briefly shimmered before fading away once more.

Gabriel paled, his eyes focused on where the connection between them had disappeared. "We really need to get out of here. Whatever that is, it's only here, right? Not in the real world?"

Mira took a few deep breaths and tried to sound sincere. "Sure. Have you ever seen a silvery cord between two people in our world?"

"I don't know why you bother lying," Gabriel snapped.

"The truth is, I don't know." She tried to take a steadying breath before going on. "I don't know what it is. For now, why don't we just agree not to make promises to each other?"

Gabriel nodded.

Confident that Gabriel wouldn't let her secret compartment become public knowledge, at least not before she had time to make another, Mira opened the hidden latch and started pulling items out onto the counter.

"What's this?" Gabriel asked.

She glanced at the floor where he was kicking at a piece of glowing tile.

"That's one of my circles. I guess it's glowing because I put a lot of magic into it over and over again. Well, my partner and me. She's a witch as well. There are several other hiding places throughout the store."

Gabriel sat his sword and shield aside, and left Mira sorting through items while he stalked around the store, checking out the imprint of magic.

"I just can't wrap my head around all of this," Gabriel said when he returned.

"You just got sucked into the Ether with a witch that you thought was a murderer. You found out you're an angel ready for battle and you're not sure if you can get home. I can't imagine what's tripping you up."

Gabriel burst out laughing and Mira joined him a beat later. It felt good to laugh. The atmosphere seemed to be momentarily lifted.

The ground turned again, shaking everything. Their laughter died quickly, and they held onto whatever was close until the earthquake was over.

"Right," Gabriel said. "I'll contemplate my newfound knowledge when I'm safe in my own bed. In my own world."

He came over and poked through Mira's supplies. When that bored him, he leafed through one of her spell books. "How come all your stuff is here?"

"Not all of it. Not by half." Mira sighed. "It's only the stuff that I've had for a long time or that has been magicked in some way."

"Isn't that all you need?"

"It doesn't work like that. What you start out with, the base ingredients, they usually aren't magical in nature."

"Anything in these books about this place?" Gabriel asked.

"Only a few spells that affect what a person sees or feels from here. All other knowledge of the Ether was stripped away centuries ago." While Mira looked over the contents of her hiding place, she explained to Gabriel about the disappearances of witches. "It's forbidden for anyone to enter the Ether."

"So we have nothing in your books, and no one from our world could help us, even if we could somehow contact someone?" Gabriel asked.

"Right," she said.

"Why did we come to your store?"

"Just because it's not written down doesn't mean we can't figure it out," she said. "We've been here for a while. What do we know about this world?"

Gabriel pulled out two stools, and they sat and contemplated what they'd seen.

"The air isn't clear here and the place is filled with monsters," Gabriel said.

"Well, they don't like me, anyway," Mira said. "They were more than willing to let you go in the beginning. They may not be complete monsters."

"Yeah, right," Gabriel said with scorn.

"Fine, it's filled with strange mean creatures that eat their wounded." Mira shivered. Picturing the beasts eating was too unsettling. She tried to steer the conversation away from monsters. "We know things line up, at least mostly, with our world. Same buildings and stuff."

"Buildings and streets, but no glass in the windows, no food, and no water," Gabriel said.

"Magic is strong here, or at least it has a physical presence. I mean, things don't glow in our world just because they have magic."

"What does that tell us?" Gabriel asked.

"No idea," Mira said. Then she grinned. "It means you are an angel here. Does your sword or shield say anything?"

Gabriel turned to where he had set them down, but they were gone. He rolled his head on his shoulders and held out his arms before closing his eyes and concentrating.

Nothing happened.

"Come on," he muttered.

"Maybe think about attacking something?" Mira suggested.

Eyes still closed Gabriel tensed, and out of nowhere, appeared his sword and shield. Both gleamed of shiny silver. After taking a moment to marvel over their appearance, Gabriel passed over the shield while he inspected the sword. After a while, they traded. Besides an inscription on the inside of the shield and along the hilt of the sword, the items gave no clues. The inscription was in another language, so they were both at a loss.

"Maybe I can think of other things and have them appear." Gabriel set the sword and shield aside.

Neither one of them took their eyes off the weapon, which remained solid.

"Maybe," Mira said. "The only thing we've had a chance to do here is fight."

Watching Gabriel for a while was amusing. His face scrunched up in concentration, but nothing happened. Mira started flipping through her potion recipes for something that may help them out. Specifically, she reviewed the recipe made for seers to keep the Ether away and thought about the recipe that she had created for Emmit. Her mind worked furiously as she thought about each ingredient and its purpose.

"Do we know anything else?" Gabriel asked. He seemed to give up on producing anything out of thin air.

"No cars," Mira said absently.

Gabriel thought that over while Mira stared at the book.

"No cars, no food. Maybe that means nothing temporary," Gabriel suggested.

Mira looked up at him, impressed.

"Maybe it has to be in our world for a long time before it appears here. Unless it's magic," he said.

"You're right," Mira said. "That might help us figure this mess out. Nothing temporary is in this world, except magic. That could be why there are no mirrors or glass?"

"I don't think so," Gabriel said. "The glass in most of the shops and houses we passed has been there as long as the buildings."

"It has to be because of the reflections."

"You think a reflection could get us out of here?" Gabriel asked.

She blinked at him, her tired mind grabbing hold of his idea. Her face split into a smile, and she hurried to her hiding place and dug everything out, setting each item on the counter. The last thing she pulled out was a black velvet bag a little wider than her hand.

"Cross your fingers," she said. Carefully, she opened the bag and pulled out a flat round mirror with a smoky black reflection.

"It's here! It's really here! It showed up in this world!"

Gabriel went over to see what the fuss was about and whistled as he looked at the mirror. The mirror, like the rest of the ingredients in her magic kit, glowed softly.

"You're a witch with a magic mirror," Gabriel said. "Naturally."

Mira ignored his jibe. "Okay," she said, placing the mirror carefully on the table. "We have a reflection. It's obviously too small to step through, even if we had a spell that would allow us to move between worlds like that. Still, I think this is our key out of here."

"Is there any hocus-pocus to make this thing bigger?" Gabriel asked.

Mira raised an eyebrow at him. "No," she said dryly. "Hocus-pocus will not make this bigger."

Gabriel shrugged and examined the large kitchen circle again.

"What do you think these creatures did to pull us through?" Gabriel asked. "I didn't see any magic around at the police station. Apart from what you and I had."

"I've never heard of anything like that happening."

The earth rumbled beneath their feet again. The trembling stilled, but only momentarily. Mira gripped a wall and held on tight to the mirror until the ground stopped moving.

"It's like something in the ground is rolling over," Gabriel said.

Blood rushed from Mira's face. "Don't say that!" She started shaking again, even though the ground was still.

"I just meant—I mean I've never—" Gabriel stammered. "It couldn't be that. I've just never been in an earthquake before. It startled me."

Trying to push the idea out of her mind that a giant creature was under her feet was like trying to turn iron to gold. Some people had a knack for it, but Mira wasn't one of them.

Gabriel mumbled to himself a bit. She thought she heard "couldn't be" come from him again.

"Right," Mira said, trying to pull Gabriel back to the problem at hand. "There was no magic except what we had. They weren't trying to pull you through, so it had to be something on me. I had my necklace and my string. You had already taken my rock away."

"Your rock was magic?" Gabriel shook his head.

"Never mind that. It wasn't on me. These things don't like the necklace, so it has to be the string."

"What is so special about the string?" Gabriel asked.

She was about to tell him that she had no idea why the string was special. Then the truth hit her.

"I used the string in one of my last spells." Mira licked her lips nervously. "I used it to balance the ethereal and physical planes. It was only on the ground to mark the circle, but that has to be it."

Gabriel looked confused and encouraged at the same time.

Something banged against the back door and they both jumped. Gabriel's shield and sword once again appeared in his hands, but he looked weary.

They both were. It was past time to get out of this world.

"So, I balanced the physical and the ethereal earlier. I also have a potion to block the Ether. Maybe if I combine the two?"

"Do it," Gabriel said. He shifted his focus from the back door to the front as something began to slam itself repeatedly against it.

Mira grabbed a few bottles and started throwing together a potion. Thuds upstairs interrupted her work.

"They're in the building," she said, staring at the ceiling.

"I didn't see a staircase. Where is it?" Gabriel asked.

"Outside. It doesn't come into the store."

"I've got this," he said. "Do what you need."

There was no time to worry about measurements. There were a few ingredients missing, but Mira made substitutions as best she could.

"Get into the circle," Mira said.

Gabriel glanced at the lines for a moment before moving with her. Mira wove the braided silk around the edge just as she had for Emmit the previous day.

Had it even been a day yet?

Raising the protective barrier around them, Mira gave the bottle to Gabriel.

"Drink half and then touch the mirror," Mira said. "Think firmly of our world."

Gabriel shifted his sword and shield to the same hand, as though he were afraid to let either of them go. "Shouldn't we do this together?"

"I'll be right behind you. Think of nothing else," Mira stressed. "Don't let another thought sneak in."

He hesitated, looking at the back door, which was being repeatedly hit.

"The faster you go, the faster I get to follow," Mira snapped. "Think of *nothing* else."

Gabriel looked at her, half-glaring. Then he downed his part and handed the bottle to her. He touched the mirror.

Mira held her breath and watched, counting down the seconds.

He closed his eyes. Mira's stomach was clenched so tightly she thought she might be sick.

There was a flicker.

Gabriel grew misty and faded away.

"It worked!" Mira punched the air in celebration.

The back door split open, cutting off her cheer.

The two creatures from the station, the ones that had followed her through the streets, walked in. Behind them, other creatures jostled each other to get a good view.

"Your protector is gone, witch," the moldy-looking creature said.

"Hiss sstrength will not help you," hissed the other.

They moved forward as one, but they were forced to stop short. Her protective barrier pushed back the hazy air and stopped the beasts several feet from her circle.

The ground trembled again.

Mira crouched down to keep from falling out of the circle. The creatures didn't look like they could break through her magic, but Mira was sure they'd love it if she ruined the protection herself. When Mira looked up, however, she saw that they were not concerned with her.

They looked as fearful as she did as the ground rumbled.

"Stupid witch," the green creature said once the shaking stopped, "you have chosen sides with Harkers, which will not go unpunished."

"I'm afraid that's not up to you," Mira said, and then drank the other half of the bottle.

The creatures growled and tried to move forward. Mira grabbed the mirror. Knowing she had only one chance at this, she closed her eyes and thought of nothing but the physical world and her shop.

Nausea rolled over her. Somehow, she felt real and unreal at the same time. Then a heaviness grew from her stomach out. When she opened her eyes, there were no creatures, but if anything, the haze was thicker. She spun around and bumped into Gabriel.

"What went wrong?" Mira cried.

"We're home," Gabriel said.

"But…" Mira gestured hopelessly at their surroundings.

"Let's get out of here," Gabriel said, dragging her by the arm.

"But…"

"Mira, your store is on fire."

CHAPTER 26

GABRIEL STARTED COUGHING, BUT STILL grabbed Mira and pushed her toward the back door. Her mind was fuzzy, but when Gabriel shoved her outside the frigid air jumpstarted her brain.

"Are you okay?" Her voice was much higher pitched and louder than she had intended. "How long were you in the smoke?"

"Forget it," Gabriel said. "We're home."

The words settled over them like a blanket.

Home.

It was hard for her to take in. "It's over," she said out loud, more for herself than for Gabriel.

"Listen, I'm not sure what's going to happen now, but you need to go home and wait there until you hear from me," Gabriel said.

"What? Why?"

"We disappeared from the police station. Someone could be looking for one or both of us."

"What for?" Mira asked.

"I know Ian, for one, will want some answers, especially since your stuff is probably still at the station. If anyone asks, we went for a walk. That's it. Say nothing else."

"I... okay," she stammered. This wasn't what she had anticipated.

"I'll call this in," Gabriel said. "You should go."

"How am I supposed to get home?"

"Is there anyone you can call?"

"With what?" She was close to yelling now. This was supposed to be over. They'd get back and everything would be fine. Now her store was burning and Gabriel was pushing her away as fast as possible.

"Everything I had in my pockets when we went away, it's all back." He held out his phone. "Is there anyone you can call that won't ask a ton of questions?"

Was there anyone? Her family would never let her hear the end of it if they found out. Even Della was bound to push. She didn't know Emmit's number.

Mira dug around in her pocket and pulled out a business card. "There's someone I can call."

"They won't ask a lot of questions?"

"They're discrete," Mira said, feeling defeated.

She called Reinfield Concierge service, giving them an address a few blocks away. When she slid the card back into her pocket, her hand found something else.

Feathers. Gabriel looked at them mutely.

"Never mind them," Mira muttered, shoving them back in her pocket. "We'll talk later."

Gabriel nodded. "I'll get in touch with you as soon as I can. Tell no one anything about what happened." He didn't wait for a reply before he strode away in the opposite direction. Mira could hear him calling in the fire.

Wanting to put distance between them, Mira hurried away. She went a block before she heard the sirens and she slowed down. Freezing, she rubbed her hands together before hugging herself against the cold.

The street was dark. She had no idea what time it was. Noises from the bustling city life only a few more blocks away were muffled. A few sounds made her jump. Not knowing what they were made her mind leap straight to thinking monsters were lurking in the dark, ready to grab her.

However, the monsters weren't here. Not in this world. When she arrived at the address she had given the car company, she leaned against the wall and shivered. The cold, brittle night would make anyone shiver, but Mira's nerves had been pulled so tight for so long that she was having trouble letting go of that tension.

An Escalade pulled to a stop in front of her, but the sight didn't register immediately. Cold and exhaustion were dragging her down. A man jumped out of the front seat and opened the back door. She pushed away from the wall and got in without a word.

The warmth actually hurt when it started to thaw her face. She said nothing when she put her seatbelt on. The man that had opened her door got something out of the back before getting back into the front seat again. He gave the driver a look. The driver looked intently in his rear-view mirror before he nodded.

They hadn't said anything.

The man in the passenger seat turned around and passed something back. Mira blankly took it. The soft dark fur unfolded into a blanket, which she gladly wrapped around herself.

"Can I get you anything else?" the man asked quietly.

She felt numb. "No." Rubbing her hands over the blanket reminded her of Gabriel's feathers. "What time is it?"

"Four-fifty-eight AM," the man said.

They had been gone for over half a day.

It had felt like much longer. Laying her head back on the seat, she watched the city lights. She closed her eyes, meaning only to rest them, and listened to the sound of the cold air whisking by.

It hadn't been cold in the Ether. It hadn't been warm either. No breeze, no sun, no clouds, just that persistent haze and light that didn't seem to have a real source.

Maybe this world was the source, she mused.

When the vehicle pulled to a stop, she bolted up in the seat and grabbed her necklace. Breathing hard, she looked around. Home. They had taken her to her apartment. She took a deep breath and tried to slow her racing heart.

"We've reached your destination," one of the men said.

Slowly, she unsnapped her seat belt. Her cheeks felt like they were on fire, and her stomach clenched at the idea of stepping back out in the cold. But it was only until she was upstairs.

Except she had no key.

"Shit," she said under hear breath. She looked toward the main house and saw no lights.

"Is there something you need assistance with?" the driver asked.

"I don't have my key," Mira said rubbing her head. "I'm sorry. I didn't even think about it."

"We can take care of that," the man in the passenger seat said. "Wait here."

Mira rubbed her face, trying to wake up and figure out what to do. She couldn't wake up Della, and she definitely wasn't going back to the station.

Before she had mentally gone through the list of things she wasn't going to do, the passenger returned to the front seat.

"Your door is unlocked," he said.

"Oh." Mira wasn't sure what else to say. What do you say to someone who took only a minute to break into your house?

"Would you like extra security until Mr. Harker arrives?" he asked.

"I forgot he was coming over," Mira said, more to herself. "I'm fine. Thank you, though, I just want to go to sleep."

The man stepped back out into the cold and opened her door. She shivered and stepped out. When she started to unwrap the fur blanket, he stopped her.

"Keep it," he said. "Please let me see you safely inside."

"What?" she asked, confused. "Oh, no. I'm fine. Thank you." She looked at him, really looked at him for the first time. "Thank you." She repeated. "Both of you."

"It's our pleasure."

Despite her reassurances, he walked upstairs with her.

"You really don't have to do this," she said, feeling exasperated.

He gave her a weak smile. "Mr. Harker might disagree and we'd rather avoid that if possible."

"Mr. Harker has a lot of explaining to do," she mumbled.

He held the front door open for her. "If you need anything from us, don't hesitate to call. Mr. Harker should arrive in less than an hour."

Mira frowned. "An hour?"

"Our apologies, but he would insist on knowing about this."

Mira groaned. She wanted nothing but sleep.

"Again, my apologies."

"It's fine," Mira said, not really meaning it. "Thanks again for the ride."

Mira leaned against the door after the man had gone. She thought about curling up on the couch until Emmit arrived. Then she remembered the monsters from the Ether and shivered. She went room by room and turned on every light she had. When she was certain she was alone, she opened one of her hiding spots. She had no idea what to do with the feathers, but above all else, she knew that no one else should get their hands on them.

Once she knew that Gabriel's feathers wouldn't be found, she decided to scrub her skin and burn her clothes. Not wanting to sit on anything that couldn't be scrubbed, Mira tried to remove the shirt that Gabriel had tied around her leg.

Gabriel had been amazing in the Ether. What had she done? If he hadn't been there, she would have died; she knew that.

The knot Gabriel had tied wasn't budging. She sighed and let her shoulders fall. She couldn't even remove his knot. There were scissors in the kitchen. It wasn't as if she was going to give his shirt back anyway. The creatures had pulled her in by a string that had touched a hint of the Ether. She had no idea what they would be able to do with something that had actually spent time there.

Her step quickened at the thought.

The clothes weren't magical, though, right? They wouldn't be able to use those. Right?

Either way, Gabriel would need a new shirt. She was pretty sure it wouldn't take much to convince him to burn his own clothes as well.

By the time she was in the kitchen, her hands were shaking again. She dug through two drawers before she found what she was looking for.

She immediately started hacking away at the shirt.

"Good lord."

Mira jumped and had the scissors pointed out as a weapon before her brain had registered that it was Emmit, even with his beautiful British accent.

"It hasn't been an hour," she accused.

"I didn't need an hour," he said. "Please lower the scissors."

"Oh." She blinked at the scissors and was surprised she hadn't lowered them automatically. "Sorry."

Once they were lowered, gentle fingers pried them from her hands and she jumped again. She hadn't even seen him move. It had to be the lack of sleep.

"What happened?" Emmit asked, leading her to kitchen chair. "Who did this?"

"I... it's a long story," Mira said.

He pushed her into the chair and started to untie the makeshift tourniquet. "Do you need to see a doctor?"

"No!" She said it too quickly and forcefully. The idea of particles of haze from the Ether being spread across the city made her grip the edge of her seat.

Under Gabriel's shirt, her jeans and skin had been torn by talons. The material was stiff with dried blood and it was sticking to her skin. Although his touch was delicate, she winced when Emmit lifted the pants away from her leg. Without seeming to use any effort, Emmit tore back the material and inspected what remained of the cut.

"Wait here," he said.

Looking down, she saw that the cut had started bleeding again, but in a sluggish way. The wound itself was red and angry, even where it wasn't covered in blood.

But it was also partially healed. It was bleeding because it had been torn back open again. Gently, she drew her fingers over where the cut had been. Whatever else that could be said about the Ethereal Plane, magic was stronger, worked better, and did the job faster than it ever had in this world.

At least not in her lifetime.

Emmit returned with a towel, and what looked like the contents of a first-aid kit. Did she even have one of those?

"Tell me what happened," Emmit said while he started to clean the area around the cut.

How do you even go about approaching a subject like this? Mira thought of and discarded several ideas. Gabriel had said not to tell anyone until they had spoken, but she had questions for Emmit and had no intention of listening to Gabriel where Emmit was concerned.

"How is the spell I did working?" Mira asked.

"I hardly think this is—"

"*Emmit.*" Her voice was sharper than she had expected. How long had it been since she slept? She tried to lighten her tone. "Just tell me. Please?"

Emmit's lips twitched into a semblance of a smile. "It is working beautifully. I felt twinges from the Ethereal Plane late yesterday, but after that, I have been balanced." He stopped long enough to take her hand. "I cannot thank you enough for what you have done."

He looked at her, and there was something in his eyes that she had seen hinted in the past. Even after she had performed the spell and he had kissed her, it was only a glint compared to this.

Love may be a strong word, lust as well. But they were there. She wanted to keep them there.

When he tried to let go of her hand, she gripped it, not wanting to lose contact with him. It was a comfort, and one that she wanted, needed, right now. She wanted this less guarded version of himself that he now showed.

She wanted him.

But she also needed answers.

Emmit gently removed her hand from his, but he maintained in contact. His hand rested on her thigh beside the wound. Goosebumps rose when he rubbed the area gently, almost unconsciously, as he finished wiping the blood away.

"I believe you were picked up downtown," Emmit prompted in a low voice. "No coat, freezing, and bleeding. I have people searching the area for your things." His eyes began to turn gray and his voice hardened. "And to find who did this."

"What?" Mira snapped. "Tell them to stop."

"Mira, your store is on fire. Well, it's been put out by now. You were only a few blocks away. It's not hard to put the two together."

She closed her eyes and rubbed her head, trying push the fog away. "Put what two together?"

"You being injured and your store on fire. Whoever wrote those letters has become more adamant about wanting you to leave."

Mira let out an exasperated sigh, which Emmit must have mistook for something else.

"Don't worry." Emmit's voice was soothing and he rubbed her leg again before bandaging it. "I'll stay with you today, ensuring nothing happens while other arrangements are being made. I'll take care of this."

"You'll take care of this?" The idea made her irrationally angry, which was good for her on multiple levels, the best being that she wouldn't fall apart in front of him if she were mad enough.

"Do you have any other injuries?" Emmit asked.

"The two aren't related," Mira said, ignoring the question. "My store and this," she gestured to her leg, "are two different things entirely."

"Tell me," Emmit said, not rising to her anger. "We'll work it out."

This would have been tricky if she wasn't upset. "Why do the creatures from the Ether hate you so badly?"

There was a long pause before he said, "I'm not sure what you mean."

Mira dove in with the truth. "They said I had placed myself on the side of the Harker family. What exactly does that mean?"

Emmit's face paled. "You talked with something from the Ethereal Plane?"

He sounded accusatory, which Mira didn't appreciate. "I guess you could say that. Mostly, I ran from them."

"You walked on the other side?" He stood up abruptly. All of Emmit's usual grace and good manners were gone. "I should never have asked for your help. Had I thought you would actually attempt to go there—"

"Hey!" Mira balled up her fists and tried to reign her temper in. "For your information, I didn't try to go there. I was sucked over there by creatures that you seem to be dealing with!"

Emmit started pacing the room. "That is not possible. They could not have pulled you there without help from the Elders, and the Elders are sound asleep. Besides, had you been drawn to the other side by the creatures, you would not have survived."

Mira glared at Emmit. "I'd say I'm insulted, but after being there, I agree. I wouldn't have survived—not long, anyway—if I had been on my own."

"You took someone over with you?"

"Took?"

Emmit looked away and tried to compose himself. "Perhaps you should start from the beginning." Apparently, composure wasn't an easy task when Emmit was upset.

The beginning? He wanted to hear what happened?

There was no way she was going to relive the full nightmare right now.

"I'm not sure exactly what happened, but I can take a good guess," Mira said, deflating a little. "I went to the police station this afternoon. The silk we had used to mark the circle was in my pocket."

"That's how they pulled you over?" Emmit asked.

Now that she had said it out loud to someone beyond Gabriel, it sounded crazy. "It's the only connection I can think of."

Emmit looked like he was adding pentagrams and getting crosses. "Why did you have it with you?"

"After you left, I performed another spell. Nothing to do with the Ether—or you," she added quickly with an edge to her voice. "It was a perspective spell."

Emmit looked confused.

"For the case," she said. "I was trying to find out who is killing people." Mira tried to think back to why she had been at the police station in the first place. "Anyway, I thought Tyler was in trouble... or something." She shook her head at the foggy recollections. "I was with Gabriel when those, those things, started to come into focus."

"Gabriel? They took him as well?"

"He's the only reason I'm alive."

"What did you see?"

Mira closed her eyes and shook her head. "I don't want to go into details right now."

"Anything you say or heard could be important!"

"The only thing important to me, right now, is making sure it doesn't happen again."

Emmit opened his mouth to say something, then stopped and looked her over. When he approached, Mira wasn't certain if he was walking with exaggerated slowness or if her brain had decided to start processing things slower. He took her hand and drew her to her feet.

His eyes still had a hard edge to them. "I can assure you that you are safe right now. I'm sorry I pushed. You obviously need some time."

CHAPTER 27

I NEED A SHOWER AND SLEEP."

"Of course," Emmit said. "You should rest."

She tottered on her feet. "And Gabriel?" she asked. "He'll be safe?"

Emmit pulled her tightly to him. "He is."

Feeling grimy, she wanted to push him away, but somehow that never happened. She closed her eyes and embraced him, leaning on him for support more than she thought she should, but again, her treacherous body didn't listen to her.

Closing her eyes was a mistake, and opening them was harder than she had anticipated.

"Is there anything I can get you?" Emmit asked. "Anything you need?"

"I need to get clean and burn my clothes."

Mira squeaked when Emmit picked her up without warning. It was involuntary and should have been embarrassing, but she was too tired for that.

Emmit put her back on her feet outside her bathroom. He spent time looking over every inch of her that he could see. Mira suspected Emmit could see a lot more than she did.

"When you wake up, there are a lot of questions that I'll need to ask. You understand that, right?"

"I do," Mira responded, "because I have a lot of questions for you as well."

His eyes hardened again for a flash, and then he shook his head. "You continuously surprise me."

It was Mira's turn to look confused. "How so?"

"People don't demand answers from me."

"Demand?"

Emmit looked frustrated. "Let me know if you need anything."

Mira tried to get her tired brain to say something, but it was rebelling.

When she looked in the mirror, she regretted it instantly. How had she not cleaned up before Emmit came over?

Remembering what happened before Emmit came over, she realized that there had been no time.

Mira couldn't remember ever being this tired, but she found, as she methodically scrubbed herself of all remnants of her ordeal that she was trying to think of what she could have done differently in the Ether. The feeling that she had been almost completely reliant on Gabriel didn't sit well with her. She had never been a fan of offensive magic, but once upon a time, she would have been prepared at least to fight back long enough to get away.

She wasn't exactly sure what had changed, but she was certain that she had become too complacent.

It was time for that to come to an end. Once she had scrubbed herself twice, she decided there was nothing she could do about it tonight. Or was it morning?

When she thought about the haze clinging to her skin, she scrubbed herself all over again and surprised herself by reversing that decision. Gabriel wouldn't always be there and she had no idea if Emmit could tether her in this world. Relying on him to do so didn't sound like a recipe for keeping herself safe.

Going straight to bed sounded divine, but she didn't think she'd be able to sleep if she didn't have something prepared. Sadly, her mind wasn't functioning on higher levels, and the only thing she could bring to mind was Spark. Essentially, it caused glitter to glimmer for a few moments.

She almost didn't put the effort into the spell, because it certainly didn't seem worth it.

Nevertheless, it was something, and she had everything she needed close at hand.

When Mira came out of the bathroom, the blinding sun was leaking through the shades. Emmit was in living room, pacing and talking with someone. Mira was glad to see, when she poked her head out of the bedroom, that he was on the phone. Company didn't sound appealing right now.

When he saw her, he stowed the phone in his pocket without a goodbye or 'talk to you later' sentiment.

"You don't have to stay around here all day," Mira said, leaning against the doorframe to her bedroom. She mentally crossed her fingers, because she really didn't want him to go. "I'm sure you had other plans."

"I'd prefer to stay. If it's alright with you, that is," Emmit said.

She gave him a tired smile. "I'd like it if you stayed, although this isn't exactly how I pictured us spending the day together."

"We'll have to keep practicing until we get it right."

"I'd like that," Mira said.

Her smile grew, which pulled Emmit closer. He put an arm around her, settling his hand on the small of her back.

"You should get some rest," Emmit said. "Is there anything you need?"

"You keep asking that."

"I'm afraid I'm not very good at this," he said.

"At what?" Mira asked.

"Knowing what to do for someone."

She looked up at him, thinking of the different roads this could go down, depending on what she said. Since her tongue, along with her brain, felt clumsy, she settled for repeating his sentiment.

"This will be good practice," Mira said, resting her head on his chest.

Comfort was exactly what she needed to push the beasts of the Ether out of her head. Eyes closed, she soaked up his warmth and somehow fell asleep.

When Mira opened her eyes, hours later, she saw that the room was still brightly lit. Looking around, she tried to find what had woken her up.

A thick shadow loomed in the corner. She grabbed her ward and screamed. Emmit was immediately beside her, seemingly appearing from nowhere.

Breathing heavy, still pressing her ward tight to her skin, Mira's brain caught up with what she was seeing. A thin bookshelf took shape in place of the figure in the corner.

"Mira?" Emmit's concern was almost palpable.

"I don't—something—" She shook her head and tried again. "Sorry. I don't know what…"

She didn't know what she was saying or even what she was trying to say. The aftereffects of the jolt of adrenaline left her shaky, and she was feeling stupid for screaming about a bookshelf.

"I'm okay," Mira said, letting herself fall back in the bed. "Bad dream, I guess."

"That's understandable," Emmit said. After a moment, he added, "It's okay, though. You can drop your ward."

Mira nodded. When she let go of the necklace, Emmit stepped closer.

They were both quiet, each unsure of what to say.

"Would you like some tea or something to help you sleep?" Emmit asked.

"I should get up," Mira mumbled.

"It hasn't been two hours yet. Get some rest."

"We're alone, right?"

"Yes. Are you expecting anyone?"

"I suppose Gabriel might stop by. We didn't get the chance to talk when we got back."

They looked up when Mira's home phone started ringing in the kitchen. Mira yawned and ignored it. The shaking had died away, leaving her feeling worn.

"Get some rest," Emmit said. "I'll be in the living room if you need anything."

She wanted him to stay, but couldn't say it. "Thank you."

Emmit hesitated before leaving.

Had he wanted to stay? As much as Mira wanted him there, she didn't want him to remember their first time in bed being because she was sleeping, scared, and twitching at shadows. Besides, what would he do? Lie there and stare at the ceiling?

For that matter, what was he doing in the other room?

The phone in the kitchen rang again. It was probably her mother or her sister, trying her home phone since she wasn't answering her cell. She pushed it out of her mind and attempted to sleep.

It might have been her business partner. Mira blinked at the ceiling. Her store had been on fire. She should be doing something about that. Instead, she rolled over and pulled the covers up around her. It's possible that she should get up and face the world, but she was already feeling the pull of sleep.

A knock on the front door made her blink. It was probably Gabriel. She should get up for him. They needed to talk, and Gabriel might be aggravated that she had told Emmit about the Ether.

It wouldn't be her mother, would it? Could she have heard about the store?

Mira's eyes snapped open. Crap. It could be her mother.

It could be Ian or any number of other people.

She tossed back her blankets and heard Emmit answer the door. Not wanting to leave him with her mother for long, she got to her feet as fast as her tired body could be forced.

Halfway across the room she registered that Emmit was talking with someone that had a male voice.

Gabriel? Her dad wouldn't have heard about the store, right? She picked up her pace.

A deafening blast filled the apartment the moment she stepped out of the bedroom.

Mira froze.

Emmit fell back.

Mira screamed.

The shotgun swung in her direction. "Don't worry, this isn't for you," John Parnell said. "Not unless I need it, anyway. And I don't see that in the next few minutes."

John kicked Emmit's leg back so he could slam the door shut.

Emmit. She stared at him lying motionless on the floor.

He hadn't even needed to be here.

"He shows up unexpectedly," John said. "Well, he used to, anyway. Now, I guess not so much."

"John?"

"I might get into a little trouble for that."

Mira's brain tried to catch up, but it was having a hard time.

"We've got work to do," John said.

"What are you talking about?" Mira managed.

What did she have? It was hard to get past the thought that what she had was a gun pointed at her.

"Well, I had a message for you," John nudged Emmit's leg a few times, "but that may be a moot point now."

"What kind of message?" Mira asked.

Spark. Had she really expected to feel any safer with Spark? What the hell had she been thinking? Her kitchen phone began ringing again.

"A message from the Ether," John said. "The acolytes pieced it together this morning."

"From the Ether?" Mira snapped. The fact that anyone from that world would try to send her a message lit a small fire inside her. "How? Why?" The phone stopped ringing, which was good, the shrill noise was distracting her further.

"The how is easy. PostsFromTheEther gets updated and the acolytes interpret. The why is problematic." John nudged Emmit one last time. "Let's go to the kitchen. Even with him being dead I don't want to be around a Harker."

Mira looked at Emmit again, tears welled up, unheeded in her fear. Her heart felt like it was being ground under John's shoe.

"The kitchen!" John yelled.

Mira jumped. She didn't care about any message. Nothing

John could say had any interest to her. Slowly, she moved in the direction of the kitchen.

There was Spark and her ward. The kitchen was full of things she could make, but nothing was ready. Nothing planned.

She needed Della. Something fast that didn't need to be prepared would be helpful. Or Gabriel. He wasn't an angel here, but he was a cop.

Emmit. She was sure Emmit could have taken care of this. Even without knowing what he was, or what he did, it always felt as though he could take care of anything.

What she had, though, was Spark, and herself.

It would have to do.

"What was the message?" Mira asked without turning to see if John was following. It was a struggle to keep her voice level, but she had a feeling that John wouldn't notice.

"They wanted a sacrifice," John said casually. "They always do, but now I can give them a Harker."

He was right behind her.

Her heart pounded faster in her chest and her hand twitched.

"For some reason," John said, "they made it sound like he'd be hard to kill."

Mira glanced back. As before, the gun wasn't pointed at her. Not directly.

There was a knock on her front door.

If anyone else came into the apartment, they wouldn't survive long. Mira felt sure about that.

John frowned back at the living room. "I don't see this in the future either," he muttered.

Mira let loose with her spell. It was stronger than she anticipated. A flare, brighter than any that came from a camera lit in front of John's face. The flash brought heat with it, which was an unexpected bonus.

"What the hell?" John staggered and tried to rub his eyes.

Surging forward, Mira bowled into John, trying to push the gun aside.

He was bigger than she was, but distracted and partially blind. The gun clattered loudly to the floor.

"Mira?" Gabriel called from the living room. "What the hell?"

From his tone of voice, she figured he must have seen Emmit.

John lashed out. With one hand pressed against his face, he used the other to hit Mira. Pain exploded from the side of her head and she fell to the ground.

Right on top of the gun.

She had no idea how to use a shotgun, but she was hoping the usual point and click approach would work. Scrambling away, she aimed the gun.

"Stop!" she yelled.

"You're not going to shoot me," John sneered.

"If she doesn't, I will," Gabriel said.

John looked panicked, but it quickly passed into a snide grin. "There's no stopping them."

"Put your hands up," Gabriel said.

John closed his eyes and started muttering under his breath.

Mira got shakily to her feet. It started to feel as though she was being watched. The cool, misty feeling that she associated with seers and the Ether began to gather in her apartment.

"Gabriel, get back," Mira said, afraid to raise her voice.

Gabriel didn't say anything, but he didn't move, either.

Being sure to stay as far from John as possible, Mira circled wide and joined Gabriel. Her eyes never left John.

She tugged on Gabriel's arm. "I think we need to move back."

He glanced at her, but again said nothing.

John's eyes popped open, though only the whites showed. His head turned, taking in the whole room until he ended up facing Mira and Gabriel. He couldn't see. It would have been impossible for John to see with his eyes rolled back into his head.

But something was looking at them all the same.

"Ahh, it'ssss good to sssee thiss world onsse again."

Mira shivered at the sound of the voice and gripped Gabriel's arm. "You can't be here."

"It's that thing?" Gabriel asked.

Mira could tell that he was looking for confirmation, rather than asking a question. "That black, leathery monster. Yes."

Gabriel fired his gun.

Mira's ears rang from the noise. John, or the thing inside John, looked down at his chest, which was quickly turning red.

John leered at them. "He wasss dead when he invited me in."

"Mira."

Mira spun around at the sound of Emmit's voice. Relief washed over her.

His shirt was shredded, but there was very little blood. Emmit was alive.

Moreover, exceedingly pissed off—so much so that he was shaking. His pupils were so gray that they almost looked black. Anger radiated from him in waves

Emmit didn't look at Mira or Gabriel. His eyes were locked on the thing that used to be John.

"Your ward," Emmit said, "use it and get back. Gabriel, stay with her." He stepped in front of them, facing John.

Gabriel seemed conflicted with the order before grabbing Mira's arm and glaring at Emmit. "We're going to talk about this."

"Later," Emmit snapped.

"Drop the gun," Gabriel said, pulling Mira back.

Mira let go and gripped her pentagram. Around them, anything not attached to a wall began to rattle.

"You are weak and pathetic in this world," Emmit said, fury behind every word. "And you have no right to be here."

Gabriel managed to get Mira out of the kitchen, but she refused to let Emmit out of her sight.

"We belong to thiss world," John spat in the voice of the creature.

The atmosphere became charged. Malice clung in the air around them.

"Leave now!" Emmit yelled.

Mira felt her own feet want to move away. Emmit's words felt like an order, much like Gabriel's had been in the Ethereal Plane. She poured more power into her ward.

"We want the witch," the creature said.

For a brief, hesitant moment, everything in the kitchen went silent. The rattling stopped and Emmit even seemed to stop breathing.

"No," Emmit said.

The apartment erupted. Wind ripped through the rooms, picking up smaller items in its wake. Mira never knew she had so much stuff until it began banging into them from all sides.

Several voices together screamed, but in a whisper, as though they yelling from a great distance.

"We're not far enough away," Gabriel said.

Mira barely heard him as the cyclone in her apartment picked up its pace. Her flat screen TV slammed into Gabriel who cursed at the impact.

"Get down," Gabriel yelled.

Emmit and what used to be John stood in the eye of the storm, neither saying a word.

The screams continued.

Chanting blew in on the wind. Mira looked to the door, expecting to find the source, but there was nothing there. Individual words couldn't be heard, but the dark intent was heavy in the air.

Mira grabbed her arm when her marble mortar tried to fly by, hitting her instead. Gabriel pulled her onto the floor.

"Get off me!" she yelled, trying to push Gabriel aside.

The angel didn't budge. She could still see the back of Emmit, but John was blocked from her view.

Windows shattered. Glass mixed with the other debris and Mira was forced to shield her face from the hundreds of tiny, razor-sharp pieces of glass joining the maelstrom.

The apartment wasn't moving, was it? A larger crash came from the kitchen. Mira chanced looking up, seeing that Emmit still stood in calm air.

Gabriel pushed her head back down. "Are you crazy?" He put an arm over her head. "We need to find a way out of here."

A sound like the tearing of wood joined the wails. The floor shook under them and pressure began to build.

Mira could sense the base source of the pressure building around Emmit. He was speaking in another language now, but rage and a harsh bite to the words told her it was nothing friendly.

The worrying part was the tinge of fear that had entered Emmit's voice.

Was he losing? Gabriel wouldn't let her look up, but she didn't have to. She clung to her ward, squeezed her eyes shut, and concentrated on the circle in the garage below them. Having been called to action recently, the memory of protection still clung to it.

Without the connection to the ground, it wasn't enough. She couldn't force the circle to expand.

Eyes still shut tight, Mira tried to move toward Emmit, but Gabriel wasn't exactly light, and he definitely wasn't cooperative. "I have to get closer to Emmit," Mira hissed.

"Not a chance," Gabriel said.

"You can't stop me," Mira said, pushing against him.

He was like marble.

"Look, unless you want to get sucked back into the Ether, I need to get closer to Emmit."

She could feel Gabriel's hesitation.

"There's no time!" Mira was turning frantic as the increase in volume rose and the chanting took on a higher pitch.

When she struggled forward, Gabriel let her go. She could hear him cursing under his breath, but she continued forward, trying to stay as low to the floor as possible. Stinging bites cut into her arms.

Gabriel moved up beside her, clearly pissed off. "You have one minute, then we're out of here."

Mira ignored him, but it didn't matter. She couldn't get any closer to Emmit. When she tried to edge forward, she felt as though someone was grinding her into her carpet.

Easing back slightly, Mira frantically tried to come up with a new plan. She couldn't get close enough to put a circle around Emmit in order to connect with the one in the basement.

But there were other ways.

She tore her necklace off and wiped her hand down her arm, which was oozing blood. Clutching her ward, she began to draw symbols on the floor. First the pentagram for protection, then her own sigil, rarely used and never shown to others. She ended with a symbol of the Ethereal Plane and slashed through it.

The wind began to slow. Larger objects dropped. The chorus of chanting became lighter, farther away.

But the pressure didn't lift.

"That's it," Gabriel said, "we're going."

"Wait!" It was working; she knew it was. If she had more power, or maybe if she was less worn down.

Whatever else, she knew she didn't want to lose Emmit. Whatever he was, whatever he could do, he needed her help and she would do this.

Gabriel grabbed her arm. "Let's take the chance while we still have it." His own blood was running freely in several places.

Without even thinking about it, she reached out to a cut on his neck, pressing hard until she knew his blood was mingled with her own.

Using Gabriel's blood, her protector throughout their journey across the Ether, she slashed through the symbol of the Ether once again.

The rushing air stopped. There was no slowing to a breeze. Instead, the air froze, deadened, everything fell to the ground, and the pressure lifted. The chanting was gone, but the memory of it still echoed in Mira's head.

A screech from the kitchen replaced the noise. Thin, high, loud, and extremely angry, it filled the space. Emmit said a few tight words and the wail ended.

The lifeless feeling of the room disappeared, leaving them with a normal stillness of slow-moving, shifting air. The smell of burnt hair curled through the freezing room.

Mira let her head drop and worked to catch her breath. She hadn't even noticed when she'd lost it. Lying still, she tried to relish in the feeling that she was alive.

Beside her, she heard Gabriel get to his feet. "What the hell just happened?"

Mira had no idea if he was directing the comment to her or Emmit, and she couldn't bring herself to care.

"Mira?" Emmit's voice was controlled and stark.

"I'm okay," she said, dragging her head up to look Emmit over.

He was leaning against the wall, looking as out of breath as she was. Taking a moment to close his eyes and lean his head against the wall was the only reaction to what had happened. Except for his clothing, Emmit looked unruffled, and his face was as empty of emotion as his voice.

"Someone had better tell me what the hell just happened, and now." Gabriel's anger seethed out of him.

"Hell is exactly what happened," Emmit said, not opening his eyes. "Or was prevented from happening."

"I'm going to need to know more than that," Gabriel said, sounding as though Emmit had taken the wind out of his sails. "Where did that... guy go?"

When Emmit didn't answer, Mira took a stab. "I think he went to the same place we were. The Ether."

Emmit nodded dully.

Gabriel looked like a million questions had just come up and he was struggling to pick which one would be first.

Mira sighed and braced herself before getting to her feet. Even then, she winced and sucked in a sharp breath as red pokers of pain stabbed into her. Emmit was beside her, but she was too tired to feel startled. He began to look her over.

While he did so, Mira put a tentative hand on his chest. Tattered remains of his sweater clung to him, held to his skin by drying blood.

He gently moved her hand away, intent on her injuries.

"I thought you were dead," Mira said. She shivered as the adrenaline started to wear off and the coldness of the room started to sink in.

Emmit's face softened and he started to say something. Then he glanced at Gabriel and seemed to change his mind. "I'll be okay. You, however, need medical attention."

"I'm okay," Mira said.

"Huh." Gabriel shook his head at the obvious lie.

Her eyes narrowed, but she was too tired to pull off a real glare. "I'll be okay."

"I'll call this in," Gabriel said. "An ambulance can pick her up."

"Call in what, exactly?" Emmit asked.

Gabriel's eyes hardened. "This whole mess."

"You're calling in a rift between dimensions?" Emmit asked.

"I…" Gabriel stopped and tried again. "An attempted murder."

Emmit shook his head. "That would be unwise. This will be taken care of by different means."

Crossing her arms and rubbing them to ward off the cold, Mira watched the two of them argue. At this point, she didn't care what happened. Looking around the room, she had trouble bringing up any remorse over her apartment either. The only thing that broke through the fuzziness that threatened to swamp her mind was the fact that she had drawn symbols on her carpet in her own blood.

Then it hit her. She had also used Gabriel's blood. She sighed and rubbed her head, thinking about the consequences of taking someone's blood and using it in a spell without permission. With a human, it wouldn't matter, not really, anyway. Saving the person's life would cancel that out, but an angel's blood? She wasn't too sure of what the consequences of that would be.

"I'm sorry, Gabriel," Mira said, interrupting whatever they were saying.

Both men looked up at her and Mira waved at the ground.

"I didn't ask," she said as way of explanation.

Gabriel looked confused, but Emmit knew exactly what she meant.

"You don't have to worry about the repercussions," Emmit said, taking her hand. "Gabriel would never begrudge that if you used it as a way to protect yourself." Then he frowned. "You are freezing." Emmit checked his watch. "They'll be here in less than two minutes."

"Maybe because he doesn't really understand what I did," Mira said, watching Gabriel. "And who is they?"

"As far as anyone else knows," Emmit said, "John arrived and attacked you. When Gabriel arrived to tell you about your shop, John fled."

Mira nodded.

"It's important that only the three of us know," Emmit pressed.

"I get it," Mira said. "What would I even say? Something came here from the Ether? Della and Tyler would both freak out and try to get to know more."

"You've seen Tyler?" Emmit asked.

"Not in a few days." Mira said. "That's why I went to see Gabriel in the first place."

Through the open door, sounds of boots on the wooden staircase blew in with the frigid air.

"I need a moment with them," Emmit said to Mira, "then you and I will leave."

"She'll need to be questioned," Gabriel said.

"We'll stay close by," Emmit said.

"Della will know things aren't right if she sees me like this," Mira said.

"Lance's is only a few blocks away. We can wait there," Emmit said. He raised a hand to the three men that appeared in the doorway, motioning them to stop.

Mira was too tired to feel any real panic, but she managed to remain leery. "I'm bleeding. I don't think Lance will appreciate that, or me, after he sees me."

Emmit smiled and squeezed her hand. "You don't need to worry about him."

"Who's Lance?" Gabriel asked.

"We'll go over together," Emmit said, ignoring the question. "It may be best for you to stay a few days. This will be a crime scene after all."

"What about Alchemy and Oracle?" Mira's hand flew to her mouth when she realized she hadn't seen the cats since John had entered the apartment. She looked around frantically and moved towards her bedroom.

"Don't!" Gabriel shouted at her.

Mira only looked at him, confused.

"The glass," he sighed.

She rubbed her forehead. "But—"

"I'll grab your shoes," Gabriel said, looking hopelessly around the debris.

Emmit started talking to the men at the door. Once he had passed Mira her shoes, Gabriel stood over Emmit's shoulder.

Mira went straight to her bedroom, the last place she had seen her cats. Now that she had a focus, she moved with purpose. She was relieved to find that her bedroom hadn't sustained as much damage as the main rooms.

When Mira called for the cats, she heard a mewling that she hadn't heard since Alchemy and Oracle were kittens. Dropping to the floor, she lifted the bed skirt, and found two frightened sets of eyes peering out at her.

Mira reached under the bed. "Are you two okay?" Even though she stretched her arms as far as she could, she couldn't reach the cats. "Come here. Alchemy, Oracle, come here."

They only stared at her. Mira knew that the cats understood her magic, but what happened tonight was something beyond anything either of them had ever seen. She didn't blame them for staying hidden.

While discussion went on in the other room, Mira stayed put and talked to Alchemy and Oracle, until she could finally coax them out from under the bed. When Mira sat up, they both laid on her lap. She stroked their fur until they were calm, even though she could tell that neither was happy.

Someone had placed a pet carrier in the room with her coat on top. Neither Alchemy nor Oracle fussed about going in the carrier, which spoke volumes about how unhappy they were about what was going on. Apparently, they were as ready as she was to leave this nightmare.

Mira hunted down a change of clothes and a few other things, tossing them in an overnight bag. Emmit was waiting for her at the door.

"You're sure going to Lance's is a good idea?" Mira asked.

"Are you comfortable with her being at Lance's?" Emmit asked Gabriel.

"You said it was only a few blocks away," Gabriel said. "This is going to be a shit storm no matter where she is."

"You don't feel anxious or agitated about it?" Emmit asked.

"Why should I?" Gabriel asked.

Emmit shrugged. "Lance's will work for our purposes then."

Mira took one last look at the junkyard her apartment had become, and emotions twisted together and squeezed her heart. It didn't look like anything had survived. She had no idea how they would pin all this on John, and at the moment, she didn't really care.

Lance looked uneasy, but Emmit had a chat with the vampire, and Lance agreed to let Mira stay for as long as she needed. The room he gave her was about the size of her apartment and had its own bathroom, but she felt out of place in the mansion.

Even so, after letting Oracle and Alchemy out of their carrier, she left Gabriel and Emmit discussing what they were going to do next and she locked herself in the bathroom. With cuts and scrapes covering her, not to mention bloody clothes, getting clean was her first priority. She felt numb, so she tried concentrating on one thing at a time.

It was going to take more than fresh clothes and a shower to settle her nerves. From the way Gabriel talked, though, she would have to face the police sooner rather than later.

After her shower, Mira saw that her cats had found a comfy place in the middle of the bed, so she went looking for Emmit and Gabriel. She found the two men in an extravagant living room sitting on plush couches. Somehow, they both seemed to fit the room, each man looking as though they owned the place, although Gabriel looked unhappy with the company he was keeping.

"We have a plan," Emmit said when she joined him on the coach.

"For what?" Mira asked.

"Reporting the incident," Emmit said.

"We're really reporting this?" Mira said.

"Gabriel is quite insistent," Emmit said. "It's very simple, though, and mostly the truth. John attacked you at your apartment and was frightened away after Gabriel showed up."

Mira blinked at him, waiting for more.

"No one outside the three of us should ever need to know he moved into the Ether," Emmit said.

"But… my apartment doesn't exactly—"

"That's being taken care of as we speak," Emmit cut in. "The scene will reflect what you are reporting."

"I'm still not convinced we should be doing this," Gabriel said.

Emmit gave him a hard look and Gabriel sighed.

"But it's the best we can do at the moment," Gabriel added.

"Gabriel will ask the police to meet you here," Emmit said. "He'll stick with you."

"I want Della here as well," Mira said.

Emmit looked like he was going to argue.

"She's going to be here," Mira pressed.

"But I shouldn't be," Emmit said, standing. "You can stay here as long as you need."

"You're leaving?" Mira asked.

"There are things I need to do," Emmit said, "and with me being here, it will only confuse the story. Too many people will ask too many questions."

"Oh." It was the only thing Mira could think of to say.

"Gabriel, you're sure you feel comfortable with her staying here?" Emmit asked.

"I don't feel comfortable with any of this," Gabriel said.

"What I mean is, do you think she will be safe here?" Emmit asked.

"Why do you keep asking him that?" Mira asked.

"I want to ensure that you'll be okay if I am away for a while," Emmit said.

"He barely knows me," Mira muttered.

"Yes, but he's bound himself to you," Emmit said. "He'll know if something is wrong."

Mira stared at Emmit, but didn't get a chance to say anything.

"What the hell are you talking about?" Gabriel asked.

"You didn't know?" It was Emmit's turn to look confused. "It's not something that typically happens on accident. I assumed it was intentional."

"That's ridiculous," Gabriel said. "You don't know what you're talking about."

"You knew to show up at her apartment today," Emmit said.

"That was…" Gabriel seemed to lose some of his steam. "A coincidence."

Emmit chuckled, which only seemed to aggravate Gabriel. "I assure you, if Mira is in danger, you will know, and you will feel the need to go help her."

"But it'll go away, right?" Mira asked.

"I shouldn't think so," Emmit said as he stood. "I should leave."

"You can't go," Gabriel said, standing as well. "You have to fix that bond thing you're talking about."

"Even if I could, why should I?" Emmit asked. "John was not the beginning or end of this. Mira is safer now than she was before."

"But she's not my responsibility!"

"Don't I get a say in this?" Mira asked, feeling her own blood pressure rise at the accusation that she was anyone's responsibility. "I don't want him traipsing after me."

"I'm sorry," Emmit said, "there is nothing I can do."

"That's crap!" Gabriel snapped.

Emmit lost any trace of amusement. "I don't know why you did this, but you cannot blame Mira or me."

Gabriel clenched and unclenched his fists.

"Besides," Emmit said, seeming to relax a bit, "it could be that with John gone, she will no longer be a target. I'm sure Mira is safe for now, with or without you. The whole community should be safer. Now, I really must take my leave. You should be able to call this in anytime."

Gabriel and Mira were quiet when Emmit left. Minutes ticked by and Mira was glad for each one of them. Gabriel's reaction had hurt and aggravated her far more than she thought it should have. The time gave her a few moments to calm down.

"Listen," Gabriel said, interrupting her thoughts, "about this—"

"It's been a long day," Mira said. "A long two days. Can we just get this over with?"

"Yeah," Gabriel said, sounding relieved, "I'll make the call."

Creating a new series has been nerve wracking and a lot of fun! Mira was a fun character to write and I love watching her work with Emmit, Ian, and Gabriel. If you enjoyed this book, please leave a review on the site where you made the purchase.

Leaving a review helps the reader and author in many ways. Your support is appreciated!

Thank you for reading!
Amanda Booloodian

Hidden World Newsletter Sign-up:

ACKNOWLEDGEMENTS

This new series has been loads of fun! Spellbound Murder started out completely different. The original idea was to have a supernatural support group, but it morphed drastically from there. Special thanks to Adria Waters who read the book early on and helped me make it a stronger book!

I'd also like thank Tamera Walton, who took the time to read the book and give me quick feedback! This helped calm my nerves and reassure me that fans of AIR will like the new series. I also need to thank JD Book Services and Frankie Sutton, my editors, for their feedback on the book.

Deranged Doctor Design has done another amazing job with this series! They've provided the entire series with wonderful covers. I love their work and their flexibility.

Many, many other family, friends, and acquaintances have been incredibly supportive.

For all the people who gave reviews online, you are amazing! Thank you so much for taking the time to leave a review.

ABOUT THE AUTHOR

Amanda Booloodian lives in Missouri with her loving, and often times peculiar, husband. Amanda has been passionate about the written word throughout her life. Now, much of her spare time is spent at the computer, delving into worlds accessible only through vivid imagination. In warm weather, when she isn't pounding on the keyboard, she can often be found wandering through the wilderness. Occasionally she gets it into her head to SCUBA dive or to sit back at home and make wine, which can have interesting results and inspire her writing.

You can find out more about Amanda and her writing, including upcoming releases, on www.Booloodian.com. You can also find her on Facebook: Amanda Booloodian - Author, Twitter: @ajbooloodian, and Instagram: AJBooloodian.

www.ingramcontent.com/pod-product-compliance
Lightning Source LLC
Chambersburg PA
CBHW050340190726
48284CB00007BB/2082